Maroons

A Human Epic

NO FEAR IN LOVE

To Steve
Enjoy the journey

Randy Luallin

ISBN : 1-4392-4275-5
ISBN-13: 9781439242759

To order additional copies, please contact us.
BookSurge
www.booksurge.com
1-866-308-6235
orders@booksurge.com

acknowledgments : I want to thank my loving and supportive friends and family, many of whom I have used for character traits and names. You know who you are!

A special thanks to Sue Schmidt (Williams), my fellow traveler and inspiration for the book; Leanette Tarply Ashcraft, fellow author and confidante; Kathy Leftwich, my editor who took on a total unknown without judgment and encouraged me along the way.

Table of Contents

The Maroons

Sheila Lincoln b. 1985; Gary Llewellyn, b. 1974; Neville Lincoln, b. 1978; Sue Pratt, b. 1977; Jung-suk Go, b. 1980; Mandy French, b. 1976; Marcus Suffern, b. 1981; Cyndra Dietz, b. 1985; Nathan Pierce, b. 1999; Gretchen Pierce, b. 2000; Sharon Thompson, b. 1975; Roy Strecker, b. 1942.

Important Dates:and Births

2005 Zero year

	Paul & Mitch Thompson
01	Caleb Pratt/ Llewellyn
	Acoba Go/Lincoln
02	Lori Dietz
	Nicole Suffern
	Wendy Llewellyn
03	Joan Hannum
	Jacque French/Lincoln
04	Lee Pratt/Lincoln
	Peggy King
	Anna Go/Llewellyn
	Abel Dietz
	Mariza Vasquez
05	Fredrick Suffern
	Nile Fukanaga
06	Sarah Smith
15	**Leave Dominica**
16	Joshua Pierce
	Liberty Hannum
	Freedom Vasquez

Chapter 1
The 17th Colored Regiment
1780

Acoba flicked the pebble with his big toe, watching it skip over the parapet of the thick stone walls. Guard duty was never very exciting. Fort Shirley had seen no attacks and probably never would.

He flexed his strong toes, feeling the warm stones beneath his bare feet, and wondered if the English would ever get around to issuing shoes. Not that they were necessary. His feet were callused from walking barefoot all his life. As a black man, he did not expect shoes.

Nonetheless, Acoba was proud of his bright red British uniform and especially the three chevrons adorning his sleeves. It was a distinction to be a soldier instead of a slave who worked long, hot hours in sugar cane fields under the oppressive whip of the master. When the British army had decided that the black man was better adapted to the monotonous heat and rain of Dominica than the British regulars, many slaves rose to the rank of soldier.

Not too long ago, the island had been occupied by the French—or so Acoba's parents had told him. His parents still spoke in that strange tongue along with words haphazardly retained from whatever tribal African language they spoke before being enslaved and brought to this Caribbean island. Before the coming of the Europeans, Dominica had been the home to brown-skinned natives called Caribs. Now only a few remained.

There was so much Acoba did not know about Dominica, the place of his birth. The scars of agriculture and any pursuit of man were quickly erased by the verdant growth of trees. Only the names of places survived to speak of those who had come before. Just names.

Acoba did not know the meaning of his own name. He liked it, it was his, but its past was unknown. The English had started the practice of naming people to keep some kind of record. They were a conquering people of strange dichotomy. Considering themselves civilized and having the only true God, they used other human beings for their greedy end. They are just like everyone else. Acoba thought, smiling to himself.

It was all too big for him to ponder at times. Some things did not have to make sense, he supposed. They just were. That's why when the opportunity to be a soldier came, he grabbed it. He would be something more. His strong mind and stature made people take notice. It was obvious that he possessed great intelligence. He was twenty- five years old, over six feet tall and well muscled. If you looked into his large brown eyes you knew he was someone to be reckoned with. The women loved him and he took advantage of this often, spreading his seed whenever he could. How many children had he fathered? It was hard to say, but his lineage would live on.

He looked up at the Cabrits, two hills that made up the isthmus that protected Portsmouth Bay and the town. It was an ideal spot for a fort. The white man had denuded the hills of vegetation for the wooden beams that supported the ceilings of the buildings. The walls were made of stone.

To Acoba, it was a place of wonder. The beautiful walls were amazing works created by stone masons from England. They constantly worked on improving and adding to the basic structure of the fort.

Masons...now that was a breed of men...working the stones, shaping them and carefully placing them to produce eternal works of art. Acoba had wanted to learn this trade, but the slaves' place was only to mix the mortar and do the bidding of the prima donnas of art. You could tell the masons were men of pride, and were easily noticed in the crowd of white men of all trades when they went into town to drink the rum and sample the women available for their hard-earned pay.

The transition from building the fort for white soldiers to black soldiers had not been easy for the masons. The blacks were considered inferior by most white men. But shipping slaves from Africa was considered a good alternative to bringing white men from England. Only the officers were white now...and they had shoes.

Acoba turned and gazed out to sea. It was coming on evening and he loved the way the sun sent its rays into the cloudless sky that had held the day. The sea had always fascinated him and scared him at the same time. It gave life through the bounty of fish and refreshment swimming in its warm waters. He welcomed its embrace at the end of the day. But it could be quite violent and the stories of serpents and monsters told by the sailors kept a healthy fear alive in him. Good and bad always came from the sea and from mankind.

Acoba's former master had whipped him often and had sold his parents when they were older to another plantation on the island. Good men like Lt. Lincoln had immediately seen the potential in Acoba and made him a sergeant over the other black soldiers. Lt. Lincoln was a young man Acoba's own age and they had come to know each other well. They even had become friends in a way. Lt. Lincoln was far from his home and did not share the same desires as his fellow officers in pursuing fleshly pleasures or strong drink in town. Often he and Acoba would sit and talk for hours about everything from his strange God to their personal lives.

Lt. Lincoln was a Rasta, at least in Acoba's book. Rastas were a people respected by all because they truly loved everyone. They would give food, clothing and the shelter of human kindness to anyone in need. Rastas were held in high esteem by Acoba's people and, although it was not an official office, everyone knew who the Rastas were.

Lt. Lincoln must have some far distant African root he was unaware of, Acoba thought. Yes, Lt. Lincoln was a Rasta, he just didn't know it. He had even decided to teach those slaves interested to read and write. Most of the black men couldn't have cared less, but Acoba was fascinated. He had already decided that when the Brits required him to take an English name, it would be Lincoln.

The blare of a bugle shook Acoba out of his thoughts. It was time to change the guard. He stood tall and erect so that when the next shift came he would look smart and ready to salute Lt. Lincoln.

When Colonel Cornwallis appeared, Acoba was surprised. Rarely did the Colonel make his presence known. Acoba snapped a smart salute, which was returned slovenly by the Colonel.

"Sergeant Acoba you will take yourself and your entire company to my plantation this evening. That is all," Cornwallis barked.

Acoba saluted again and watched as the Colonel waddled away. Cornwallis was a glutton for food and his leisure. His body was amorphous, highly irregular in an officer, but Cornwallis was the commandant and one does not question that kind of authority.

Acoba gathered up his company and started the march towards the commandant's plantation. His soldiers had come a long way in the last year. They now marched in formation and in step. They took a lot of pride in their discipline. After all, they were the pick of the Island and Acoba considered his men the best in the regiment. He loved them all and made it a point to know each man not just by name but everything about them. They never questioned him when he gave an order. Like Acoba, they felt privileged to wear the British uniform as soldiers. They were something more now, not just beasts of burden, but a part of something. They had uniforms and duties. They had rifles and knew how to shoot them.

Acoba marched his men through the streets of Portsmouth and the slaves and people of town stopped to watch. Nothing could be grander than this. The women were clucking and ogling these splendid men, his men. It was strange, however, that Lt. Lincoln was not present and that bothered Acoba. He swallowed and lifted his chin higher. Life was grand.

When they neared the entrance to Cornwallis' plantation, another company of the 17th Regiment passed them on their way out. Their uniforms were stained with sweat and they looked dog tired. Acoba saluted his fellow sergeant as the two companies came alongside. Not a head turned. They had been trained well. Acoba marched the men to the front of the Colonel's small building. Cornwallis had a monumental house of stone at the post but preferred to stay here. He was rarely seen at the fort. No one knew if he was married, one did not ask such questions, but everyone knew he called for women from town. The soldiers made many jokes about copulating with such a fat man.

It was not Colonel Cornwallis who materialized from the building, but Captain Wilson, the adjutant. "Sergeant Acoba, have your men stack arms and then assign men to the proper tools and begin clearing the forest behind the building," he ordered.

Without question Acoba gave the relevant commands. The men worked diligently until dark, far past the normal meal time. Water that had been carried was gone and many asked to go to the stream nearby to drink. But without orders, Acoba could not let them. Finally, Captain Wilson appeared and gave the order to regroup and return to the fort. It had been a long day with guard duty and then this. The march back to the post was far from grand but the need for food and water seemed to be the only thing on everyone's mind. Sleep was immediate.

To his great relief, Acoba saw Lt. Lincoln after the morning call to breakfast. He petitioned the lieutenant to speak freely. He acquiesced, looking very surprised. When Acoba described yesterday's activities, Lt. Lincoln's face changed from surprised to stunned. The adjutant had ordered his men on an errand without his knowledge! The lieutenant became livid as Acoba described their long hours without water or food. This was a complete breach of military protocol and a personal affront to use his company without his knowledge and without his supervision. Lt. Lincoln would look into it.

Lt. Warren Lincoln had come from a family of military men and to him the military was a career and a passion. His father had been distinguished and achieved the rank of Lt. Colonel through many campaigns. His mother was a devout Christian woman and had drilled the scriptures into him. She was an adamant subscriber to charities for the poor and downcast much to his father's chagrin and pocketbook. Lt. Lincoln loved his mother and strove to be like her. Dominica was a difficult assignment, but he was determined to make his father proud and put into practice what his mother had taught him.

Then came the harsh realities of life. Despite its regiment and ceremony, the military was filled with graft and corruption just like any other part of society. He had witnessed incredibly harsh punishments for minor infractions and whipping that could almost kill a man. Like any organization, there were good officers and there were tyrants. Cornwallis was a tyrant of the highest order. Warren had to respect the man's rank, but he despised the man. He was a glutton in all the ways of the flesh, especially food. He stank of undigested food and decaying teeth. It was everything he could do not to vomit when they spoke. Cornwallis must have had connections somewhere very high because as a soldier he neither deserved the rank that was bestowed upon him nor did he take it seriously. He had acquired land near the fort and was determined to have his own plantation. This was not out of line, but it was odd that he spent all his time there and rarely came to the fort. He had acquired a few slaves and treated them horribly. It was obvious what he was up to. He used the government-paid soldiers under his command as his personal slaves to further his ends.

Lt. Lincoln visited Captain Wilson that day. Wilson was much older and his thin, gaunt face was in complete contrast to Warren's youthful features. In fact, with his long brown hair and boyish face the lieutenant looked like he could be Capt. Wilson's son.

Wilson looked over his hawkish nose at Lt. Lincoln and returned the salute as if he was too tired to pick up his arm.

"I am inquiring as to the use of my company during my absence yesterday, Captain," Lt. Lincoln said.

"First of all lieutenant, you may say it's your company but as you know this post is under the command of Colonel Cornwallis and we all are under his orders," Wilson responded.

"I understand Sir. However, it is military protocol that the chain of command be used and I be informed to the use of those under my direct command." Lincoln said.

"Well, you are duly informed, lieutenant, that your company and the two others are assigned to work on Colonel Cornwallis plantation when not on duty," Wilson said.

"This is highly irregular and the Colonel's plantation is not government business," Lt. Lincoln said.

"Dear boy," Wilson said, as he gazed into Lincoln's green eyes, "This is not a regular post and these are not regular soldiers; they are glorified slaves, nothing more."

"I object," Lt. Lincoln blurted. "I request to speak with the Commandant."

Wilson sat back in his chair. "Objection duly noted and I will deliver your request to the Commandant. In the meantime, lieutenant, you will carry out any orders issued by the Commandant. You are dismissed."

That went well, sighed Lincoln as he walked into the bright sunlight of a hot Dominican day. He must write home immediately and to Headquarters in Bristol. It was against protocol to jump command, but he did not have a good feeling about this and a letter would take months to be delivered and answered. Until then, he would just do what he could.

His request to meet with the Commandant went unanswered, but the orders to march his company to the Cornwallis' plantation to work came regularly. He had a hard time obeying this order and would often march his company in circuitous way, taking more than the normal number of breaks along the way.

The lieutenant explained everything to Acoba. As the weeks went by, it was obvious that nothing was changing and the men were grumbling. His rapport with his fellow lieutenants was not good to begin with, and for their part they saw no problems. Of course, they did not work alongside their men as Lt. Lincoln did.

When a man from another company refused to work on the plantation anymore, he was severely beaten as an example to the other soldiers. Two days later he died from his untreated wounds. Lt. Lincoln wrote letter after letter to headquarters, and to the Commandant. The Commandant completely ignored him.

Finally orders to reassign Lt. Lincoln to the marine company in Roseau came. It was a major blow to Acoba. He had truly believed the lieutenant was the answer to the problem of working such long hours for Cornwallis.

At their last meeting, the two men walked down to the wharf late at night and sat by the water. The constant breaking of the waves on the shore was the only thing that seemed never to change.

"I won't give up, I will work until this is rectified," Lt. Lincoln said, looking into Acoba's eyes.

They both turned and looked out to sea. They said nothing for a long time. Friends sometimes don't need to say anything to communicate. Acoba finally broke the silence, "You were the only thing keeping us from revolt. With you gone, I don't know what will happen."

Lt. Lincoln did not answer and Acoba continued. "I have thought about joining the Maroons, many of us have. You, my friend, have given me a glimpse of true freedom and I can't go back to being a slave now."

Maroons were escaped slaves. The island was 26 miles long and 10 wide. It did not seem possible men could escape on this small island, but the interior was almost impenetrable. Many whites had gone in pursuit of their slaves but had come back empty handed. The only thing that made people believe that these Maroons had not perished was an occasional theft of livestock or kidnapping of young slaves.

"I can't blame you for wanting to become a Maroon," Warren finally said. "Please, give me a little more time." His eyes were sad and tears glistened in their corners.

Acoba did not respond. They stood up and Acoba wrapped his black muscled arms around this little white man in an awkward embrace.

Two weeks later the soldiers of the 17th Colored Regiment took control of Fort Shirley in a well-planned coup. It was bloodless. The soldiers captured the officers in the middle of the night. In the morning, the white officers and masons were marched to the front gates minus their shoes. The regiment now had control of one of the most secure forts in the Caribbean along with arms, ammunition and supplies for at least a year. The island was in an uproar and many slaves thought this was to be emancipation. It was no surprise Acoba was selected to be their leader.

Acoba maintained discipline among the soldiers, but there was pressure to do something more. In a meeting with the other former sergeants they tried to decide what should be done next. Keya, the acknowledged second in command, wanted to comb the city and countryside, liberating all the slaves and executing the whites.

"How far do we go?" Acoba asked. "At some point the British will return and the bloodshed will be enormous."

"They would come anyway," Keya answered. "Let us die fighting like men."

Others wanted to just disband and melt into the forest with the Maroons. In the end, Acoba persuaded them to wait a little while longer.

Cornwallis wasted no time in fleeing to Roseau. There he found refuge with Governor Smith, who had been appointed by the Crown. Governor Smith was relatively new to his post but an adept man of higher learning. He was well informed and knew the situation in Portsmouth and Ft. Shirley. He also disliked Cornwallis. At his disposal were the 3rd Marine Regiment and several ships. Smith knew that he needed to contain the uprising immediately and that there was only one person capable—Lt. Lincoln.

Smith called for Lt. Lincoln and received him immediately. Lt. Lincoln did not know what to expect when he entered Governor Smith's office. He stood at attention until the door was closed. The governor smiled and Warren immediately felt at ease. Smith had a full head of dark hair and a handsome face. He and Warren were about the same height, five foot seven inches, and looked directly into each other's eyes.

Warren was given room to speak freely and he told the Governor everything he knew about the situation and Acoba. The Governor's response was both brilliant and resourceful. Lt. Lincoln would sail with the marines to Portsmouth Bay and without prejudice demand they shoulder arms. If they did as they were asked, they would be offered total amnesty. They could remain soldiers or take their freedom. If they did not shoulder arms, the lieutenant was to lay siege and upon surrender execute ever last soul in the fort. The ship left the next day.

It was the longest voyage Warren had ever made. He did not sleep or eat for the day and a half it took to reach Portsmouth Bay. The residents came out to watch as he landed. The air was thick with the electricity of foreboding and malice. The fort did not open fire with the huge 10- pound cannons that could have easily made splinters of the three ships at anchor while the marines offloaded. It was all very queer. All exits from the Cabrits were sealed off. The only thing the lieutenant could do was to attempt to open dialogue with Acoba's men. He approached the main gates with only a small squad of marines. He had chosen to wear his dress uniform and hoped that it would inspire some loyalty to the British army. When he saw Acoba approach from the gate, his heart sailed into the clouds like the huge navigator birds overhead. It was a cloudy day, humid and hot. Acoba walked alone, his uniform clean and wearing shoes. They saluted each other. Everyone was watching and in the dead silence Lt. Lincoln reached out his hand. They shook hands heartily, glad to see one another even under these tense circumstances.

"We can put an end to all of this today," Warren said. He explained the Governor's message and Acoba listened. He loved this man.

"I must go back and hold a meeting," Acoba said. "It will not take long. Can you wait?"

"Of course," Lt. Lincoln said.

As Acoba turned to go, he heard the report of the rifle from the wall and caught a glimpse of the flash. When he turned around, his friend was on the ground, blood spurting from the wound in his neck. "Cease fire!" Acoba yelled.

In a strangled voice, the lieutenant ordered his men not to return fire. Acoba knelt beside him and cradled his head in his lap.

Warren could see every blade of grass and feel every atom of wind that brushed his cheek. He looked up at Acoba and smiled as his life slipped away.

Acoba wept as he closed the lifeless eyes. He gently laid him down and walked back inside the fort gates with bloodied hands outstretched.

Later that night Acoba slipped away to the interior with his rifle, uniform and shoes. The 17th Colored Regiment would accept the terms and shoulder arms; no more blood would be shed. As for him, he had made his choice. He would be a Maroon.

Chapter 2
Allah Be Praised
March 2005

Osama looked around the austere environment that had been his home for so many months. It was the end of February in these high mountains of the Karakorum. He had never gotten used to the cold. As one of the highest ranges in the world, these mountains had always been a barrier for everyone, conqueror or trader.

He reached out and touched the cold stone walls. What a strange and majestic place this was, he thought, looking down at his now-threadbare shoes. He remembered the days when he had really nice shoes. It was hard not to reflect on better times, especially right now. Any minute, any hour, any day, the American soldiers would arrive.

George Bush had been steadily losing popularity and he needed to capture Osama to boost his political career. George Bush needed Osama Bin Laden. He needed the capture and prosecution of this most heinous criminal ever to live, at least in American eyes. And with his capture, President Bush could turn the focus away from all the other woes that besieged the United States. The Americans would be placated once again with a common villain.

Osama knew the Americans had always known where he was. George Bush was using him just like he had used George Bush. He knew that this small man did not have the ability to see beyond the tragedy of 9/11 and direct the country for its greater good. He knew that Bush would never turn against the corporate powers that put him in place. And his own family dynasty was built on oil from the Middle East. Osama chuckled at the irony of it all.

He remembered the times he had done business with the Bush family. He had worked with the Americans just as he had with the Saudis. In fact, he even recalled the time the Taliban had been invited to the governor's mansion in Texas. It was all so very strange and quirky the way life turns out. But he knew the Americans would come. There was no doubt about that.

Yes, Osama had worn better shoes. He had come from a wealthy family. He had been reared in luxury. He had been educated partially in the United States. But there was something about Osama that didn't let the wealth of the West, nor the ideology, nor the infidel freedoms, deter him from his Muslim roots. He was a true Muslim. And over and above that he was Arab. Soon he would be welcomed into the gates of heaven. He would become one of the greatest heroes in the history of the Middle East. Upon dying a martyr's death he would be immortalized forever. Of course, at the moment that was really no comfort. He was cold. Food was short. And the austere environment had begun to crowd in on him. The cave was a prison, more than the comfort it was meant to be. He wondered, why had it all come to this?

He was tired. But the anger in him lived on, fueled by his belief that the West had manipulated his people. He believed that the Americans were determined to change the very core faith of the Muslim people with their decadency. The power of the United States had infiltrated his world. The need for cheap fuel that let the Americans drive their big cars and carry on their lifestyle oblivious to the rest of the world had corrupted his people.

How had the American people, living in a country that was a beacon of freedom, been so easily duped as to become nothing more than the masses that fueled corporate greed, this corporate greed that now encompassed the entire world?

The anger still burned when he thought about it. How could the American people have let this happen? How could they not see? His rage had become all consuming and 9/11 was nothing compared to what he had in mind next. It hadn't been easy, but he had found the ultimate revenge. With funding you can do anything. And he had the funding. His family, the Saudis, other groups, were all there to help him in his cause—the destruction of the West.

Osama had been working on this project for a long time. It was a very sensitive, diabolical scheme. He planned to annihilate the people of the entire world except for the Arabic and Muslim people. Then there would be harmony. There would be only one race of people and only one religion. It was only an idea, at first. He had dreamed of producing a virus for which he had an antidote to inoculate the people of Islam, and then setting it loose to annihilate the rest of the world. If done properly, there would not be enough time for the victims to figure out how to inoculate their own people. So the quest had begun.

He had selected a site in Iran for a laboratory. He chuckled. It certainly would not have been in Iraq. He had no love whatsoever for Saddam Hussein or any other person that worked outside the Muslim faith. The fact that the American people even considered that he was in collusion with Saddam Hussein was laughable.. But of course, it was an easy sell for the Bush administration to link Osama and Hussein. Iraq had the second biggest reserve of crude oil in the world.

Additionally, Iran was off limits to the United States and most intelligence agencies. And the Iranians were glad to help him. There were many places to hide a lab in Iran. They had focused on blood. They wanted to develop a virus that would attack the blood and work quickly to kill the victim.

Osama was an intelligent man but he was not a scientist so he left it up to those qualified to work out the details. They had created a virus, but they weren't sure how it would operate or to what extent. They had not found an antidote. This was a problem. The days were numbered. Without Osama at the helm, they would be compromised eventually and the lab would be discovered. No one knew that Osama had forced the scientist in charge of the project to give him a vial of the virus. This was his ace card.

The scientist who had given him the vial had expressed grave concern. But Osama had insisted. He needed the vial as an ace card. Because the military might that was bearing down on him now was not something that he or anyone or any country in this world could resist. He needed a bargaining chip. He was in the process of making a video to be sent out on the air. It was his last hope to stave off his capture. His last chance to tear victory away from the Bush administration.

How long had it been since he bathed? He couldn't remember. He'd been in this cave so long. Of course, when you've been together with a group of men you get used to the smell. It was hard for him as a Muslim to not be clean. The one thing they had not forgotten was their daily ritual prayers. There was a red mark on the wall that indicated the direction of Mecca. They bowed in that direction three times a day. Their feet, hands and faces were supposed to be clean. That was the hard part. Fresh water was used sparingly. It was a rough existence. It was not what he wanted. It was not what he had dreamed of. It was what they had given him. THEY. He couldn't stop thinking about them...the infidels. How much he hated them. The capitalists...the Christians.... They had tried to foist their way of life on him and then wrest his riches away.

No, he was not altruistic. He did not want everyone to be happy. He wanted everyone to worship Allah. He couldn't figure out how Allah had allowed all this to happen.

Maybe I am the tool of Allah, he thought. Maybe I am Allah's soul. He looked down again at the vial. They weren't really sure what this stuff was. They hadn't had enough time to learn about it. They were working in Iran even as he spoke. But communication had been cut off. They had told him it was something that would affect the blood. And because blood had different types it would affect people differently. But even that, they weren't sure of. They did know that it was volatile and once it reacted with air it would spread across the globe at a rapid rate. In fact, they'd estimated it would cover the globe within a month.

It scared him, just a little to think that he held the future of the world in his hand. The only part of the world he really cared about was the homeland of his own people. The Muslims and Arabs. Yes, it was a diabolical plot. Only a madman would consider doing it. Osama smiled. He was a madman for Allah

He was so hungry. Oh...for a nice meal. Nice, clean clothes. How long had it been since he'd seen relatives? He couldn't remember. He sat down on a rock and leaned against the wall. He lifted up the vial and gazed at the innocuous looking liquid. He imagined the world purified of decadence.

The American people were not united against Osama. They had finally gotten tired of the fiscal drain that the war had brought and the unending line of deaths, injury and psychological trauma. They weren't sure what they were sending their sons and daughters to their deaths for anymore. This really was worse than the Vietnam War. If the war were to continue the Americans needed some sort of victory and capturing Osama would be that victory.

Osama knew they would capture him so that's why he had to make the video. That's why he had to tell the world of his plan. But of course the question remained...would they believe that he had it?

His quest to get the West to see his dilemma had been a failure. Thirty thousand people had been in the Trade Center and a few thousand had died. That was nothing compared to the hundreds of thousands of Muslims who had died in the holy war...innocent civilians, men, women, children. That didn't matter to the American people. It was Muslim blood, not American. Why was American blood so much more valuable than anybody else's? Of course, if he had his way Arab blood would reign supreme. He was tired. He was cold. He was hungry. When were his people going to get here with that video equipment?

The weather outside was bad. It was always bad up here......blizzards and cold. The cave temperature remained a constant 67 degrees Fahrenheit. It was funny...he still thought in English terms. He bent his turbaned head back against the stone wall. He started to drift off to sleep. Sleep was the only escape and it didn't come very often. He began to dream about those days when he was young and innocent. When he didn't have this consuming hatred inside of him. He thought about his mother, his brothers and sisters. It was a good feeling. Good feelings did not come often.

Suddenly, he heard the sound of machine gun fire—the U.S. soldiers had arrived. He heard the yelling. He instinctively knew what was going on. Here they were. There was no time for the video. He could not bargain. In the midst of a storm they had found him. The only thing he knew for sure, he did not want to die by the hand of an American GI. He stood up calmly. It wouldn't take them long to mow down his men. They had been here so long...so many had died...

resistance would be small. He straightened his robes and his turban. He would look his best. He held the vial in his hand.

The American soldiers burst into the cave. Time stood still. A soldier looked at him. He had to know that this was Osama. This wasn't Saddam Hussein hiding in a hole in the ground pleading for his life. This was Osama Bin Laden. Osama stood erect and looked the soldier straight in the eye.

"Get down on the floor!" Sergeant Miller yelled. He really hadn't been prepared for this. Osama stood there straight and erect. He did not obey.

"I will shoot," Sgt. Miller said, although he knew he had orders not to shoot Osama Bin Laden if at all possible. Osama didn't have a weapon. Osama and the soldier just looked at each other for what seemed like forever.

Finally Lt. Kennedy came around the corner. Lt. Kennedy was in the Special Forces and was a very educated man. The Special Forces typically drew upon the educated populace especially for their officers. He was one of the elite. He hadn't been with the Special Forces that long....six years. Long enough to be hardened. He knew what was going on. He knew what was going to happen to Osama Bin Laden. He too ordered Osama to go down on the floor. Osama did not budge. He had a peculiar look in his eyes. Almost a glaze. Maybe he really was a madman, Lt. Kennedy thought.

There was a small smirk on Osama's face. The corners of his mouth curled up. He lifted up the small glass vial. He looked both soldiers in the eye. "Allah be praised!" he shouted. He smashed the vial on the stone floor.

Almost immediately Sergeant Miller began to breathe more rapidly. It was as if he couldn't get enough air. A look of fear came into his eyes. His breath came harder and harder. He couldn't get enough air. He dropped to his knees.

Lt. Kennedy looked down at him. He ordered him to get back up. He couldn't respond. He was breathing so hard he couldn't speak. As the other soldiers arrived some of them also began to breathe rapidly. Osama stood erect, looking proud. There was a gleam in his eyes still. He stared at the soldier on his knees and at the lieutenant, who did not seem to be affected. He didn't know exactly how the virus was going to affect these people. He wanted them dead. He thought he would die first.

Lt. Kennedy stepped forward and knocked Osama across the head with the butt of his rifle. Osama fell to the floor. Lt. Kennedy put his foot on his neck. "What the hell was in that vial?" he yelled.

Osama did not respond. He would never respond to infidels.

About this time, Sgt. Miller passed out on the floor. Corporal Scott ran into the room and reported to Lt. Kennedy. "The cave is secure, sir, but there seems to be a problem. People are passing out."

Lt. Kennedy was not prepared for a situation like this. "Tie that son of a bitch up over there," he said. "That's Osama Bin Laden. I'll get on the radio and call in for Med Vac immediately."

The lieutenant kept his rifle aimed at Osama. They tied Osama's hands. No one cared how tight. The son of a bitch was going to hurt. Lt. Kennedy went to the entrance of the cave and called Med Vac for the soldiers that had passed out. What the hell was going on, he wondered.

Most of the terrorists that had not been shot initially had passed out. Lt. Kennedy didn't know what to do. He just knew they needed to get out of there.

By the time the helicopter showed up, all those that had passed out, both terrorists and American GIs were dead. The medic was still working but when asked for information just stared blankly. He had no idea what was going on. Why were these people passing out and dying. Obviously, they were suffering from a lack of oxygen, but why? And why did it affect some people and not everyone?

Lt. Kennedy wasn't sure what to do. Should he quarantine the area? He called into headquarters on the radio. Since this was not a standard request it would take a tremendous amount of time to encode the message. And then a long time to get a response from headquarters. He aborted the encoding and just called. The response did not come initially. Of course, he was not surprised since he did not use radio protocol. But when it came the response was simple. "Remove the dead and the living. Blow the cave. Return to base. We will quarantine the people here." They set the dynamite charges and as the helicopters took off just as the whole side of the mountain caved in.

They barely made it into the air and Lt. Kennedy heard someone gasping on the radio "Can't get air," As he looked to the right, an Apache Escort helicopter, a machine worth $40 million dollars veered to the right and crashed into the mountain. It was just the first. One of the transport helicopters also veered and smashed into the mountain. Fortunately, the pilot of Lt. Kennedy's aircraft was still alive. They headed directly for base. Once again, Lt. Kennedy broke protocol. "Mayday!" Mayday!" he barked into the radio. "We are carrying a biological agent. Make appropriate arrangements at the air field."

Just then Corporal Scott kicked Osama right in the teeth.

"At ease, soldier, what are you doing?" Lt. Kennedy yelled.

"That son of a bitch," Scott growled. They could barely restrain him as he lunged toward Osama, who smiled through crushed teeth. Now he knew what the virus would do to the world.

"What the fuck have you done? You asshole," Lt. Kennedy yelled at Osama.

Osama smirked. "You will never know.... infidel."

There was general mayhem in all the cockpits and all the transport ships. Soldiers were fighting, mostly assaulting the prisoners, the perfect target of their anger. But they also were fighting among themselves.

Chaos was breaking out in the cockpit. He didn't know if they would make it to the air field. He drew out his bayonet and held it to Osama's neck.

"Now, you son of a bitch," he growled. "You are going to tell us what is going on or I'll kill you right here."

"You are already dead and so am I," Osama said. "You pathetic American."

They were approaching base camp rapidly. But it was unclear whether the pilot could maintain order long enough to land the helicopter. He was yelling and screaming. Lt. Kennedy went forward. Looking down at the base he could see people running in all directions. He could see bodies on the ground. Whatever had hit them preceded them all the way to the base. He didn't know what to do. He went back into the cargo area. Corporal Scott was looking at him. Corporal Scott was a young black soldier from Mississippi. He was an ideal soldier, in top physical condition. He was a person who would rise to the top but the look in his eye at this moment was different from anything Lt. Kennedy had ever seen. It was just pure rage. He lunged at Lt. Kennedy.

Lt. Kennedy fended him off and pushed him to the ground. "What the fuck is going on here! At ease!" he screamed. He heard Osama laughing. The chopper hit the ground with a hard smash. It came to a spinning stop.

The doors were yanked open and hands reached in. They pulled Osama out and began to beat him mercilessly. They beat him to a pulp. He would surely die. Lt. Kennedy was appalled. He looked on in horror. He ran around the side of helicopter and headed toward headquarters. To his left he saw a female soldier being chased by a male soldier. She was pulled to the ground and raped. It was hideous to see what was going on! Stepping over the bodies he turned the corner only to be hit by small arms fire. It hit his protective vest and knocked him to the ground.

The last thing he heard was the butt of a rifle crushing his skull.

Chapter 3
Celtic Wind
March 2005

The seas finally calmed. Gary Llewellyn wasn't really a seaman at heart. But he was enjoying this trip. It was badly needed. At 31 years old, he'd already managed to earn several degrees and establish himself as a successful biochemist. But his work had taken a toll on him and his marriage with Amy. This voyage was to be the rejuvenation of their relationship. This was a trip of a lifetime.

It had been a long voyage. As Canadian citizens, Gary and Amy were used to the cold. But nothing could have prepared them for the cold they had experienced that January as they made their way down the St. Lawrence River. They headed south, using the winds and the Gulfstream to get them closer to their destination, the Caribbean.

Ahhh....the Caribbean...just the thought of it...going from island to island soaking up the sun, doing nothing but exploring and enjoying each other. That's what this trip was about.

But it had been a stormy voyage. Their only comfort had been the shoreline of North. America as they worked their way south from place to place. The sea was not Gary's choice for an extended vacation. It was Amy's. She grew up near the ocean and her life had always circled around the sea. Her father was a fisherman. Despite moving to the city to become a powerful attorney, she retained a passion for the sea and sailing.

Gary had learned everything he could about sailing before they left. He studied books and videos, but this voyage had been on-the-job training in terms of hands-on experience. After a bit of seasickness, he'd recovered and found his sea legs.

He looked out over the calm ocean. The sun was setting. They were getting close to the Caribbean islands they had so looked forward to visiting. They wanted to visit the original islands that Columbus had discovered. These islands had a history more ancient than any in North America.

Buying the boat had been a big decision for Gary, but not for Amy. Money wasn't a concern. His job as a professor and Amy's career as a lawyer generated plenty of income. But the decision to sell their home, buy a boat and make this long voyage was a difficult one. Gary hadn't been sure he wanted to spend so much time at sea, away from his work.

He was used to traveling. When he was younger he had traveled back to his native home of Wales. What a wonderful trip that had been. He had loved meeting the Celtic people from whom he descended. The Welsh were the oldest of the Celtic people. They were not quite as rambunctious as the Irish or as obvious as the Scottish. The Welsh were a peace-loving people and in their way had an impact on the world. The most striking thing about the Welsh people was that they loved to sing. Gary loved to sing as well and had a sweet baritone voice. It must be in his genetic code. Gary had felt a kinship and connection with the land of Wales. He had walked Clybr Glendyr, otherwise known as Glendurs Way, an ancient foot path that crossed the country. He learned a bit of the Welsh language, the language of the Cymru. Despite their subjugation by the English for so many years, the Welsh had kept their native tongue alive.

Gary's deep blue eyes gazed out across the tranquil ocean. He didn't have anything against the English, even though they had subjugated his ancestors. In fact, he had married an English girl, Amy. Her skin was pale, contrasting with her dark hair and her youthful smile. She was quite a bit older than he and more experienced sexually.

They had tried to have children, but were unable to. After many tests, they learned the problem lay with Amy, causing some strain on their marriage. Gary had wanted a family. But being childless had allowed them both to focus on their careers and now they could afford a trip such as this. And so here they were on a trip of a lifetime.

Gary didn't enjoy the raging seas or storms. But he did enjoy the cool calm evenings when he could curl up next to Amy at anchor in a safe harbor and enjoy the warmth of her body. He truly loved her and she truly loved him. This voyage was an opportunity for them to re-connect. It was also an opportunity for him to think. And boy there was a lot to think about in this world that was constantly changing.

Gary had always been politically active. He had even run for a local government office a time or two unsuccessfully. Politics was often on his mind and he shared his ideas with his colleagues and friends. They often talked about political issues in the States. How could a country so powerful, so knowledgeable, a country which had sent a man to the moon, not provide basic health care for the people?

Canada had a health plan. It may not be the best plan in the world but it was working. How is it that a country like the United States couldn't take such a plan and make it better? Of course, the answer was obvious. It all had to do with corporate greed and the medical profession. It wasn't a matter of providing care. It was about making money. The people of the United States were buying their prescription drugs in Canada because they were cheaper, even though the drugs often were manufactured in the States.

The Americans were so full of themselves. They weren't humble enough to look inward and say, "We can do better." They didn't seem to have the drive to call for change and to use their power for good. Everything seemed to be corrupted by corporate greed...politics, economics, even religion. The decisions of the government were not based on what was good for the environment or the people or education. Only decisions that would to fill the pocket books of large corporations carried any weight. And the corporations were trying to gobble each other up. Slowly, individual businesses were becoming one gigantic mega corporation that controlled not only the money but the very lives of the people. A clear example of this was industrial hemp. Canada had seen the usefulness of this plant. Hemp had been grown everywhere in the world but its cultivation had come to a stop after the '30s, when petroleum had come on the market.

But Canada had again begun to grow hemp. They realized there was a difference between marijuana and industrial hemp. This difference was easily identified. Yet the United States was the one country in the entire world that did not recognize this difference. Farmers could not grow it in the States. It was illegal. It wasn't really a drug issue. Industrial hemp threatened the paper industry. You can produce more paper with one acre of industrial hemp than you can with 30 acres of trees.

Also, the textile industry could make stronger more durable clothing from hemp than cotton. Probably most importantly, the cultivation of industrial hemp threatened the petroleum industry because of the tremendous potential for biodiesel and biodegradable plastics.

It was laughable to watch the Americans keep this wonderful plant from being utilized under the guise of narcotics issues. It was typical and sad.

The Americans were too busy suing each other and only the law community really benefited. In a lot of ways it reminded Gary of ancient Rome. In its day, Rome had kept the people pacified with cheap food and entertainment. The people turned out in droves to watch games, gladiators and chariot races. Not too different now. The United States had patterned itself after the Roman Senate and Plebian Council. They had also figured that as long as they kept the masses satisfied, the people wouldn't ask questions. As long as the people were entertained by video games, sports events, ridiculous sitcoms and silly movies, they wouldn't have to time to really think. As long as they had cheap petroleum for their cars they weren't going to ask the important questions. They weren't going to press the point. They weren't going to make the changes that needed to be made.

Ahh....he shook his head. It was hard to believe. But it was happening right in front of their eyes. In Canada they were often astounded by the way Americans acted and reacted. And yet, in a lot of ways, America and Canada were the same. The whole world was becoming homogenous. It was becoming typical for huge corporations to move in to third-world countries and use the people for labor. Nobody stood up and protested. Nobody said a word. It was just a matter of time, though, before this volatile world retaliated against corporate America. Even now the United States was in a war whose purpose was supposedly to spread democracy. America was sinking deeper into debt trying to impose the policies generated by corporate business. The blood of America's sons and daughters stained the ground.

Gary shook his head, enough of these thoughts. He needed to learn to enjoy the moment and to see the beauty that was. At 5 foot 9, with light brown hair with a tinge of red, he was a strikingly handsome man. He was not muscular, but he was fit. His efforts had been primarily aimed toward education and learning. He loved learning. He loved technology and science. And although he was a believer in Jesus Christ, he didn't adhere to any particular religion. His family had long since strayed from the conservative Christian background of the old country of Wales.

Amy's family was Catholic and she retained the guilt and conscience that was so predominant in that religion. She was slightly taller than Gary, a well bosomed woman, with green eyes. They had a good physical relationship.

He heard rustling down in the cabin below. He knew it was Amy getting up from a nap. She would be up soon. On a night like this, when the sea was so calm, it was time to break out the wine. They would have dinner and enjoy the sunset together.

They had sailed south and west after passing the Virgin Islands in their 30-foot sloop. The boat was well equipped with the latest navigating devices. They knew they were east of the islands of Guadeloupe, Dominica and Martinique. It was their intention to visit all three. But of particular interest to Gary was the island of Dominica. Different from all the rest, Dominica was largely undeveloped. It was said that it was the only island Columbus would recognize if he were to return. It had been under British control for many years and now had an independent government. Although there were many old plantations on the islands, the island had not been denuded like other islands. It had not become a tourist destination simply because it was a rugged island with few beaches and occasional volcanic activity. They would go to Dominica first. In fact, they would probably see land anytime in the next day or two.

Amy came out of the cabin, smiling. It was one of those peaceful moments. Her life as an attorney was hectic. She had been a driven woman, particularly in her 20s. Now at 39 she was ready to relax a little bit. She was ready to do some of the things she probably should have done when she was younger. She looked at Gary. He was already starting to tan. She was envious. Her pale white skin burned so easily. But she copiously put sunscreen on and made the best of it. She gave Gary a hug. They kissed and held each other for a long time.

Gary put the steering on automatic and they sat down together, just looking out at the sea. Once in a while they would see the surfacing of a large fish. It was amazing that the sea was so full of life even after so much fishing and so much pollution. It gave them hope that the earth was not destined for desolation. He got up and went down in the cabin and picked out another bottle of Merlot, Amy's favorite. He brought the glasses and the bottle up and poured them both a glass.

"Is there any man as lucky as I?" he often said. Even though he had had not wanted to go on a voyage of this magnitude, now that they were in the Caribbean, he knew they had made the right move. He looked down at his feet. He hadn't worn shoes for two weeks now. It felt good. In fact, the whole ideas of shoes gave him a feeling of restriction. Being barefoot gave him a feeling of openness, of freedom and he luxuriated in it. He put his feet next to Amy's and they curled them together. He loved the feeling of skin on skin.

Amy put down her glass as a small breeze fluffed the sail above them. "When do you think we will get to Dominica?" she asked.

"Soon," Gary answered. "Maybe even tomorrow."

God, he loved this woman. He wanted to take her right now. As he reached out to her, she suddenly looked uneasy. Her breathing became rapid. But despite her breathing, she didn't seem to be getting any oxygen. She gave him a shocked look.

"What's wrong honey?" he asked.

"I can't get air," she gasped.

"Do you think it's the humidity?" he asked. But then she passed out.

Gary was frantic. He tried artificial respiration. He tried to rouse her, but he couldn't. She began to have convulsions and foamed at the mouth. Gary was frantic. He tried to give her cardiopulmonary resuscitation but despite his efforts she would not breathe. In about

10 minutes she was dead. He was beside himself. He didn't know what to do. He had no idea what had happened. He must have taken her pulse twenty times in the next fifteen minutes. He tried to resuscitate her for a half an hour; her body was already turning cold. Even if he got to shore he knew that it was too late. Amy was dead.

How could this have happened? Was something lodged in her throat? Why couldn't she breathe? He didn't know what to do. So he did nothing. He sat down next to her body, stroking her hair. It had all happened so fast.

They had not been in radio contact with the outside world for quite a while. And they had made it a point not to listen to the radio or the news. Now he felt so isolated. Amy was all he had needed. And now that she was gone, he was so alone. He sat there all night, stroking her hair.

Should he keep the body, he wondered. What was the proper procedure? He had no idea. He was lost. Should he surrender her to the waves? He was totally unsure. A sense of hopelessness surrounded him. His whole life had changed and he didn't even know why. The next morning the sun came up and with the sun came the heat. It was obvious he could not keep Amy aboard the ship much longer. He wrapped her in the best blanket they had. He anointed her head with her finest perfume, weeping, his tears dropping on her lifeless body. When the time came to lift her overboard, he was weak from sadness and wasn't sure if this was the way it should end. Finally, late in the afternoon, he gave himself permission to go ahead. He dropped her body carefully over the side. He watched it slowly bob and then sink beneath the waves.

He thought about getting the .45 they had on board, an old army pistol, and ending his life as well. Why even bother going back? He loved Amy and at this point he didn't feel like there was any reason to live.

He went down into the cabin and picked up the gun. He looked at it for a long time. It would be simple. Whoever found the boat would find his corpse and would see the obvious head wound. No one would know what happened. Maybe he should write it down? He went back on deck and that's when he saw land. He could see the outline of Dominica in the distance, rugged and mountainous against the horizon. Maybe it was the sight of land, maybe it was the desire to live no matter what, but he decided not to commit suicide. He would tell the authorities what happened, sell the boat and go home. He would teach his classes and maybe life would go on. But he didn't know if he would ever understand what had happened. He went below and put the gun away, went back on deck and sat by the tiller. He watched the mountains slowly grow larger.

Chapter 4
Far and Away
March 2005

Jungsuk walked out on the balcony of their small apartment and looked out over the city of Roseau just coming awake in the morning light. Roseau was an ancient city on a wonderful island called Dominica. What a strange series of events had brought her to this place, she thought.

She wiggled her toes in her thongs, thinking. It had been a long time since she'd worn shoes. It was so pleasant here in the winter months. Korea seemed like such a long ways away now. So far away

She'd grown up in a wealthy Korean family. Her maiden name was Jungsuk Go. American GIs had been ever present in her life. They were always on the TV. The GIs were constantly traveling their roads. Korea had been occupied by the Americans for a very long time. Most of the people felt secure because of it. But the occupation had had a huge impact on her culture. The GIs ran freely around the country and as a result there were many orphans of mixed blood. Her native Korean people didn't accept these mixed-blood children. Many of the children born from these unions went unrecognized and were put into orphanages. The GIs did support the orphanages, but still they had no home.

Jungsuk's family wealth allowed her the opportunity to go to school anywhere in the world. Her parents chose a college in the United States for her. It was a small college in the state of Washington. It was a school they could afford and one that had good qualifications. It was there that she had learned English quite well. You would think that she would have met an American and fallen madly in love, but she did not. She knew Americans already. She didn't dislike Americans but she had seen firsthand the impact they had had on her country. And living in the States did nothing to change her opinion of these people. These were a people who were on top of the world economically, but ignorant of the rest of the world. The wealth of the United States seemed false to her. Americans had become lethargic with their work ethic. They had become apathetic in their passion for self government. It seemed like as long as they had amusement, cheap gas, and a car in the garage it really didn't matter who was in office. They did not have the passion Jungsuk did for learning and more importantly, the desire to grow and change.

She met her love in Washington. He was studying abroad too. He was from Taiwan, nationalist China. His parents had also sent him to the United States to get an education and learn English. They found each other almost immediately. They had already felt alone because they were from another country and their English was poor. The fact that they were in the same situation, threw them together even faster than the physical attraction.

Tien See Tung was his name. Jungsuk thought he was related to the great Mao. but he denied any connection. He was charming young man, well mannered and also had the same ambitious nature that Jungsuk had. They fell madly in love. Meeting each other's parents had been difficult. Fortunately, each set of parents had come to the U.S. to visit. This gave Jungsuk and Tien the opportunity to introduce their parents to one another in the American setting, so that both families were on unfamiliar turf. This lessened the tension. Neither set of parents approved of the marriage. They considered it a mixed marriage, an unnatural joining of Korea and China.

Eventually both sets of parents came to accept the union. At least their children would be Asian. Tien and Jungsuk had finished their education and then had married. Their wedding had been a big, lavish affair. They had to spend time in both Korea and China so that their relatives could get to know one another and meet the new spouse.

Jungsuk and Tien decided to settle in Taiwan, where Tien's family was well established in political circles. When there came a need for an English-speaking ambassador to the small island of Dominica, Tien was asked and accepted the post.

Dominica and Taiwan had been friends now for 25 years. It had been a good relationship. Taiwan never exerted any more economical clout over this small country than was necessary. The trade between the two countries had been free. However, things were changing. In Dominica, the Blue Party that had been in office throughout the good years of the relationship with Taiwan was in the process of being dethroned by the Red Party. The Red Party wasn't necessarily communist. But the Red Chinese government had been making overtures to the Red Party. They had promised money to develop the island. This was attractive to some of the Dominicans. Development could become an avenue to make some people very wealthy. The Red Party was making inroads. The Blue Party was trying to hold onto the friendship with Taiwan. They knew that if the Red Party came into power, they would accept money from Red China and develop a diplomatic relationship with them. Then the ties with Taiwan would have to be severed. So this is how Jungsuk and Tien had come to live in this beautiful island paradise.

Jungsuk was a lucky lady at the tender age of 25. She had traveled far and seen so much. She had a loving husband. At five foot seven she was tall for a Korean. She had beautiful creamy white skin now turning dusky brown in the Caribbean sun. She had beautiful almond shaped brown eyes and jet black hair that hung long over her shoulders, almost to her waist. Men turned their heads when Jungsuk walked down the street. She kept herself in great shape too. She studied Taoism and had blended this ancient philosophy with Christianity and Buddhism from her home country. She meditated. She practiced yoga and Tai Chi. She was the picture of physical fitness and peace. When you were around Jungsuk you couldn't help but feel peace and she gathered friends quickly among the Dominicans. She loved the Dominicans and their way of life, full of celebration.

Carnival had ended not too long ago. Carnival was the celebration of the Dominicans emancipation from slavery. The Dominicans sang and danced in the streets for three days. Everyone joined in. The smell of ganja smoke filled the air. Jungsuk enjoyed the ganja when she could. Her husband did not approve. But it gave her that euphoric feeling, that sense of loving kindness toward all people. Yah…man.

They were a wonderful, loving people and they showered their love on Jungsuk and she returned that love.

This morning, as she listened to the sounds of Roseau awakening she felt peaceful. But the peace was shattered by the clanging of a trash can being overturned. She looked down into the alley. It was Roland, her neighbor. He lay sprawled in the street. Roland was a Rasta man, totally loving and harmless. He smoked ganja all the time. Had he passed out because he was high? She wondered. He didn't seem to be moving.

"Roland! Are you ok?" she called out. He didn't answer.

She turned to go back into the house. She had to go down to the street and check on Roland. Then she heard her husband call out to her. He had been in the bedroom dressing. He always looked his best when he went to the government house. She went into the bedroom. Tien lay on the bed, breathing rapidly. "I can breathe. I can't get air," he gasped.

She ran to him. He passed out. She tried to revive him. She knew CPR. But it didn't seem to be doing any good. She checked his pulse. It was weak. Without air he would die very soon. She ran back to the window. "Help! I need help!" she screamed. But she saw no one. She tried the phone. There was no dial tone. She went back to her husband. Tien now was turning blue. It wouldn't be long. She had to do something. She ran down the stairs and out into the street. "Help me! Help me! Somebody help me!" But all she heard were the screams of other people yelling for help. What's going on, she thought frantically. She ran back upstairs. Tien was dead.

She heard more shouting, more screaming. She heard gun shots and that frightened her even more. Guns weren't allowed on Dominica although everyone knew that some people had them. She ran to her window. There were people screaming out their windows. What's going on? She wondered.

She stood on the balcony unable to decide what to do. Should she check on the neighbors? She went out into the street. She looked right, and then left down the street. She saw no one. She continued to hear shouts from all the buildings. Then a car turned the corner. It was going fast. She saw that the driver was looking right at her.

He aimed his car at her! She dived back inside the doorway just as it brushed by and scraped the building. It swerved back onto the road and headed around the corner. She'd never seen anything like that. She knocked on her neighbor's door. There was no answer. She knocked again. She turned the knob. It was open and she went inside. Her two neighbors, an elderly couple she had known since she moved in, were on the floor, they had turned blue too. Obviously the same thing that had happened to Tien had happened to them.

As if in a dream, she went back to her home, walked up the stairs and sat on a chair that looked out over the balcony. Something strange was going on that she did not understand and there was nothing she could do about it. Her husband had died so quickly. It was hard to believe that he was even dead.

The screams continued. There were more gun shots. People were driving through the streets crazily. People were chasing one another. What to do...What to do....she thought over and over. She must hide. She thought about the church. Surely she could find sanctuary there. She grabbed some food, ran out the door and headed toward the church. It was an old stone Anglican church that had been there for centuries. She had met the minister on occasion. She and Tien hadn't been members, but the minister was always nice to her. She went up to the doors and pushed them open. It seemed vacant, dim and quiet. She went to the back of the church. There was no one there either. Maybe she could just stay here. She would sit in a pew and wait. See what else happened. She sat down. She must have sat there for 45 minutes. She could still hear screams outside. It just wouldn't quit! Then she heard yelling outside the church door. She decided to take a peak. The minister was yelling at a man who was raping a woman right there in the street. He was saying, "Stop this! Stop this! What has come over you?" When he did not stop, the minister grabbed the man and pulled him off the woman. At that moment the woman got up and lunged at the minister and scratched his face with her nails. He stepped back in horror. She lunged at him again and he pushed her away. Then the man jumped on him from behind and pulled him to the ground. They pummeled him with their hands. The woman scratched him. He fought like an animal to get away and every time he got up they dragged him down. It was horrible to watch. Jungsuk didn't know what to do. Should she help the minister? She ran back and grabbed the candelabra on the altar. She ran out the church door and swung it over her head, hitting the man attacking the minister. She swung again and hit the female. They both went down. The minister jumped up and grabbed her. They ran for the church. They entered the door, and shoved the heavy bolt in place from the inside, locking it.

"What is going on? I don't understand it, these people are assaulting each other for no reason whatsoever!" the minister cried.

"My husband is dead," Jungsuk sobbed. "And many others too. They can't breathe and then they pass out. They breathe but they don't get air!"

"What are we going to do?" the minister asked. He was a small skinny black man, named John. He wore wire-rimmed glasses.

"I don't know," Jungsuk replied. "I don't know what to do. My husband is dead and people are going crazy!"

John looked at her. "I have to do what I can to stop this in the name of Jesus. You stay here and hide." He took her back behind the altar and showed her a small compartment that had been reserved for the sacraments. She crawled inside.

"Don't make a sound," John said. "If anyone comes in here don't let them know you are here." Then he left. It was dark in the compartment. But fortunately the screams outside were muffled. She tried to sleep, but couldn't. All she could do was lie in the darkness and listen to the faint screams outside. She didn't even have time to grieve for her husband.

John never came back.

Chapter 5
Her Loving Ways
March 2005

Neville walked slowly down the shaded road toward Gran Fon. He was on his way home once again to visit with his mother. Annette had 10 children, of which Neville was the middle child. They had all moved away, even as far as the United States, London and to other islands in the Caribbean. But they would always return to Dominica to see Mother.

She was the kind of woman everyone loved. Her bosom was big enough to enfold anyone she came in contact with. Everyone knew by her warm embrace that she genuinely loved. Some referred to her as a Rasta woman. Being a Rasta was about love and connection to the land.

Neville looked up at the sky between the leaves of the coconut trees. At 27 he was six feet tall and a good looking man. But a deep restlessness shone in his eyes. Even though his childhood in Gran Fon had been a happy one, he'd always felt the need to experience new things and explore new places. He often wondered what life was all about. He had wandered around the island, taking higher educational courses when he could. He had worked on almost all the islands in the Caribbean. He was fluent in French, English and the local patois. He had worked as far away as the Virgin Islands. In spite of the rich materialism of those U.S. territories he did not find any more peace and happiness there. He always seemed to come back to Dominica. There was peacefulness here. He could rest and feel still in Gran Fon at his mother's house.

His restless nature had driven him toward spirituality and recently he had decided to become a Rastafarian. He was still learning about the religion and everyone seemed to have a different interpretation about what being a Rasta meant. It was a rebellious religion. It was for the black man only, but preached peace, love and unity. It seemed to Neville that the main leader was a king in Ethiopia who was supposed to be God incarnated but yet had died. This puzzled Neville. Ganja was the centerpiece of this very new religion, Ganja and her loving ways gave the Rastafarians a way to connect to the land, to one another and to the unity of all things. Just about everyone smoked Ganja on the island. No one was quite sure where this wonderful plant had come from, but they had learned of its beneficial effects quickly. Bob Marley, the legend, had made Ganja a beacon of hope for the black man and showed him how to live in love and harmony with all living things. When Neville was high, as he was now, he didn't have that restlessness that usually pervaded his being. When he smoked Ganja he felt everything strongly—the view through the trees that lined the road deep into the jungle, the sweet smell of flowers. He felt love everywhere and that love was all that mattered. He felt that way right now. As people passed him on the road they stopped to pick him up. But he waved them on with love brimming in his heart. He just wanted to walk today, that's all, just walk.

Neville didn't have much materially. He had the clothes on his back and he wore whatever footwear he was given by Christian missions. He really didn't have a place to live. But on Dominica one didn't need much. The temperature stayed a constant 70 to 90 degrees year round so he never really got cold. And he enjoyed the feeling of the rain as it softly pattered on his light brown skin. His dreadlocks had a grown to his shoulders in only two years since becoming a Rastafarian. He was proud of his dreadlocks encircling his face. They gave him a wild, yet dignified air. He didn't think he would ever be sure what it really meant to be a Rastafarian. But it was partly the mystery that appealed to him, and it brought peace to his restless nature.

His ancestry was complicated. He was mixture of many people, many tribes from Africa and he might have had Carib Indian blood in his veins from the native people of the island. And of course there was always the possibility he had European blood from the former slave owners who took what they wanted from their female slaves.

His ancestry didn't matter anymore. The black man was free in Dominica. It was a blessed country.

A man could live wherever he wanted in the vast forest reserves in the interior of the island. The elders of his family said that at one time his ancestors had been Maroons hiding up in the forests. His mother told him he got the last name Lincoln from his Maroon ancestors. Lincoln was a strange name for a Dominican. But Neville liked it. He was proud to call himself Neville Lincoln.

He thought about his mother again. She would once again ask him if he had found a wife yet. She would ask when he was going to have children so she could have more grandchildren. She loved children. Neville had had many relationships and had sired children on the islands where he had worked. But he wasn't ready to settle down. His mother accepted him. Like most Dominicans, she felt that what religion a person was did not matter. Dominicans accepted everybody whether their religion be the conservative Anglican church that the English had brought or the strange Rastafarian religion that he now embraced. Annette just loved him. He was always glad to go home and see her. She was an anchor in a sea of life that was often stormy and without sight of land. She was that land.

His father had died some years ago. He'd been a hard working man. He had scratched a living picking cinnamon bark. He grew cocoa and fruit trees and sold the fruit. He had provided well for his children and was a good and loving father. Neville smiled as he saw his father in his mind's eye. He had been much smaller than Annette. It had been comical to see them together But they loved each other... you could tell that. He missed his father.

He continued walking along the road. A large snail caught his eye, moving slowly through the grass. It seemed to him that he was like that snail moving slowly down a very long road. Lately he had been working for a man named Fred in Wooten Waven. Fred had come from Tennessee. He had found his Shangri La in Wooten Waven and was building a small resort of bamboo cottages. He had his own waterfall and a hot sulphur spring. A beautiful river flowed through his property. Like all the rivers on Dominica, it came straight from the mountain tops pure and clean. You could drink the water right out of the river.

Fred had dreamed of this place long before he found it and bought the land. He had big plans for the place and was sure he could respect the island's beauty and make a profit. It had been amusing to the Dominicans to watch Fred transform from a driven ambitious man, full of the materialistic ideals of the United States, to someone who had given in to the softer ways of the island and its atmosphere of acceptance. When Fred had first arrived he worked nonstop, trying to inspire his workers to do the same. But as time went by, you could see him change into someone who accepted that things didn't have to get done right away. When Fred began smoking Ganja, his acceptance of a slower pace of life became even stronger. He had learned Ganja's loving ways and began to understand the true meaning of tranquility.

Neville reached up and straightened his tam. He was proud of his knit cap of black, red and yellow, the characteristic colors of the Rastafarians.

Ah...what a day it was, he thought. He came to an opening in the trees and gazed out on the Atlantic side of the island. He didn't have too far to go now to Gran Fon. He noticed a large cargo ship in the distance. It was heading across the violet-blue water toward the rocky Atlantic shore. This was quite unusual, since most ships docked on the Caribbean side of the island, where there was refuge from the storms and the harbors were deeper. This ship seemed to be bearing straight toward the shore. He watched it with curiosity. He sat down and rolled another ganja cone as the ship approached the shore, never wavering in its course. As he watched, it sailed into Rosalie Bay. Oddly, the ship did not seem to cut its speed as it entered the bay. Neville watched it head toward shore with a puzzled frown. What could the captain of this ship be thinking? He took a deep drag on the cone and the sound of a parrot behind him in the jungle distracted him. Dominica was truly a bountiful land, he thought. The euphoric feeling that came over him after he smoked a cone made him close his eyes and smile. He felt like nothing else mattered in the whole world but this wonderful feeling and this beautiful island.

He loved all the animals, plants and trees that surrounded him. His heart swelled with pleasure as he thought about seeing his mother and telling her he loved her. Neville knew he was mother's favorite. She would never say that, but he knew it all the same. Neville was her wandering, restless son and she loved him best. You could see it in her eyes when she looked at him. This evening they would sit at her table and they would talk.

A slight wind was blowing from the east today and it moved his dreadlocks, slowly caressing his cheek. He continued to watch the ship. He frowned once more. It didn't seem to be slowing at all. Now he was becoming concerned even a bit frightened. It seemed like hours had passed since he sat down to smoke a cone and watch the ship. It seemed unreal as the huge cargo ship plowed straight into the bay and incredibly beached itself on shore. Neville jumped up, totally surprised. Now this was different! He must investigate this strange thing. He walked quickly toward the bay. When he reached the beached ship, the shore was empty of people. Why hadn't anyone come to rescue? he wondered. The waves crashed against the ship's stern. The huge ship was totally beached like a giant unfortunate whale. Why had the captain drove his ship clear up into the shore? And what was such a huge ship doing on this side of the island?

He approached the ship cautiously. He yelled out, "Hello! Hello!" No response. He felt uneasy and swallowed. What was going on? There must be a way to get on the ship, he thought, even though the sides were very steep. Then he heard some movement up on the deck. Neville melted back into the foliage. For some reason, he felt the need to watch without being seen. Men appeared on deck. They were yelling, fighting and hitting each other violently. Several men suddenly jumped overboard into the ocean. They were swept by the surf and washed against the boat. They struggled to shore yelling and trying to hit one another all the while. Neville kept hidden. There was something not right about this whole situation. The men continued their fight on shore and when there was no obvious winner they ran into the forest toward town. Neville sat for a long time. There was no more movement or sound on the ship. He decided he wanted to board the ship to investigate. No one else had appeared. That was odd. There should be a crowd of people who had come to see what had happened. He had to come up with a plan. He sat for a long time contemplating how he would get on board this ship. The bow had been hopelessly dug deep into the sandy shore of the bay. When the tide went out perhaps he could throw a rope over the anchor that hung lifeless from the upper deck and climb aboard. That would mean he would have to get a rope. He looked around. There were several houses. He would ask. So he headed for the nearest house. No one was home. He went into the shed where the fishing equipment was stored and he found a good rope. He wound it around his shoulder and went back to the ship to wait for the tide to go out. When the tide finally did go out he tied the rope in a noose and attempted to lasso the anchor. He wasn't a cowboy by any means! He tried over and over to lasso the anchor. Finally, he succeeded and he climbed the rope over the anchor and fell onto the deck. An eerie silence pervaded the atmosphere. He made his way toward the aft where the steering compartment was. Rounding a corner, he saw the first dead body. It was simply lying there. It didn't take long before he saw more. Some were just lying on the deck. Others appeared to be beaten, the co-agulated blood still shining on their skin. What had happened here? Obviously some of these men had died violent deaths while others had just collapsed. He explored the whole ship. He found no living soul, only dead bodies. Something bizarre had certainly taken place here. Neville's hands shook with fear. Those people that had jumped off the ship must have been the only survivors, he thought.

Well, there was only one thing to do. He needed to get off this ship and report what happened. Again he thought how odd it was that he was the only person to investigate this odd occurrence. Usually crowds appeared when anything unusual happened.

He made his way back to the bow, where he found the anchor and climbed down the rope back onto the shore. It felt good when his feet, clad in their old tennis shoes, hit the sand. He turned and walked toward Gran Fon with fear in his heart.

Chapter 6
Exiles
March 2005

Sue looked down at the moccasins on her feet as the plane left the runway. Her moccasins always gave her comfort. Made by her great aunt, they reminded her of who she was and where she had come from. She was Tistista, the people, or better known to the whites as the Cheyenne Indians.

This was the last, long, hot flight she and Pedro would take from Miami to Dominica. So far the flights had gone smoothly. She smiled to herself as she thought about how easy her travels had been compared to the long journey her ancestors had made from the grasslands of Kansas to Florida. As the plane leveled off in altitude high above the island of Guadeloupe, she began to daydream about the long trek that had made her ancestors, and ultimately herself, exiles in Florida. Her father, grandfather and great grandfather had always spoken of the wide prairie in gleaming words. The Cheyenne had left Kansas five generations ago, but the story of their exile and been passed down through the generations. Some of Sue's relatives had returned to the northern Cheyenne reservation in southern Montana, but a group had remained exiles in Florida.

She vividly recalled the story her grandfather had told her many times. The Cheyenne's troubles began in the aftermath of the Red River War of 1875 with the massacre of the Germaine family and the capture of the Germaine daughters. It had been an epic frontier story, brutal and short. But life was brutal then, as it was now.

When the army recovered the Germaine girls from the Cheyenne warriors the whole country was incensed. Not that capture of women by hostile Indians was anything new, but this was a situation in which the white man had a controlling hand. The whites demanded justice and punishment. They were determined to capture any Cheyenne male warrior involved in the subjugation and rape of the Germaine girls. But it had proved impossible to determine who was actually involved in the horrible incident. The army simply lined up those warriors who were most likely involved, along with innocent bystanders and numbered them from left to right until they felt like they had enough. There were many legendary names in that ill-fated group. And there were many warriors who would never be known like her great-great-great-grandfather, Manibata, Young Bird. He was one of the unlucky Cheyenne who was shipped off with forty-two other tribal leaders for imprisonment in Fort Marion in St. Augustine, Florida. It had been a brutal imprisonment. Ft. Marion was one of the oldest buildings in the northern hemisphere and was not equipped to house prisoners. The fort had been built by the Conquistadors and been inhabited on and off ever since. It was a Bastille made of stone, built carefully by the masons to last forever. It had hastily been remodeled for these new prisoners, but was still damp and dark.

The hot, humid environment was completely new to these free roaming people of the plains and they suffered greatly. Some warriors had chosen to sacrifice themselves by stabbing the guards, or were shot trying to escape or simply ended their suffering by taking their own life. Manibata had watched his friends die. It was a sad time and he did not know what would happen. He made a friend in a white officer named Lt. Pratt and that good man was a comfort to him and all the Indians. Lt. Pratt was the only officer the Cheyenne trusted. They knew the lieutenant truly felt for their cause and empathized with their suffering. He made every effort to make the warriors comfortable. It was a difficult task. The whites treated the Cheyenne inhumanely. They were shackled, thrown into box cars and jostled for days on end without enough water or food. These men had no idea they were being sent to the east coast of southern Florida.

Lt. Pratt still had a conscience. He truly wanted to do what was right for the Indians. It always seemed that it was the lieutenants who were the conscience of the army. They were the lowest ranking officers and still had dreams of what was ethical and right. They hadn't been ground down by the need to climb the ladder of rank or to unquestionably obey unethical orders. That disillusionment came only with time. He saw the grief and despondency of his captives and he had petitioned his superiors to allow the wives and children of the warriors to come to Ft. Marion and join together to make the warriors' lives a little bit easier in this strange land. Some of the families chose to join the prisoners, others decided to stay on the reservation in Montana with their people. But Sdasdona, Manibata's wife, had decided to come to Florida to be with her lover. Their love was strong and in a society like the Cheyenne where sex was bound by taboo, their relationship was an unusually passionate one. Unlike many of the other captives, who in their despondency either died or continually begged to return to their homeland, Manibata decided to resign himself to his position and tried everything he could to learn the white man's ways without forgetting his own. He and Lt. Pratt became fast friends. They were about the same age. Lt. Pratt took great pleasure in teaching Manibata all about the U.S government and taught him to read and write. Manibata, or Young Bird, would in turn share his new knowledge with Sdasdona.

When Manibata had served his time, he and Sdasdona decided to take the name Pratt and remain in Florida. Throughout the five generations that would follow, they maintained the Cheyenne or Tistista ways and language as well as learning the customs and language of the white man. They would often send their sons and daughters home to the Cheyenne reservation in Montana to find husbands and wives. Some would return and some would not, but there was always a lineage that remained in Florida and the names Manibata and Sdasdona were carried down through the generations as a middle name of at least one child of every union. And so it was with Sue. Her name was Sue Sdasdona Pratt

Sue often traveled to the reservation to visit her relatives. She had a favorite great aunt named Owl Woman, who would take her into the fields and show her the many medicinal plants that grew there. Owl Woman would teach Sdasdona the old songs and they would listen to the soothing melody of the meadowlark together. Owl Woman was the person who explained to Sue that her middle name,

Sdasdona, meant Meadowlark in Lakota, the language of their al-
lies, the Sioux. Those were the times Sue loved. Owl Woman sparked
Sue's interest in healing. It was that interest that drove her to enlist
in the Navy and learn the nursing occupation. She understood the
20th-century way of medicine. She liked to couple western medicine
with her knowledge of the natural medicinal herbs her ancestors had
used. She was still in the reserves when the war broke out in Iraq and
she suspected that soon she would be called back into active duty.
At 28 she wasn't ready to go back into the Navy. She had gotten used
to civilian life. She was a plain woman, with long, light brown hair
and the characteristic high cheekbones and brown eyes of the Cheyenne. Her hawkish nose gave definition to her face and a dignified,
distinguished countenance. She was 5-foot- 6 and slightly overweight,
but she had perky breasts and smooth brown skin. At birth she was
pulled from her mother's womb with forceps and that had damaged
a nerve in her face, giving her a slight downward curl to her lower lip.
Her crooked smile was a characteristic all her own. Sue had a beauty
that surpassed pure physical attractiveness. Her beauty was spiritual
and hard to define externally. She had had many relationships and
loved men.

She looked across at Pedro sitting next to her. He came from
a Cuban family. A family that had been refugees themselves, exiles
from Cuba set adrift in a foreign land. Although she was attracted to
him partly because of his exile status, she also was fiercely attracted
to him physically. God how he could do the salsa, the way he could
move..... The thought made her wet even now. Pedro didn't know that
Sue was carrying his child. She had discovered her condition herself
only very recently. She was hoping they would be able to discuss this
situation on their trip. In any case, she felt good about the pregnancy
and she certainly loved Pedro.

Suddenly, the plane began to bank left and right erratically.
Even though the small airport was clearly visible the pilot appeared
to be having difficulty deciding which course to take. Pedro awoke
suddenly. He began to gasp with a look of panic in his eyes. He didn't
seem to be able to get any air.

"What's wrong Pedro?" Sue asked quickly.

"I can't breathe," he gasped.

He tried to gulp air for a minute and then passed out. Sue hit the button to call the flight attendant. No flight attendant came. There were other people who were having trouble breathing. People began to yell and scream. The flight attendant ran down the aisle and then collapsed on the floor. The plane bucked left and right as if the crew was fighting for control of the plane. The plane swerved to the right heading toward a very large mountain, glowing green in the afternoon light. They were heading straight toward the tallest mountain on the island!

Sue didn't know what to do. None of her Navy training, or any of her training as a nurse had ever prepared her for a situation like this. There was nothing she could do anyway. She realized that they were going to plow into the trees near the top of the mountains any second. She braced herself. She looked over at Pedro. He was turning blue. She pulled his head down between his knees so that he would be protected on impact. She put her head between her knees, clasped her hands behind her neck and began to sing her Cheyenne medicine song. And then she blacked out.

Chapter 7
Zero Year

It was getting close to evening. Neville was still wondering what had happened on the ship as he walked toward home through the lengthening shadows. Maybe someone at home will know what happened, he thought. He hadn't smoked a cone in a while and the shipwreck and the fact that no one had come to see it began to seem stranger.

Then he saw the first body. It was an older man, an elder he had known. He could still recognize the man's face even though the body had started to bloat. The man lay sprawled in the main street of Rosalie. He edged around it. Suddenly a girl he knew named Zoe staggered out into the street. Neville had known Zoe while growing up in Gran Fon. She was a large gal, always had been, but she had a pretty face.

She ran up to him. "Neville!" Neville! You're my man."

"What do you mean, Zoe?" Neville asked, startled.

"You know what I mean." She turned around, bent over and pulled her pants down, revealing her large black ass. "Hump me! Now!"

Neville was shocked even though desire was beginning to well in him. Suddenly, he was pushed from behind and hit the ground rolling. He looked up. One of the sailors he had seen jump off the ship had pushed him. The sailor was a big, Germanic white man and he was coming toward Neville with a sinister sneer on his face. Neville reached over and grabbed a large branch. As the sailor came close, Neville swung the branch with all his might. He hit the sailor at knee level. He heard the audible crack as the bone gave way. The sailor went down, groaning.

Neville ran into the trees and hid. He looked through the branches. He saw the sailor get up and hobble toward Zoe. She bared her ass toward him. He pulled out his large, erect penis and thrust it inside. At first Neville thought he should stop the sailor. But it was obvious that Zoe was enjoying it. She was laughing and smiling.

Neville felt like his mind was slipping. It was all too weird. He ran through the woods and headed up the steep, rutted road to Gran Fon. Gran Fon sat on a plateau high above the ocean. The land was fertile but it was a difficult place to get to.

In the waning light, the images of all he had seen this day raced through his head. The ship, the dead bodies, the old man in Rosalie, Zoe and the sailor....it didn't make sense at all. He wanted to light up another cone, but he thought he better keep his wits about him. He needed to find someone to talk to. He had to tell someone about what he had seen to get the images out of his head.

He heard shouts and screams periodically coming from town. It didn't sound natural at all. Usually in the evenings it was quiet except for the occasional car, a dog barking. He was wary as he walked along the road. He didn't see anyone and as he entered town it suddenly became quiet, too quiet.

He went to his Mother's house, but there was no one there. He knew where she would be. She would be at her sister's. His mother and her sister were twins and very close. Twins were a rarity on Dominica and even more unusual was that his mother and her sister had married twin brothers. It had been the talk of Gran Fon for years. It had been a good union and they had all become very close. Both his father and his uncle had passed away. His mother and his sister were the closest two human beings could be and not be husband and wife. Yeah, she'd be over at Maud's, Neville thought.

When he entered Maud's house he knew something was wrong. It was a simple house, like everyone's house on the island, with little furniture. It was built of concrete block, stucco and with a tin roof. Most people didn't even bother with windows. The weather didn't require it. They only needed shutters to block out the hurricanes that came each year in the summer months.

The house wasn't right. Furniture was thrown everywhere. He heard a small rustling noise in the back bedroom. He peered into the dim room. Maud was on the floor. She groaned and tried to move.

"Maud!" Neville cried. Her eyes opened. "What happened? Where's my Mother?"

She beckoned him to come closer. Speaking in whispers she told him that she had been raped, beaten and left here to die. With tears running down her face, Maud told him his mother had suffered the same fate. She had not lived. Maud pointed out into the garden with a shaking finger. That's where his mother lay. He wanted to go to her immediately. But Maud grabbed him and held on. "The world has gone mad, Neville," she whispered in a strained voice. "You must save yourself."

He tried to ask her questions about what had happened. But she was too weak to answer. She drifted in and out of consciousness.

Neville made her as comfortable as possible. He brought her a cup of water and held it to her lips. "Do you need something to eat?" he asked. She shook her head. Neville knew that in her old and frail condition she may not make it. She slipped again in unconsciousness and Neville went into the garden. He found his mother lying beneath a flowering bush. She had been severely beaten. She was sprawled on the ground and her body had begun to bloat. He dropped to his knees and wept. Who would do this, he wondered. Who would do a thing like this?

He was beside himself. His mother was the only anchor he had in this very volatile world. And in this moment, when it seemed the world had gone mad, he needed her more than ever. He jumped to his feet. He had to save Maud! He ran into the house. He heard a rustling from the back bedroom a scream, then silence. He ran into the bedroom. Sheila, a girl he had grown up with, stood over Maud with a machete in her hands. She raised it over her head and drove it through Maud's skull.

She turned toward Neville. "Now you are all mine. You are mine alone," she muttered. Neville couldn't believe the young, pretty girl he had grown up with had turned into this animal. He punched her square in the face. She went down like a sack of potatoes, unconscious. He bent over Maud. She was gone. Now what he was going to do? He looked over at Sheila. He didn't know what to do with her.

He pulled her onto the bed and tied each hand to the posts. He had to find someone, someone who could tell him what was going on. After he had tied her securely he grabbed the machete. Everyone owned a machete on the island. It was a common work tool. The Dominicans called them cutlasses. A machete could cut vegetation, grass and lumber and could be used as a weapon as well. Neville recognized this machete. It had been his father's. His father had engraved his initials in the handle. This same cutlass had been used to kill his aunt. "The world has gone crazy," Neville muttered.

Sheila was still unconscious so he decided to go outside and look around. Night had fallen and the full moon was out. There were fireflies everywhere. They looked like little fairies bobbing through the air. They reminded him of stories his mother told him as a young boy and fresh tears wet his cheeks.

He went down the street and into the store. It had been ransacked. It was mostly empty but he found some canned goods and headed back to the house. He heard movement, but he didn't see anything in the dark. He didn't want to encounter any living thing in this house. He closed the door and shutters. It was stifling hot, but he didn't want anyone to know he was there. The electricity was off so it was completely dark. He was alone in the house with his aunt Maud on the floor and Sheila on the bed. He lit one small candle.

Sheila awoke and smiled at him. "Come over here. You can have me right now," "What is wrong with you?" Neville asked. "Why did you kill my aunt Maud?"

"I had to," she replied. "You have to be mine, and only mine. And I will kill any woman that gets in the way."

"You are completely mad!"

"Just come over here," she said. "That's all I want. If you don't, I will get another man."

She began to yell and he put his hand over her mouth. Her skin felt rough and as Neville peered at her in the candlelight he saw sprouts of hair like a man's beard covering her face. It was strange and horrible.

He grabbed a bandanna from around his neck and used it as a gag. "I don't know what's going on," he snarled. "But you are going to give me answers." He sat breathing heavily while she thrashed. Finally she stopped moving and simply stared at him. "Do you think you can talk without screaming?" he asked.

Sheila nodded.

He untied the gag. "But fuck me first! Fuck me!" she said.

"I am not going to fuck you. You are going to talk to me and tell me what is going on. What happened to your family?"

"Dead," she said. "Dead. Some died right away. Others were beaten and killed."

"Is there anybody else left?" Neville asked, horrified.

She shook her head. "I don't know. What matters is I'm here and I'm alive. And I'm hungry. Let's eat."

He opened up the cans. She seemed to have no remorse or sorrow for her family. After she had eaten she started yelling at him again. He gagged her once more. Neville was tired and needed to sleep. Sheila seemed to need no sleep at all. She struggled against her bonds on the bed.

Neville slept fitfully with the machete in his hand, Maud's blood still on it. He didn't know what to do. In his restless sleep, he had nightmares of what he had seen that day.

When the sun rose in the morning it was stifling hot. Even though he was still very tired, the heat drove him awake. He rose and opened the shutters. The smell of Maud's body decomposing was horrible. He couldn't bear it. He needed to bury Maud and his mother. He looked toward the bed. Sheila was finally asleep. He took the gag off. She didn't even respond but continued to sleep.

Neville went to the shed in the backyard and found a shovel. He began to dig a grave next to his mother's dead body. He wasn't going to bother taking Maud or his mother to the church. There was no one around to give a service anyway. He dug two shallow graves. Then he began the laborious task of pulling his Aunt Maud's body out of the house. She was his aunt no longer, only an empty shell.

He wanted to clean their bodies but he knew the best thing to do was to get them in the ground. He placed them side by side in their graves and began to shovel the dirt on them. He began to weep uncontrollably. What was he going to do? There was no one around, only Sheila and she was crazy. He lay down by the graves and slept for a while. When he awoke he knew he needed a plan. He went back in the house. Sheila was still sleeping. It was midafternoon by then. He opened a can of tuna. He had to find more food. He was hungry, tired and lost in this strange new world.

Finally, he decided to go through town and see if anyone else was around and if not he would go to Rosalie and try to find someone there. Gran Fon was not a big town, just a village really, and he knew everyone who lived there. He looked from house to house and as he did he discovered more bodies. Some were mutilated; some people looked as if they had died peacefully. The bodies were in different stages of decomposition and the smell was becoming unbearable. Dogs had begun to feed on the bodies and the vultures darkened the sky above the village.

He went back to the house and woke Sheila and untied her hands and legs. "Wake up," he said. "We have to leave."

She was so drowsy she could hardly open her eyes. "I don't want to go anywhere," she said. "Just stay here you and me. We'll be fine." She went back to sleep.

He shook her. "You murdering bitch, we need to get out of here and I am taking you into the authorities." He grabbed her and pulled her to her feet. He walked out of the house and she sluggishly followed him. He picked up the bag of food he had collected and grabbed the cutlass. He and Sheila walked toward Rosalie.

When they rounded the bend, he could see two pairs of legs sticking out from under a bush one male and one female. It was Zoe and the sailor. The sailor's leg had already blown up to twice its size and was red and puffy. When Sheila saw Zoe she screamed and ran towards her. Zoe and the sailor woke up. Upon seeing Sheila, Zoe jumped to her feet and ran toward them, waving her arms. Neville noticed that Zoe had hair on her face like a three-day growth of a man's beard.

Zoe and Sheila began fighting, scratching and biting, rolling on the ground. The sailor leapt at Neville, swinging his cutlass. The sailor's face and arms were completely covered with a mat of brown curly hair.

"Brother, let's talk," Neville pleaded. He was exhausted and sick of fighting. But the sailor kept coming. He raised the cutlass, dark with coagulated blood and swung it at Neville's head. Neville veered to the left and the cutlass came down on the upright wooden post that held the road guard. The cutlass buried itself deep in the post and the sailor struggled to pull it out.

Neville swung his cutlass and severed the sailor's hand from his arm. The sailor roared and grabbed Neville around the throat with his good hand. His stump squirted blood and it splashed into Neville's eyes. Neville struggled to free himself from the sailor's monstrous grip, closing his eyes against the stinging blood. Neville began to lose consciousness and darkness closed in on him. Suddenly the sailor let go and fell to the ground unconscious from the loss of blood. Neville knew he would soon die.

Neville got shakily to his feet. He turned just in time to see Zoe hurl Sheila over the road guard into the deep valley below. He was appalled as Zoe turned toward him and said, "Now you are my man," and bent over to receive his phallus. Neville ran into the woods. Because of Zoe's large bulk, he quickly outdistanced her. He collapsed in the jungle, panting.

I need to go back and get the cutlass, he thought, and the food.

He tiredly got to his feet and circled around to the road. Zoe was no longer there. The sailor was lying in the road, dead. Neville picked up his father's cutlass and the bag of food and slipped into the forest. He would stay in the woods until he got to Rosalie. Maybe in Rosalie he could find a car and get to the next town. He didn't often drive but he knew how.

When he got to Rosalie he searched the buildings In vain. He found one vehicle crashed into a tree, it was unusable. He decided to go on to Petit Soufriere. This time he would take the trail along the ocean shore and maybe he would find someone there. He went down the cliffs to the bay. Once again he saw the large cargo ship shipwrecked on the shore. The waves crashed against it. The beautiful day and blue calm ocean lent a surreal feel to the events Neville was experiencing. The birds were singing but there were no people. He realized suddenly he was covered with sticky, dried blood. He stripped off his clothes and dove into the sea. The waves washed over him and he closed his eyes in the warm water. It began to all seem like a nightmare, a horrible dream.

Maybe he should go home and his Mother and Maud would make him a nice meal. But he also knew it was not true. He staggered out of the water and pulled on his tattered shorts and old tennis shoes. He walked silently into the forest. When he came to Petit Soufriere, once again he saw the bodies strewn everywhere in various stages of decomposition. He wished he was back on the trail.

He looked in the garages of several homes and finally found a vehicle that was not damaged. It was a Honda Accord, black and sleek. Obviously, the owner had taken good care of it. There were no keys. He looked though the house. The inhabitants were dead, bloated and stinking. He gritted his teeth and held his breath and looked through their pockets for the keys. He found them in a man's pocket. He ran out of the house. He wanted to throw up, but couldn't. His stomach was empty. He threw the bag of food in the back of the car. He had to get more food. He had to force himself to enter the empty homes. He found more canned goods, plantains and coconut. He threw the food in the back seat of the car and started it up. He never imagined he would drive a car like this, and now he could not enjoy it. He headed down the road to Castle Bruce. "Please God," he whispered, "let my other relatives be alive."

He had a brother in Roseau, John. He had become an Anglican minister, which had pleased Neville's mother greatly. Perhaps John was still alive. Perhaps he could get help there. He also had a brother Samuel in Calibishie who ran a small store. He decided to go to Calibishie first to find Samuel and then if he were still alive they could go together to Roseau and find John. The rest of his brothers and sisters were working on other islands or had gone to the United States or to England. He hoped they had been spared this horrible misery. It may be a long time before I see any of them, he thought anxiously.

He drove down the road and saw many cars along the road. They had crashed into trees; the drivers slumped at the wheel. It was a world gone mad. Here on his blessed island. How could this happen?

When he got to Castle Bruce he didn't slow down. He wanted to get to Calibishie. He drove through town looking from left to right for any signs of life. He saw none. He didn't even slow down for the dead bodies in the intersection. He had to find someone he could talk to.

Chapter 8
Gathering 1

Gary's global positioning device told him he was entering Calibishie Bay. The air was soft and warm, the water a deep turquoise. If only Amy could be here, he thought as he sailed into the beautiful bay. But she is gone.

His charts told him the bay was shallow, so he circled in carefully. He ached to find another human being and tell them what had happened. As he approached the shoreline, he noticed that there was no activity along the beach or in the town. That's odd, he thought, his anxiety mounting. I don't see any cars or people. It's as if there's nobody here.

Fishing vessels moored along the shore were unoccupied and silent. He got in his dinghy, started the engine and motored away. He looked over his shoulder at the boat. It wasn't a yacht by any means, but it had been his home for a long time and had served him well. Gary had named their boat Minnow, after the television show *Gilligan's Island* that he had watched as a kid. It had been Amy's and his joke.

He headed into shore in his little rubber dinghy and as he powered up on shore he became painfully aware of the horrible smell. What is it, he wondered. It smells awful here.

After tying up his dinghy, he headed into town looking for a grocery store. Calibishie was a small town strung along the coast. He came upon the only grocery store quickly. He banged open the door and saw that it had been ransacked. Shelves had been knocked over; powdered milk covered the floor like snow. He looked around for a moment and then yelled out. "Hello! Hello! Is anyone here?"

He heard a low moan coming from the back of the store. He made his way through the wreckage to a back room. A black man lay sprawled across a narrow bed. He had been badly beaten. His eyes were black and blue and his nose broken.

"Oh my god," Gary cried. "What happened?"

The man opened his eyes slowly. "I don't know. They came and they beat me and they took my daughter."

"Who is they?" Gary asked.

"The men of the village," the man answered and his eyes closed.

"What can I do to help you?" Gary asked.

"Water."

Gary found a bottle of water and held it to the man's parched lips. He coughed and water ran down his chin. His head fell back weakly.

"What's your name?" Gary asked.

"Samuel," he whispered. "The world's gone mad, mon."

He picked the man up and arranged him more carefully on the bed. "My name is Gary. I am from Canada."

Samuel looked at him. "You're certainly not from 'round here, mon" he said. "Or you would know what has been going on."

"What is going on?" Gary asked. "Where are the authorities?"

"There is no one. You have to fend for yourself."

"What do you mean?" Gary asked.

"There is no help. Everybody went crazy."

"Look," Gary said. "I'll go back to my boat and get a first aid kit. Those cuts are going to get infected. I'll be back Samuel."

He went out the back door and ran down the beach. He fired his dinghy up and shot off toward the Minnow. He boarded the ship. This doesn't make sense, he thought. Amy's dead. The whole town is deserted. A storekeeper beaten almost to death, his store ransacked. What's happening?

He grabbed the first aid kit off the wall of the cabin. It was well stocked. Amy had made sure of that. He was about to jump back in the dinghy when he stopped. He went back into the cabin and grabbed the pistol. I might need this, he thought. He got in his dinghy and headed back to shore.

Maybe this is just some strange horrible nightmare, he thought. Here I am in this island paradise and yet all I see is destruction and violence. He jumped off at shore and tied the boat. It was beginning to get dark. He entered the back door of the store and heard a noise. It sounded like a man grunting. He heard a thumping noise.

He noticed a young girl, maybe 15 years old, standing in the shadows. She smiled at him with large white teeth. He couldn't help but smile back. The thumping noise continued. He went to the back room and saw a man chopping at the storekeeper's body with a machete.

"Stop!" Gary shouted. "What the hell are you doing?"

The man turned. He was monstrous. He stood over six feet tall and was wearing a police uniform. He carried a sidearm. He pulled it out, aimed it at Gary and pulled the trigger. Gary heard a click and the gun did not go off. Gary's legs turned to water and he almost fell to the floor. The policeman was out of ammunition. He threw the gun on the floor and grabbed the machete. He came toward Gary waving the machete in front of him. Gary pulled out his .45. He wasn't familiar with it at all. He fumbled with the safety. "Stop or I'll shoot!" Gary yelled. "Stop right where you are!"

The policeman kept coming. He didn't hesitate for even a moment. Gary pulled the trigger. The gun went off. The loud crack shocked Gary. The noise was deafening and his wrist kicked back with the recoil. The large man fell backwards and red blood oozed out over his chest.

"Oh my god," Gary muttered.

The policeman was dead. The wound was huge and bleeding profusely. Gary wanted to yell and scream. He turned and saw the girl.

"I just killed this guy," he cried. "I had to. He was going to kill us! We have to get out of here. We have to get help."

The girl didn't answer him. She walked slowly toward him and put her arms around him and hugged him tight. Gary shoved her away.

"Are you crazy! There's no time for that," Gary said. "I don't know what is going on here. But we have to do something."

It was dark outside and all he wanted to do was get back to his boat. "I am going back to my boat," he said, "You are welcome to come with me."

She simply nodded and followed him out the door. They spoke very little on the trip out in the dinghy. Gary couldn't get the nightmarish image of the policeman chopping Samuel out of his mind. He managed to tell the young girl his name was Gary Llewellyn from Canada.

"My name is Mona," she said softly once they were onboard the Minnow.

"I live in Calibishie." She was silent for a moment and then said, "Much fighting. Much fucking."

Gary was taken aback by her harsh language and didn't know what to say.

"We'll be safe on the boat," he said after a few minutes. "At least for now."

"Are you hungry?" he asked.

"Yeah, mon," she mumbled.

They went down into the cabin. He turned on the lights and shut the windows so that the lights would not be visible to anyone on shore. He began to cook a meal. When he turned around Mona was taking off her clothes. "Ah, young lady that it is not necessary," he mumbled. Her lithe young body was covered with soft downy hair.

Gary was shocked. "Is there something I need to know," he asked. "I mean, the hair. Is there something you need to tell me about?"

She shook her head. "Only that I want you."

He was repulsed by her hairy body. "Look, let's eat and then get some sleep. We'll find your folks in the morning. We'll figure out what's going on. "

"Well after I eat, I wanna fuck," she said.

Again he was appalled by the language and the mannerisms of this young girl.

"That's not going to happen," he said exasperated. "You've been traumatized and so have I. We need to eat and get some sleep. You are way too young to be talking this way." He patted her shoulder awkwardly. "You'll get through this."

She grabbed his hand in a vise-like grip. He yanked his hand back suddenly afraid.

She stood staring at him, her eyes flashing angrily. "If you don't want me, I'll find me a man who does," she said. She ran out of the cabin.

Gary heard the splash as she dove overboard. Should I go after her, Gary wondered. He shook his head. There wasn't anything he could do. If she wants to go, she will, he thought. She is obviously disturbed.

He slept fitfully that night. He didn't know if he would be boarded by the strange inhabitants of this place. He kept the .45 next to him all night. In the morning, bleary eyed, he made coffee. It was one of those rituals that made the day what it was. But he missed the true half and half that made coffee special. He wondered if it had all been a dream. But he knew Amy wasn't there. Mona's clothes were still on the table. It was hard to believe all that had happened. He realized he needed to go back on shore and try to find help, food and water. He ate and the food sat heavy in his stomach

On shore he went back to the store. The policeman lay rigid on the floor and Samuel was on the bed. Their bodies were beginning to bloat in the heat and Gary realized the horrible smell he had noticed when he first came to shore was bodies decaying. It didn't take long before he found other bodies in various stages of decay strewn in the alleys and streets of the village.

He took his time going from house to house looking in the windows. If he found an open door he would go inside. Sometimes he would find bodies. All the houses had been ransacked; food scattered, clothes, bedding on the floor, dishes broken. The pickings were pretty grim with the bodies and rotting food. But he put whatever edible food he could find in a small sack. I need fuel, he thought. Diesel fuel for the dinghy and the Minnow's engine. He walked to the gas station. But the pumps would not operate because there was no electricity. I need some sort of gas-powered generator, he thought, to get the gas out of the tank. He sat down in the shade of a tree and tried to think. But his sleepless night caught up with him and he dozed. He awoke suddenly with a start. This is not a safe place, he thought. He looked around the deserted town blearily. What happened to Mona, he wondered.

He walked tiredly into the house across the street. He looked in the window and saw a couple lying on the bed sleeping. They were naked and their bodies were covered with nubs of hair. They curled around each other, snoring peacefully. He silently moved away. Something told him that these were not the kind of people that could help him. He began to walk south out of town. Through the haze of heat he saw a car, a black Honda Accord, slowly approaching. Gary stepped off the road. The driver looked at him. It was a young black man with dreadlocks. Gary put his hand on his gun. He waved with his other hand. The car slowly pulled to the side of the road and the driver's door opened. The young man looked at him.

Neville wasn't sure this white man who looked like a tourist was safe. He wasn't sure anyone was safe. He kept the car between himself and the white man. The white man spoke first.

"My name is Gary and I'm from Canada. Something terrible has happened in this town. We need to get help immediately."

"Yah mon," Neville replied. "That's the truth." He looked Gary up and down thinking that this man looked normal. The first normal person he had seen in a couple of days.

Gary stared back at him. Finally, Gary broke the silence

"What's your name?" Gary asked.

"My name is Neville. There has been a really bad thing. The island has gone mad. People killing each other, raping each other. My mother and my aunt are dead. I came to find my brother. He runs a store here in Calibishie."

Gary looked down at his dirty sandals. "Was his name Samuel?" Gary asked.

Neville looked surprised. "Ya mon."

"I've met your brother," Gary said. "I am sorry to tell you that he's dead.'

Neville hung his head in sorrow and tears slid down his face. After a bit, he came back to the moment and saw Gary still standing at the side of the road.

"A policeman killed him," Gary said. "I had to kill the policeman when he came after me with a machete."

Neville took in a deep shuddering breath and motioned Gary into the car. "Take me to him," he said. Gary walked over and opened the door. "Now don't try anything funny," Neville said. "I've got a machete.

"I'm cool," Gary said and raised both hands in the air. He got in the car and they stared at each other.

"You're the only human being I've seen that didn't try to kill me or have sex with me," Gary said.

"All right, mon." Neville said quietly and they shook hands.

They drove in silence back to the store. Gary escorted Neville to the back room, where they looked at the policeman with the hole in his chest and his brother who had been hacked to pieces. Neville staggered out of the store and threw up on the beach.

Gary watched him and kept one eye out for danger. Neville sat in the sand. Gary quietly approached. "What should we do now?" he asked.

Neville shook his head. "One thing I know," he said. "Is that the crazy people come out at night and not during the day. We should find a safe place for the night."

"I've got just the place," Gary said. 'If you'll trust me, we can spend the night on my boat."

Neville went back to the car and grabbed his machete and his keys. He got in the dinghy with Gary and they motored across the bay to the Minnow. As they climbed on board, Gary noticed that they were far enough from shore that they would know if anyone approached.

They spent the evening talking, crying and sharing their stories. It was awkward at first. Gary and Neville did not trust each other completely yet. So much had happened. Gary had never been around black people before and this younger man was drastically different. Gary had a hard time understanding Neville's patois, but they persisted in their desire to communicate.

Neville sensed Gary's uneasiness. As they exchanged stories and told of their experiences they grew more trusting of one another. When he got to the part about Mona, Neville asked him, "Did she have body hair?"

"Yes," Gary replied.

They began to piece together at least some of what they had observed.

"Why were you and I unaffected?" Gary wondered out loud. "And my beautiful wife Amy died. And others have gone crazy."

They didn't come up with any answers. But they did have some facts. They guessed that whatever it was that immediately killed some people also made the others violent and aggressively sexual.

Since Gary and Neville were unaffected it made sense that others would be unaffected as well. There had to be some connection between Gary and Neville. It certainly wasn't race. Gary began to logically piece through it. But he could not come up with any similarities that linked him and Neville. He did realize that Neville and his family, his mother and aunt, although killed by the crazy ones, had not died or gotten violent. So there had to be something in Neville's genetic code that made him and his family immune to whatever killed some people and made others into monsters. And whatever that genetic factor was, Gary had it too.

Neville was sure that those affected were active only at night and slept during the day. They decided to keep watch off and on through the night. Gary realized that he had to trust this young man. In any case, they both were glad to have someone to talk to. They came to the conclusion that they would drive to Portsmouth the next day and look for other survivors. Then they would head to Roseau where Neville had a cousin named John who was an Episcopalian minister. Maybe the plague had not hit Roseau or Portsmouth yet. They would find out tomorrow.

Before he went to sleep, Gary fumbled through his luggage and found his running shoes. He had run all through high school. Running was something that he relied upon to calm him and help him think. Yes, he would need these to get through this trauma, he thought. He would run in the daytime when it was safe from the crazy ones.

Chapter 9
Gathering 2

Sue awoke to the sound of the rain pattering on the fuselage. Her body hurt from being in a cramped position on the floor of the wrecked plane. She didn't know how long she had been unconscious. She moved her head, her neck muscles screaming, and looked over at Pedro. He had already grown stiff. "Pedro," she whispered and began to sob, knowing that he was dead. After a while her sobs burned themselves out.

At last, she unhooked her seat belt and heard a low moan. The fuselage compartment was a jumble of seats and bodies. She glanced out the window. The wings were gone and all she saw was the green jungle like a dark shroud around the plane. She made her way toward the moan. It was a man. A white man. She had seen him at the airport in Guadeloupe. Definitely an American. He and his girlfriend were traveling together. He was slightly overweight and balding. She bent over him and said in a quiet calm voice, "My name is Sue. What is yours?"

"Paul," he groaned.

A small trickle of blood dribbled out the side of his mouth and Sue knew he had internal injuries.

"Get me out of here," he muttered.

She unhooked his seat belt and moved him onto the floor. She noticed a bulge in his crotch. He had an erection. His face was covered with hair, like he had not shaved for weeks. My god, Sue thought, this is strange.

He asked her for water and food. She put a pillow under his head and covered him with a blanket and climbed out of the plane through a ragged hole. The plane was destroyed. The fuselage had snaked its way through the trees and was lodged in a small saddle between two mountains.

She rubbed her aching head. I probably have a small concussion, she thought. She was also famished and thirsty. There wasn't any running water nearby but rain fell from the sky. She went back into the plane and began searching the kitchen galley. She found some bottles of water, crackers, a cracked coffee pot and packages of nuts. She grabbed a handful of the nuts and began to open them one by one. She filled up her paper cup and then went back to take care of Paul. He looked up at her with his pale blue eyes.

"Is help coming?" he whispered.

"I don't know, Paul," Sue said. "The forward cockpit is completely crushed and both pilots are dead. I don't know what happened, but I would think help is on its way."   Paul closed his eyes. "I'd like to kill those pilots," he muttered angrily.

"Try to sleep," Sue said. She sat back on her heels and looked around. There were bodies strewn everywhere. Cell phone, she thought, I've gotta find a phone. She sorted through the luggage and quickly found two phones. But neither one picked up a signal.

What am I going to do, she wondered. At the moment she didn't have the strength to do anything. She found several blankets and pillows and despite being in a morgue of bodies fell asleep.

She awoke in the morning to sunlight and birds singing. She was hungry and thirsty. A good cup of coffee would have been nice. She felt her stomach, concerned about the baby in her womb. Now I can't tell Pedro he is a Dad, she thought, and two fat tears slid down her cheeks.

Surely the rescue teams should have been here by now, she thought. They must have known the plane went down. She reflected on the whole weird scenario. When they were leaving the states she had heard that Osama Bin Laden had been captured. Bush's poll ratings had skyrocketed. Bush had held a press conference on TV and told the people that terrorism was on the run and Americans should once again feel free to travel freely and go to Disneyland. He must have had stock there.

But there had been no confirmation from other countries and rumors spread that Bush was lying or simply misinformed. Sue had felt uneasy. She sensed something wasn't right. But she and Pedro had gone ahead with their plans. Now here she was in some mountain-ous island in the Caribbean surrounded by the bodies of her traveling companions. She stiffly got up. She looked at Paul. He looked peace-ful. He had died sometime in the night.

She realized at that point that if no help came she would have to find her way out. She knew that Dominica was not a large island, perhaps ten to fifteen miles at its widest point. She went to the cock-pit to look for maps but found none. She got out the small map of Dominica she had gotten in the airport. It would have to do. She left the map in the plane and went outside the craft. She crawled up on the fuselage and looked around. The saddle the plane had crashed on was flanked by tall green mountains. She chose the one on the right. They were both about the same height.

It was hard going through the heavy, dense vegetation, almost impossible to make headway. She found herself crawling through and over branches. She stayed on top of the ridge line so she knew she was going the right direction. When she broke out of the vegetation to the top of the mountain it was a wonderful feeling. She could see the Atlantic Ocean to the east, the Caribbean to the west. She could pick out small villages and towns and even a road far in the distance. She also saw that the clouds were rolling in from the Atlantic.

She decided to head back to the plane. As she was turning she saw a small metallic disk attached to the rock. She bent down to read the writing. Mt. Diablotin, she read. The highest point on the island, she thought, remembering what she had read on her small tourist map. It felt good to know where she was. She made her way back to the fuselage. It took her most of the rest of the day to work her way back.

Well, if it is the highest mountain there has to be a trail some-where, she said to herself. Someone had put the plaque there. If res-cue doesn't come by morning I'll go back up and work my way down.

She spent the rest of the day searching the wreckage for sup-plies. She and Pedro had come prepared for a vacation, not survival in the jungle. She found water bottles and a jacket. Even though the idea made her feel sick, she went through people's luggage and was able to find long pants, several candy bars, fruit and more nuts and crackers in the galley. She found a small backpack and stuffed it with her food, blankets and a pillow.

She looked down at her moccasins. They gave her reassurance. They were made the way of the Cheyenne with a rough rawhide sole and beautiful beadwork on the top. These moccasins would have to carry her and the baby to safety. It wasn't just her life, it was her unborn child's life as well and that made her even more determined to survive.

The next morning, when rescue did not arrive, she climbed to the top of the mountain and found the faint trail that headed west toward the Caribbean. She followed the trail, losing it and finding it, again and again. She realized that through all the trauma and the need for survival she had not let herself fully grieve for Pedro. But now was not the time to let go. A sense of hopelessness washed over her and she began to weep softly as she walked through the rain forest. In some part of her mind she knew the jungle was beautiful: the flowers, the verdant growth, the shrill song of birds and the squawk of the parrot. But she couldn't enjoy any of it. Her whole life had changed. She wanted someone to share with and she felt very much alone. Soon she had consumed all of her water. A warm rain came through the canopy of the jungle pattering on the leaves and dripping to the forest floor. She realized that at some point, she had completely lost the trail. All she knew was that she had to keep moving and had to keep going down. After a while, she heard the sound of water running over rocks. The inviting sound was too much to resist. She also knew that if she followed the water downhill she would eventually find the ocean. She veered off to the right and followed the sound of the water crashing over rocks. It was a steep descent and often she would fall and slide down the side of the bank. When she came to the fast flowing stream she plunged her face in the water and splashed it over her hair. She drank freely of it. At this point she didn't care if there were microorganisms. It was good to have a drink. She moved downstream. The main stream joined small rivulets of fast clear water and eventually grew into a river. She had to continually cross from side to side following the twists and turns of the river's path.

She realized that although it was a safe assumption the river would eventually reach the ocean, it was going to take a very long time. The boulders were round and slippery with moss and spray and the river's path was tortuous.

She decided to make her way back up onto the ridge. She filled up her bottle and moved and climbed upward. Night started to fall and she realized that once it did she would not be able to see anything. Night in the rainforest was complete and total. She broke a few branches from a broad leaved shrub and stacked them against a huge tree trunk. She crawled in her shelter and pulled the blankets over her and listened to the crickets and frogs. Clouds of fireflies swirled through the blackness. She watched them dance, growing sleepy. Tomorrow I will find civilization, she thought.

She awoke in the morning to sunshine and realized that this was the weather pattern: sun in the morning, rain in the afternoon and evening. She packed up her few belongings and made her way up along the ridge following faint trails. She didn't know if the trails were made by animals or people but she was grateful to have any path at all. She came upon a two-track road that was overgrown and no longer used. But she took it as a sign of civilization and was overjoyed. It became more defined as she followed it and her heart was happy.

She reflected as she walked that if it hadn't been for the trauma that had taken place, this would have been a most enjoyable experience. The smells of the forest, the green canopy that offered shade from the blazing sun, the occasional bright splash of color from a flower in the greenery were soothing to her mind and spirit. But the dull ache of losing Pedro was like a blanket over her mind. Now, every once in a while she could hear the ocean in the distance and that gave her the energy to keep going. She wondered again why she heard no planes, no choppers looking for the plane crash. It seemed very odd. Well....she would find out what was going on soon.

She came through the trees and suddenly saw the ocean. She could hear the faint roar of the waves but could not hear any cars or other sounds of civilization. In the late afternoon, she stepped out of the high grasses onto a paved road. She decided to wait. When a car came by she would flag it down. She waited for about an hour and no one came. Strange, she thought, and her uneasiness grew. I'll have to walk, she decided. Right or left, she asked herself. Right or left. It was all up to her to decide. She chose left because, according to her map, that was the direction that the capital city Roseau lay. She didn't know what point she was on the road but she knew that if she went to the south she would eventually hit Roseau. So she began to walk. It was evening when she saw the first car. Instead of reassuring her, she felt afraid. It was so odd to see no cars at all and then suddenly see one.

She could see that the passenger side windshield was completely bashed in and she couldn't tell who was on the passenger side, but a white male was at the wheel. She stood frozen, torn between wanting to hide in the trees and aching to yell for help. The car slowed and the white man waved. She waved back. He nodded and she felt reassured. She waved her arms. "Stop!" she yelled. "Please help!" They approached slowly.

It had been a long day for Gary and Neville. They had gone back into town and then headed north to make a swing around the island through Portsmouth to see if anyone else had survived. An eerie silence hung over the island and the smell in the air was ghastly. At one point, they drove into a small village and honked the horn repeatedly to see if anyone would come out to investigate. The only person that appeared was a hairy half-naked man. He ran at them waving his arms. They locked the doors and rolled up the windows. As they took off the man hammered at the side window then threw a heavy rock. The rock smashed the passenger side window. They hit the gas and he chased them down the road out of the village.

Gary looked over at Neville, "I guess we better be more careful." He laughed nervously. Neville laughed as well. The world had gone mad.

"Do you want to drive?" Gary asked. "I am not a very good driver."

Neville nodded and they switched places. When they finally reached Portsmouth they realized they were low on fuel. But there was no electricity and so no way to pump gas. There was no living person there, just dead bodies.

"I think the only thing we can do is siphon gas," Gary said. "I used to do that when I was a kid and had no money."

Gary cut a garden hose he found at the back of the station. He inserted the hose into the tank of a car. His first attempt at siphoning was horrible and all he got was a mouthful of gas. He tried several times and got the siphon to work. "I've got to find something to rinse my mouth out with," Gary said.

He made his way to the local store and cautiously went inside. He found bottled water even though the store had been thoroughly ransacked. He swished the water around his mouth and spit it out. He went back to the car. Neville had filled up the tank and several gas containers, which he put in the trunk. "Well," Gary said. "It doesn't look like there's anyone here, let's head on down to Roseau."

When they saw the woman waving in the middle of the road in the evening light they were not sure if they should stop. It was obvious she was alone. "What do you think, Neville," Gary asked.

"I think she is ok," Neville said. "She is out in the daylight and she's alone."

By now they had figured out that it was rare to see a woman alone. Most women seemed to be with men. Meeting the same sex erupted into violence and the hairy violent people seemed to get along only as couples.

Gary and Neville had discussed many theories but had come to no conclusions. All they knew were the patterns they saw. Gary glided through a stop sign. The woman came up to the passenger door. Gary did not roll down the window. "She's ok," Neville said again. She did not have body hair and was not acting at all aggressive. Slowly, he lowered the shattered window and pieces of glass fell on the road at her moccasins.

Her long hair was ratted and her face dirty. She did not appear hysterical, but was visibly upset. "There was a plane crash and I have been walking for two days. Can you help me?" she asked. "Lots of people are dead." Tears splashed down her face. Gary looked at Neville and nodded. "Get in," he said. She got in the back and they drove off. They each introduced themselves.

"I'm Sue Pratt," she said. "I was coming here on vacation when the plane went down. My fiancé was killed." She looked out the window and tried not to cry.

Neville and Gary waited silently. They knew she needed to tell her story. She gained control and went on in a shaky voice. She told them everything that had happened. Gary and Neville listened silently.

Finally Sue stopped talking for a moment, then asked, "Why haven't we seen any people or cars?" she asked. "I was on the road a long time."

Neville turned and gently put his large black hand on her shoulder. "Something terrible has happened." Gary and Neville told Sue everything that had happened to them as well. She listened with shock and horror on her face, but she did believe them because it all fit.

"It's getting dark," Gary said. "We have to find a safe place for the night. That's when the beasts come out."

They slowly pulled into a small town consisting of a few houses and a store. They pulled up to a house with a garage and they parked. Gary and Neville went inside the house and checked it out. It was empty. They went back out and got Sue. They barricaded the windows preparing for the coming night. It would be a full moon tonight. After they had settled on the floor and eaten, they discussed various theories as to what had happened. Gary was beginning to think it had been a plague and Sue agreed. Neville felt it might be some horrible spirit or craziness. Sue felt that if it were a plague of some kind that eventually they would be rescued. Obviously, the plague did not affect everyone and she could not imagine that it spread too far. Neville just didn't know and badly wanted to smoke a cone.

Sue felt safe with these two men and felt comfort in their companionship. She offered to take guard duty. She was used to keeping watch in the Navy, she told them. When Gary showed her the .45 she told him she was familiar with this weapon. It had been standard issue in the military. It shot a large slug and had great knockdown power. She slept well knowing that she was being watched over. When

Neville woke her she took her position at the window. She peered through the slats. Soon both men were snoring. They had lost loved ones too, she thought. Neville lost his mother and aunt, Gary lost his wife like I lost Pedro.

She had not told them yet that she was pregnant. She sat in the dark room gazing out through the slats. In the moonlight, she saw a man and a woman approaching. The man was tall and muscular with dreadlocks. The woman was chubby but moved easily beside him. They were only half clothed, which struck Sue as odd. The woman's pendulous breasts swung as she walked. Sue didn't know what she should do. She kept silent and watched. Another man came out of the bushes. Sue could tell he was older by his posture and movements. The older man attacked the young man. The younger man was able to throw him off easily and then beat him mercilessly. The woman just watched passively. The old man howled and the young man beat him until he was senseless. He turned toward the woman. The woman bent over and the man thrust his erect penis in her. The whole act was unbelievable to Sue. I have to be dreaming, she thought and felt sick. It was time to change the guard. She awoke Gary and tried to tell him what had happened. He motioned her to be quiet.

"Be quiet now," he said. "Tell me in the morning."

Sue had a hard time going to sleep. She kept seeing what had happened in her mind.

They awoke groggily with the heat of the day. They found the stove had propane and made coffee. They found some eggs and ate breakfast. Sue believed Neville and Gary completely now. She had seen for herself the horrible barbarity. After their meal they went outside and inspected the old man's body. He must have been at least 50 or 60 but he had attacked a much younger man.

"Probably to get the woman," Neville said. He couldn't believe that Rastafarians would do a thing like that, but then again, nothing was as he expected it to be. The whole world had gone mad. He hadn't had a cone for a long time. He was afraid to light up. There were just too many bizarre things happening to go into the spirit world now.

They got in the vehicle and headed down the road to Roseau. They did not know what to expect. All they knew is that they wanted to find Neville's brother John, the minister, and perhaps other survivors.

Chapter 10
Gathering 3

Jungsuk rustled in her hidden compartment fervently hoping morning would come soon. She had learned that the hairy people did not roam about in the daylight. She felt safe enough to leave her sanctuary in the daytime to forage for food and water. It had been several days since she had gone into hiding and she was wondering if her plight would ever end.

All night she had heard shots and screams and occasionally people coming into the church. She held her breath, hoping to God that nobody would find her. She wanted to make contact and talk to someone about what had happened. But the memories of the violence she had seen the first day lingered.

Finally, the stifling heat and with it the smell of dead bodies let her know that daylight had come. She left her sanctuary and stumbled outside, the bright sunlight blinding her eyes.

She smelled smoke and saw several buildings in Roseau burning. Fortunately the city was made of block and clay tile so the buildings would burn without spreading to the other houses and the rain that fell every afternoon put the fires out. Between the masonry and rain, she was relatively safe from fire.

The overnight rain helped with the smell. I have to get out of here, she thought. She stretched her aching joints and cramped muscles. I need food and water and then I'm getting out.

She had been pillaging food from houses, being very careful not to disturb the sleeping hairy people. Their sleep seemed abnormally deep, almost as if they were unconscious, and she had learned that she could move about freely.

Few of them wore clothes anymore. It was appalling to see their bodies being slowly covered with hair. She shuddered. This has got to be a nightmare and I am going to wake up sooner or later, she thought. Today, I will collect as much food and water as I can and tomorrow I will leave but where?

She heard a car coming and instinctively stepped back into the darkness of the church. She saw a black Honda Accord moving slowly down the street. She hadn't seen a vehicle operating for a long time. All the cars she saw now were smashed into walls and trees or just sitting idle. The strange hairy beasts did not seem to know how to drive. The black Honda had a broken windshield on the passenger side. She saw a white man in the driver's seat and a woman in the back. People, she thought, her heart beating rapidly. People driving in the daytime! But still, she did not trust them. As the car slowed to a stop in front of the church, she ran back to her cubbyhole to hide.

As she pulled the door shut behind her, she heard them come in. God, please don't let them find me, she whispered.

Neville opened the door and walked into the church. "John!" he called. "It's Neville. Answer me mon! We need help!"

Jungsuk felt a surge of excitement. They were not acting like beasts. And they were active in the daytime. Should she say something?

"John, mon," Neville called again. "Please tell me you are alive!"

She made her decision. She climbed out of the cubbyhole and stood behind the altar. Neville, Gary and Sue jumped, startled, and instinctively backed away from her. She looked at them, smiling tentatively. "Are you one of the beasts?" she asked in a quiet, shaking voice. Neville shook his head. "No mon, we are just like you."

She practically jumped over the altar and ran down the aisle. She ran into Neville's outstretched arms crying. "I thought I was the only one left! My husband is dead. It's total madness here. People are killing each other, raping each other." She sobbed, all the fear and anxiety of the last few days flowing out of her.

Neville held her for a long time as she cried. "I can't say it's going to be all right," he said. "But we are here now." He patted her back, "Is there anyone else alive?"

"No," she said. "Was John your brother?"

He pushed her gently away so that he could look at her face. "You knew John?" he asked.

"Yes," she answered. "He saved my life. He told me to hide here in the church. He said he would come back but he never did."

Neville looked at Gary, who said what was on all their minds. "You mean you don't know anyone normal that is alive? "

"No," she replied. "I've looked around as best I could. I haven't found anyone else. It doesn't mean that there isn't anyone, but I haven't found them."

There was a moment of silence. "I think we all need to leave town and find a safe place and wait this out. I think we should find shelter, food and water and go into the country," Gary said quietly.

"I know exactly where," Neville said. "A place no one will ever find us. It's called the Jacko Steps. It's where the Maroons used to hide from the slave traders. They never did find them."

"All right then," Sue said and looked at Jungsuk. "Where can we get blankets and food?"

"I'll show you," said Jungsuk.

They went out into the carnage of the city. There were dogs feasting on the bodies and vultures flapped their dusty wings fighting over scraps.

They went to the large hardware store. Its windows were broken and the goods were strewn everywhere. They found camping gear in good condition: propane stove, sleeping bags, tents, flashlights.

Then they raided houses and stores for food. The car was full of supplies now and they barely had room for the four of them.

"I think we need to go," Sue said. "Let's find a place where we can be safe at least for a few days."

They drove to the road that crossed the island from west to east. They drove slowly through the jungle on the two-lane blacktop roads. When they came to the national forest sign, Neville said,

"Not far now." After a few more hairpin turns, they saw the sign for Jacko Steps. They parked, packed everything into their backpacks and headed into the forest.

Chapter 11
Remembrance
02-03

Gary sat beneath a banana tree savoring the warm evening. Whatever had affected this island and turned most of its inhabitants into hairy beasts had affected the entire planet, he thought, as he gazed at his worn sandals. That is the only reason why we haven't seen any lights or ships or received any radio signals. We are just a small group of Maroons, Gary mused. All alone on this earth.

I guess man had become like a bacteria and the earth had decided to beat that back with its own antibiotic, he thought. The earth destroyed man before man could destroy it.

I wonder why we were not affected. Why did Neville, Jung-suk. Sue, Sheila and I survive when so many perished or turned into beasts? Gary shook his head.

The beasts had almost become non-existent. They came out only at night. They were so brutal and aggressive that they had wiped themselves out, killing each other and even their young.

When the survivors happened upon one of the dead beasts on their forays into town, they were amazed at their hairy bodies and carnivorous fangs. These beasts had no reason or logic. They had no ability to hunt only to lust and to kill. There had even been indications that they had eaten their own young. . They certainly had the ability to breed and children were born to them. Some of them died immediately from the same symptoms, being unable to breathe. Some became beasts themselves shortly after birth. The females seemed to be somewhat protective of their young but they were no match for the larger males.

It had been difficult at first, in their forest hideaway. For the first month or two they had decided to stand watch, on guard against the beasts. It was taxing for everyone. They knew they had to protect each other. But the beasts never came and after a few months they relaxed. The beasts stayed primarily in the cities and did not have the drive nor any reason to explore. So as time went by they began to sleep through the night peacefully, knowing they were well hidden. Just like the Maroons before them had hidden from their slave masters, they knew that they were safe here.

When was it that we decided to move into town, Gary wondered? In just the last few months they had all come to the conclusion that they needed to move. It would be much easier to live on the coast instead of high up in the jungle. Having to make periodic forays into town to find food and other things that they needed took a lot of energy.

Two years of rough driving in the old Mercedes Benz that they had acquired had taken its toll and someday the old monster would not run. They had discovered that the shelf life of gasoline is about a year. But Gary had learned to make biodiesel and so they had an unlimited supply of fuel. But car parts were difficult to find and the old Mercedes was becoming more difficult to repair.

Yes, Gary thought, we need to move to town to be closer to the ocean to fish and to grow crops where the land is flat. Gary felt good about the fact that they hadn't seen any beasts alive for quite some time. It was an indication that they should move.

It's like the life before zero year never really existed, Gary mused. They had to think anew and make their own rules to survive together. They had had to become a community.

After the first year, any hope of rescue or contact with the outside world had begun to diminish. They all began to think only of the here and now. There had been hours of discussion, endless talks. Gary could not have imagined this lifestyle before zero year. Their days were filled with interaction and the quest for survival. It had simplified all their lives and the world they lived in had become small yet rich.

Gary loved Jungsuk, Sue, Neville and the children. And being the eldest he felt somewhat of a fatherly attitude toward them.

They had not chosen a leader. They decided by consensus. They took action communally. This was something only a small group could do. It took time to come to decisions they could all agree upon. It was at times awkward for the four of them. They were very different people.

Sue had been pregnant by Pedro when the plane crashed in the jungle and the plague took his life. Gary remembered the great anticipation that filled them when it came close to the time for Sue to give birth. A small girl had been born seemingly healthy until quickly she began to choke. She exhibited the same symptoms they had seen so many times before. She had quickly died. There was nothing any of them could do.

It seemed that Sue would never recover. Her sorrow struck everyone else as well. It wasn't just the death of this baby, although that was tragic in of itself. But with its death hope was lost that children would ever live again. The idea crossed their minds that they were the last human beings on earth. They despaired that civilization would never begin again.

Things had seemed so hopeless. They felt so alone and isolated. But as time passed they began to mend. And that enduring glimmer of hope within each heart could not be snuffed out. They began to talk of what they were going to do to survive without any hope of outside help.

Gary breathed a sigh. Yes, it was time to move back down into town. This would be a monumental occasion. Sue came out of a hut carrying her baby, Caleb. His child. He smiled and realized that he felt hopeful. Hope had been born with the birth of his child.

***

Jungsuk was full of energy. Her keen and astute mind was always analyzing every situation. She was in charge of deciding what was essential for them to take to the coast and what they should leave behind. She had always been the thinker of the group. Her reserved nature had begun to change since the plague had destroyed their world. She began to open up in this small community that had become her family. She chewed on the end of her pencil, making what seemed to be an endless list. She was careful to include items she knew would be important to each person. It is amazing, she thought, how we have managed to get along. Four very different people from four different cultures.

She rubbed her naked belly absently, thinking. They did not need to wear clothing in this warm tropical environment. Jungsuk's natural reserve and shyness had melted away. They all were naked before one another and thought nothing of it. Neville was the father of her child. They had become extremely close and now slept together all the time. Her breasts were engorged with milk. She suckled Acoba and also Caleb, Sue's baby, and little motherless Wendy. Sue nursed all the children as well. It gave Jungsuk great joy that she and Sue could take care of all the children in this way. I would never have experienced this feeling before zero year, she thought.

Looking at her list, with the things each one of them made and taken responsibility for, she realized how they had all brought their skills to this new life. She had used her writing skills and taken it upon herself to keep a detailed diary. She was continually fascinated by the fact that even though there were so different, they had managed to co-exist and even to love. She liked to think about the social implications for the world, if there was a world, at their success.

She was fascinated with the way things had blended. We all smoke the ganja now and revere it, she thought. And Gary has taught us much about Christianity. I erected a shrine to the ancestors the way my family taught me. They all stopped before the shrine and meditated on their loved ones occasionally. Sue brought a respect for all living things from her Native American tradition.

It was fixed in Jungsuk's mind that she and Neville were a pair and Sue and Gary were a pair, but even that definitive border was only a minor one. They all loved one another freely and there was very little jealousy.

She looked down at her bare feet, calloused from not wearing shoes for so long and she thought back to her childhood and how life had changed. She smiled. We have an opportunity to do something different here, she thought. Something better. She was full of hope. And if we can survive and learn to live with each other and love one another then there must be other communities on this planet. There must be.

She picked up Acoba lying in the crib Neville had made and suckled him. This is my life's purpose, she thought. Acoba and Caleb, and Wendy, Sheila's daughter. It will be easier on the coast, she thought. She was excited about the move.

***

Neville took a break from packing the old Mercedes. I'll be glad when we can let this old car rest, he thought. Neville and Gary had chosen this vehicle not because it was a luxury car, but because it was a diesel. We were smart to learn now to make our own fuel, he thought and felt proud.

Neville preferred the natural world. He relished the fact that after only two years the road from their remote camp to town was almost impassable. The jungle is taking over, he thought and smiled. Time to move to the coast before we can no longer get there.

Trees had fallen over the road and roots and vines had broken up the asphalt. He liked to think that in five or six years the interior would be as if no man had been there. Except for the stone buildings and walls, the jungle would take it all. Yeah...he thought it is time to move to the ocean.

He had suggested that they move to the hot springs that Fred had owned and attempted to make into an eco-tourist destination before the plague. Neville remembered working for Fred and shook his head, musing. It seems like another lifetime, he thought. It's a beautiful place, Neville thought, near the ocean with arable land. They would even have hot water in their homes for cooking and bathing. Neville visualized how he could run pipes from the hot springs to the bungalows. It's a good place, Neville thought contently. Now that the beasts are gone.

Gary and Neville had made one structure that was defensible at night just in case there were any beasts that discovered their whereabouts. Neville didn't like thinking about the beasts. They were ugly and dangerous. He didn't like having to kill them if he and Gary found one sleeping during the day on their forays into the city.

But the danger and stress of those times seemed far away. Things were much better. He and Gary had initially had an awkward and difficult relationship. They were so different. Occasionally jealousy had sprung up between them when they had paid too much attention to the other's woman. But over time, the fact that they had to work together side by side to protect this community forged a strong bond between them.

Neville depended on Gary for technological advice. Gary depended on Neville to show them all how to farm, gather food and survive, and even thrive in the jungle. And now they each felt more secure with the women, they were able to love each other and show affection for one another freely.

I am so lucky to be with my Jungsuk, Neville thought smiling. She makes me feel calm and peaceful .He had learned so much from her. Her vast experience of the world beyond the island and her knowledge always astounded him.

He was proud that he could hunt and grow food for Jungsuk and everyone. He introduced her to ganja and was happy to share its healing powers with the community. They smoked it often. Its gentle high was a vacation from the cares and troubles that surrounded them. They laughed and talked. It was a time of release. A ritual they performed on a regular basis when the work was done for the day. They were careful, however, not to let it interfere with the serious job of survival.

Neville loved and enjoyed the children very much. He thought of his young cousin Sheila, who had committed suicide and suddenly felt sad. She was so young and these crazy times were so hard on her. She was the only survivor that they had found. She had been almost unable to speak when they first found her. She trembled and cried all day. But as time passed and she realized they had a chance of survival she improved. She wanted a baby. Neville was reluctant to oblige her as he felt they were family. After great discussion, it was decided that Gary would father her child. Sheila gave birth to Wendy and they felt new hope when the baby survived. But Sheila became withdrawn and depressed again. Neville shook his head. He didn't really understand what had happened. Just too much hurt, he thought.

It had broken his heart when he found her body at the bottom of a cliff. They all knew she had jumped. They all raised Wendy as their own. The human race is growing again, Neville thought and his feeling lifted. He had hope in his heart now. Neville had finished packing the car for now. He headed back to their camp, carefully so as to not disturb the vegetation and leave a trail to their home.

***

Sue gently hummed as she rocked back and forth with Wendy in her arms. The little baby's eyes closed, sleeping contentedly. What a wonderful feeling it was to hold a small child like this, she thought. And what a wonderful place: the birds singing in the trees, the shadows moving on the ground with the wind in the trees. This is paradise in a way, she thought.

Her heart still ached sometimes for her baby that had died. But she found solace in the birth of Caleb. It had been a tremendous positive influence on her. And even now she realized that this plague was something they could overcome.

Her nursing background caused her to often speculate about the plague. What is it, she wondered, that is the same between all of us? The only thing she could think about that was similar between them was something unseen yet common to all human beings and not defined by race or sex. About six months ago, she had begun wondering if blood type had something to do with their survival. She had asked Gary and Neville to find the medical supplies necessary to determine blood type from the hospital in Roseau. Strangely enough, they were all AB. On one occasion she had extracted blood from a beast they had found and killed. And when they did that they found the blood type was A. Pedro's blood type had been O, she knew. It had to be our blood type, she thought. It must be.

Still, she could not say for sure. It was possible that it was coincidence that they were all AB. She didn't know what blood type had to do with being able to survive. She wondered if there were others on the earth with type AB blood who also survived. Of course, they would have had to survive the beasts and many other difficulties and dangers. There has to be other survivors, Sue thought. Ah well....it will be good to be close to sea, even if we never find anyone else.

It would be good to no longer have to hide in the remote jungle and to be close to the ocean. She could swim and could lounge around without any fear from the beasts. She could relax a bit. It had been so hard.

***

She and Jungsuk were the mediators of conflict in their community. They helped the men to deal with issues logically and calmly. They had had to abandon so much of what they believed and knew before and slowly they were formulating a new way to operate and survive. She found it interesting. But she found the closeness among them to be even more fascinating. She cherished it. She had spent a lot of time working with Neville to find edible plants and fruits and berries and medicines. They had experimented and they were surprisingly healthy in this environment. There was little need for clothes, and food was abundant. They never really wanted for anything. They had managed to create a small community that was compact, close and dependent on each other.

Sue had grown to love Gary although they were quite different. Wendy murmured softly in her lap. She couldn't distinguish whose child was whose, she loved them all. What a great way to grow up, she thought.

It was also interesting for her to note that with this next generation there would be no dividing line between races. All the children were mixed and they could not say they were full blood anything. This gave her a tremendous vision of the future.

She really enjoyed Jungsuk's company. The two of them talked more than Gary and Neville did about the future. Even though they were so different they talked endlessly about themselves and their past. They were beginning to work out a new way that would meld their various beliefs into a philosophy of life that would sustain them. Jungsuk and Sue understood that they may never find any other survivors, although they both hoped they would. They understood they had to make a new society. Gary and Neville seemed more concerned with the survival of the day; making sure the fire was being tended, and there was shelter and food. Although they too joined in the discussions, it was mainly Jungsuk and Sue that pondered the deeper spiritual and social issues.

Neville walked into the clearing in his slow, easy way. "Time to go," he said softly. Sue picked up Wendy and began packing a few last things. It would be hard to leave this place because it had been such a secure place for them. It had been their home for the last two years. But it would be a new beginning for everyone. They all stood together in the small clearing that had been their home. They each paid respects to the spot where Sheila was buried. They all realized that they may never return. They solemnly walked down the path to the Jacko steps to the road where the Mercedes was waiting. Neville fired it up and the familiar smell of French fries, the biodiesel, filled the air.

Neville fired up a cone and they passed it around. They began the slow journey to their new home. It was amazing to see the new growth. And they laughed as they drove the road that soon would no longer be there, engulfed by the jungle.

When they finally got to the outskirts of Roseau, they noticed that the vacant buildings were being overwhelmed by the jungle. The stench from the decaying bodies had long passed, but bones were everywhere. And here and there were remnants of what civilization had used to be. But most of it had passed into ruin. Those buildings that had survived fire were empty hulks that were slowly decaying. Only the masonry still survived.

There were many memories for Jungsuk of her husband and the life they had lived there together. A tear slid down her cheek. They drove by the old church where she had hid out.

At this point, there was no discussion in the car. Everyone was alone with their thoughts. It was always good to see the ocean again. The waves slapping against the shore was a constant force in a life where so much change had occurred.

They headed up the valley. They continued along the Roseau river toward the hot springs where they would live. They decided to rename it from Wooten Waven to Maroonville. Since they had become the new Maroons of Dominica.

It was a difficult drive as the road was steep and heavily overgrown. Occasionally they had to stop while Gary and Neville chopped back bushes and moved branches out of the road. But when they got to the springs Jungsuk and Sue were amazed at what Neville and Gary had done. The bungalows that were still intact were neat and tidy and cleaned. There was room for a large garden. Once in a while the sulphuric smell of the hot springs would waft their way. The coconut trees were ripe with fruit. The waterfall nearby gave a wonderful feeling of laughter with its pleasant sound.

The kids immediately enjoyed being dipped in the hot springs and then being doused in the cool water of the clear stream that flowed nearby. Neville thought they could drink the water from the stream that rushed straight from the top of the island without getting sick. It was paradise. They ran and laughed. They settled down in their new home and knew they would love it.

Time passed. Neville had done his best to convince Gary that they needed to hone their hunting skills and not rely on dying technology. They did continue to use the electricity generator from photovoltaic cells, saving the women the chore of making fires for cooking. They practiced making bows and arrows. They hunted the wild pigs and Neville was often successful. Gary had much to learn, but was good humored about it.

They had been able to collect chickens and goats. They milked the goats and made good use of the eggs. The women loved to till the ground and already were growing vegetables and fruits near Neville's ganja plants. It had become their sacred plant. And they honored it.

This third year was one of the happiest they had ever spent. They enjoyed talking about the religious and social issues that confronted them. They talked about the future and the possibility of other survivors. Often they would make forays into the jungle. Sometimes they would make the long trip around the island in the Mercedes to see if they could find sign of any other survivors. There was so much time on their hands to think, to be and to love. The only question in their mind was, "Is this all that there would ever be? Was there anyone else on this planet?"

Great effort was made to find radio equipment and using the photovoltaic cells they would try to rig up shortwave communications. They would broadcast but they never received a reply. It wasn't exactly a hopeless feeling, but it was a feeling of isolation.

They watched the children grow into a new world having never known of a life before zero year. It was hard to believe that there really had been a totally different world only three short years ago.

Jungsuk continued to write in her journal, collecting data and recording events. She started to paint again and enjoyed that. She taught the others Tai Chi and yoga and they often practiced together as a family. They were all fit and brown.

Sue continued her research for medicinal herbs. Gary continued trying to invent technological hybrids to meet their needs. He continually tried to make contact with the outside. Neville tended the garden and hunted. He was content with what was, and had no desire to have anything but what he had. He found in his little community the peace that had escaped him most of his life. He loved Jungsuk and Sue and Gary and particularly the children whom he lavished with affection and his time. He loved teaching them and playing with them.

When conflicts did arise between them, they always met in council. It was often the women who facilitated the reconciliation. Rarely did they go for more than a day or two with conflict among them.

Gary was always impressed by Sue and Jungsuk's wisdom. He and Neville typically would concede to their judgment. There were disagreements and those were allowed. And for the good of all, all things were discussed and agreed upon together. They had come from such diverse religious backgrounds. They decided to respect and accept any and all belief systems as long as they complied with the following rules:

They would never lie to one another.

They would never steal from each other.

They would never kill each other.

And first and foremost, everything they did must be from an act of love and never from selfishness and self promotion.

They tried hard to keep to these rules. It was not always smooth, but as long as they were able to abide by these rules they were able to overcome any obstacle. They considered year three the new beginning.

Chapter 12
Most Unholy Unions
03-05

Life at Maroonville hot springs was idyllic. Jungsuk and Sue took great pleasure in growing vegetables and flowers. Fruit trees— banana, grapefruit and mango—grew effortlessly. They raised chickens and goats, and the children loved playing with the animals. Neville tended his ganja carefully, producing plants more potent and beautiful than any he had ever grown. Gary spent a lot of his time trying to make their lives easier through technology. He worked on developing photovoltaic cells to provide ample electricity. He built a plumbing system to bring the abundant hot water from the springs into their huts. He was constantly working on the shortwave radio and trying to contact the outside world. There was time in to play with the children, to experiment with new ways of doing things, to talk, create and think. And at night there was time to make love. Their days blended and flowed together in a bright tapestry of life. Only the solstice marked the passing of the days.

They constantly wondered whether anyone else was out there. It was a question that lived in all their minds day and night. The beasts appeared to be gone. They had done an excellent job of killing themselves off. The little group of survivors no longer felt the need to sleep in the stockade Gary and Neville had built when they first arrived. Each little family stayed in its own hut.

Gary and Neville made forays into the jungle and wandered along the coast. They explored the land looking for others and for anything useful to their survival. They hunted and fished and the land gave generously. It was on one of these exploratory trips that they saw the first and only sign of another human being. They were camped on the narrow isthmus at Soufriere Bay and after a long day of fishing they decided to climb to the top of the ridge where an ancient cannon still pointed out to sea, a remnant of a fort that had been there long ago. Gary was contentedly watching the sun sink into the sea when he saw it, a bright flickering light on the island of Martinique. He grabbed Neville's arm and pointed. "Mon!" Neville cried. "A light!"

The light flickered and then it was gone. They knew it had to be another human. The beasts did not build fires nor did they use electricity.

Gary and Neville jumped up and down yelling, laughing and hugging one another. There was someone else alive in the world! They hurried back to camp talking excitedly. They would go to Martinique, right away. But there were questions. Who would go? Was the Minnow still in good enough shape to sail?

The next morning they hurried back to Maroonville with their great news. Sue and Jungsuk were elated. They celebrated that night, dancing around the fire after the children were put to sleep, smoking and laughing, wondering who this person was. Was there more than one? The next day Gary and Neville prepared for the long trek to Calibishie Bay, where the Minnow was docked. They would take the vehicle and weave their way down the overgrown road. It was an uneventful trip, but slow. They had to stop often to clear vines and plants that had punched their way through the asphalt. Often they had to drag whole downed trees out of the way. It was obvious to both of them that someday this road would be gone.

When they finally reached the bay they saw the Minnow right where Gary had docked her. Her sail was moth eaten and her hull was covered with barnacles. They beached her and scraped the hull and mended the sails. Fortunately, the boat had a diesel engine, and Gary got it running on his homemade biodiesel after much tinkering. They got the bilge pumps to work and raised the patched sail. They decided that Gary would sail the Minnow around the point to Roseau Bay and Neville would drive back to Maroonville. They already had been gone for a long time, days, maybe more than a week. They both missed the women and the children. Gary was nervous when he first set sail at dawn. It had been a long time since he had sailed. But it all came back to him easily. He enjoyed the solitude. It was nice to be alone with his thoughts. Again and again his mind wandered to Martinique and the light. Who was there? Could it have been his imagination seeing the light? No, Neville had seen it too. Was there a whole group of people? He felt a deep desire to rebuild the human race and he knew that their gene pool was not large enough to do this.

That evening as he sailed into Roseau Bay Sue, Jungsuk, Neville and the children were waiting for him. Neville had made it back much faster because of all the work clearing the road they had done. He found a place to anchor and swam to shore and grabbed Sue in a fierce hug. They were laughing and asking questions. Gary kissed Sue's full lips and stroked her long black hair. It was hard to believe he could feel so good after his world had essentially ended just a few years ago.

There was a great deal of discussion about who should go to investigate the other island. Obviously Gary should go because he could sail the Minnow. Should he go alone? Should Neville go with him, leaving the women defenseless? Should one of the women go with Gary and leave the other to take care of the three small children. After much discussion it was determined that Gary should go alone. They would attempt to maintain radio contact by way of the shortwave that Gary had been able to put together. Neville wanted to go but was convinced by all that they he should stay. The women wanted his protection. He needed to hunt for them. Who knew how long Gary would be gone? No one spoke the thought that was on all their minds, especially Sue's. What if Gary never returned? They could not risk both their men.

They all went down to the shore to wave goodbye to Gary as he left early the next morning. Gary embraced Sue one last time. He picked up and hugged each child. Tears came down his cheeks, knowing he may not return. He cast off. The others stood on the shore watching as the ship slowly became a small dot in the sea.

Gary faced the wind and felt excited and afraid all at the same time. He felt the gun tucked in the waistband of his pants. They had also decided that Gary should be the one to take the gun. They had two clips of ammunition left. The gun was reserved only for protection. Gary did not like to use the gun even when it was absolutely necessary. The few times he had killed one of the beasts he had been left with a bad feeling. Although he knew that when it came to the beasts he had no choice but to shoot. He never would have won in hand-to-hand combat with a beast. They were ferociously strong.

After about twelve hours of uneventful sailing on smooth seas with a nice wind at his back, Gary reached the shoreline of Martinique just as the sun was setting. He knew from his map that the capital city lay on the northwest shore. This is where he decided to land and search for the other survivors. He navigated by starlight now and the dark shape of the shoreline. He would concentrate his search in the capital, exploring by day to avoid any beasts that still might exist.

I'll have to find some way to let the inhabitants know he had landed if there were no people on shore in the morning, he thought. As he entered the bay he started his motor and carefully navigated through the other boats, mostly decrepit and wrecked now. He found a place to drop anchor. He was very tired and his whole body ached. But he had made it! He couldn't wait for the morning. He hung one of his biodiesel fuel lamps in the back of the boat, hoping someone would see it.

He was too excited to sleep although he was exhausted. Around midnight his eyes finally closed. It seemed that he was only asleep for an instant and when he awoke to bright sunlight pouring through the porthole onto his tiny bunk. He quickly clambered on deck. The heat was already oppressive. He raised his binoculars to his eyes and scanned the shoreline of the harbor and to his amazement he saw a woman standing on the shore! She was of medium stature and stood still with one hand over her eyes gazing out over the water toward him. He could see her fiery red hair shining in the sunlight. He waved, and after a moment's hesitation she began to wave and then to jump up and down calling to him. He started his engine and motored toward the dock where she stood. As he came close he cut the engine and tossed her a rope. She caught it expertly and tied the boat to the dock. Before he could even get on land she was covering him with kisses, speaking excitedly in a language he recognized as French. And although he could not understand what she was saying, it was obvious she was overjoyed to see another human being. He separated himself from her embraces and took a moment to look at her. She appeared to be in her mid 30s and looked healthy and strong. Her brilliant red hair contrasted with her pale white skin and Gary wondered how she had managed to protect her skin from the sun. She was almost naked just wearing a pair of old patched shorts and sandals, but did not seem self conscious at all. He made her understand that his name was Gary. She referred to herself as Mandy. She pulled on his arm, gesturing for him to follow her. Gary touched the gun and felt reassured. He decided to go with her. Perhaps she would lead him to others, maybe a whole community. He couldn't wait to find out. He took her arm and made her stop.

"Are there others?" he asked, wishing desperately that he spoke French. He repeated it over and over with gestures and pantomime and finally she got it. She shook her head. She raised her index finger in the signal of one and pointed to herself. One. There was only one.

Gary felt disappointed, but then reassured himself. If she was alive, there were others somewhere. If not on this island, then somewhere there were other human beings. He followed her through a maze of burned-out, ruined buildings, twisting and turning and climbing over rubble. The beasts had not been able to find her here, he thought. Mandy knelt at a large rock and, grunting, pushed it aside. Inside was a dark room lit only by a small hole in the roof above. Ah, Gary thought, if she stayed here no wonder her skin was so pale. It took a moment for his eyes to adjust and then to his amazement, in the corner he saw a small shape crouching on the floor. A child! He approached it, overjoyed. But the child hissed at him and retreated into the shadows. The women gestured toward the child and called, "Pierre!" The child retreated. She took his hand and let him into the light. To Gary's amazement he saw that the child looked like a beast. He was covered with hair. The child was somewhere between two and two and a half years old, Gary thought. He jumped into Mandy's arms. She cradled him lovingly, talking to him in soothing tones. When Gary tried to approach again, the child hissed at him and reaching out tried to claw at him. He backed off and Mandy's clear blue eyes showed disappointment. She carefully set Pierre down and taking his hand tried to put it in Gary's. But Pierre ran away, making an angry growling sound. Gary was shocked but tried not to show it because it was obvious that Mandy loved the strange child.

Throughout the afternoon they pantomimed and gestured, trying to understand one another. The few words of French that Gary knew and the few words of English that Mandy knew were not enough to communicate. He did try to make her understand that there were others on Dominica and that they should go back there. She nodded in enthusiastic agreement while she was fixing him something to eat. She pantomimed that Pierre would come as well and Gary readily agreed. This strange beast-child appeared to be her own. They decided to leave the next morning.

After dinner, they sat quietly in the light of candles. She is beautiful, Gary found himself thinking as he gazed at Mandy. He found himself attracted to her and unsure what to do with those feelings. She was extremely forward and hungry for the touch of another human. And before long they found each other entangled in each other's arms. They repeated their act of love throughout the night. In the morning she packed what she deemed valuable and they headed down to the Minnow. Pierre kept his distance from Gary. He seemed sleepy and rubbed his eyes and wanted Mandy to carry him. Gary had never heard the child utter a word, and he wondered if Pierre could talk.

They walked silently back to the boat and cast off. Mandy smiled often as she looked at Gary and she looked back at the shoreline of Martinique. She seemed happy to leave and seemed to trust him totally. He was surprised at how easily he had gained her trust. He felt anxious about the fact that he had had sex with her. How would Sue react? He was so used to discussing everything with his small community of survivors that he felt very uneasy at taking this action without their approval or knowledge. How much I have changed, he thought.

When they reached Roseau Bay Gary fired off one of the precious .45s knowing that the others would hear up in the valley and they would soon come down in the Mercedes to greet them. They tied up the boat and soon the Mercedes chugged up onto the shore. Everyone hugged each other and greeted each other. Mandy held back with care, waiting for the proper moment. Gary motioned for Mandy to join the others. Pierre hung back and would not leave Mandy's side. Gary introduced her as Mandy French. Everyone embraced Mandy and kissed her as if she were a long lost relative, a sister they had found. She was a fellow member of the human race, one of the few survivors left. Neville knew patois, which was a combination of English and French. So he could effectively communicate with Mandy. Soon they were talking excitedly. The women attempted to coax Pierre closer but he stayed between Mandy's legs. The sunlight seemed to hurt his eyes. The other children were afraid of him and stayed away. They all piled in the car and headed back to Maroonville. Pierre slept in Mandy's arms. The women questioned her through Neville. Were there any others? Why did Pierre have so much hair? It was revealed with Neville interpreting that Mandy had been raped by a beast and had borne this child. The others were quiet, feeling her pain and feeling their own fears of what it would be like to have a beast child among them.

The days passed and they all enjoyed Mandy's company and the novelty of a new face. Pierre, however, never did warm up to anyone. He would bare his teeth when approached. The women were concerned about the babies' safety with Pierre around. They kept a close eye on the children, but luckily Pierre just seemed to sleep all day. He became active at night. Mandy usually stayed up most of the night with him. As the toddlers became used to Pierre's presence they became more fascinated by him. But the adults kept them apart, a task made easier by Pierre's inclination to sleep all day.

Through Neville they learned about Mandy's life. The same plague had attacked Martinique. She had many of the same experiences. This created a bond between them. She too had made many attempts to find others but had no success. She had survived by hiding and using her cunning. The beasts were not able to focus on one thing long enough to discover her hiding place and they had no motivation to explore. Pierre had been her only companion. Mandy talked about how her loneliness drove her to climb a tall hill carrying a light evening after evening. One evening she had built a big bonfire and finally Neville and Gary had seen her light. She still cried when she related the story.

After the initial joy of reunion with another human being, it became obvious that having another woman in their little society raised some issues. Gary told Sue he had been intimate with Mandy. Sue cried and was hurt but also realized that she could not have the same expectations of fidelity as they did before zero year. This strange new world did not allow them the luxury of monogamy.

Mandy grew close to Neville. He was the only person she could communicate with. She asked Neville to sleep with her so that she could have another child. Neville raised the issue with the group one night as they gathered around the fire. Neville stressed that he only wanted to sleep with Mandy to produce another child. Everyone agreed to the idea, but all felt uneasy. Jungsuk cried in her hut that night as Neville went into the jungle to sleep with Mandy.

As time passed Jungsuk's logical mind allowed her to accept that this arrangement also was a part of their brand new world. The months passed and it was soon apparent that Mandy was pregnant. She allowed Sue to take her blood type and the blood type of Pierre. The results confirmed Sue's theory. Mandy had AB blood while Pierre had A. Whatever virus or bacteria was now present across the earth did not affect people with AB blood. It was her guess that people with O blood could not survive at all. And that B and A blood would be affected in ways that they could not imagine to produce the Beasts.

Nine months flew past quickly and Mandy grew heavy with child. She worked hard and was skillful at cooking and gardening. But she was never quite accepted. She did not learn English and only effectively communicated with Neville.

The women could not put aside their jealous feelings as much as they tried. And Pierre was a constant worry. One day Caleb approached Pierre as he was sleeping. Pierre suddenly awoke and chased Caleb, snarling. Caleb ran to Sue, crying hysterically. Sue was enraged that this strange beast child had threatened Caleb. What if it wasn't just a threat next time? What would Pierre be like as an adolescent or a man? He was immensely strong already. They asked Mandy to keep Pierre away from the group in a hut in the jungle. She did as she was asked, but this only reinforced her isolation. Sue promised to try and research a cure for Pierre, but in her heart she was doubtful. Sue felt the only chance was a blood transfusion. Not just a quart or two but literally replacing a great quantity of Pierre's blood with theirs over weeks and months. Mandy refused. Either she did not understand the situation, or did not trust Sue, or was just afraid for her beast child's safety.

When the new child was born there was great celebration. The child survived and when Sue tested his blood it was AB. This beautiful baby boy, with mulatto skin and pale eyes was a reflection of his parents. Mandy named him Jacque. There was much celebration and renewed hope for the human race. Everyone loved Jacque and all three women suckled him.

Tensions grew, however. Neville had continued to sleep with Mandy throughout her pregnancy. And Mandy also was very forward with Gary. It seemed intolerable to Jungsuk and Sue that they had to share their men in order to rebuild the human race. But Mandy's relationship with Neville and her advances toward Gary were not as altruistic.

The women often talked about their feelings, but still feelings of possession and jealousy remained. Finally, Jungsuk demanded that Neville stopped sleeping with Mandy until such a time came again when he might be needed to father another child. Neville agreed reluctantly.

Mandy spent more time in the jungle with Pierre. They all worried about Pierre and what they would do as he became a man. But their dilemma was solved for them. They awoke one morning and Mandy was gone. She had taken Pierre with her. She left a note in French that Neville read to the group. Mandy felt that she could not stay there anymore. She would leave Jacque to be raised by the others. But she could not bear to part with Pierre and so she had left to raise him alone and to try to find her own community of people. She said she was taking the Minnow back to Martinique. She was an experienced sailor. She asked that they not follow her and if she could not find a better situation she may return when Pierre was old enough to live on his own. At her departure, tension eased in the little community.

Neville was sad that Mandy had left, but he felt perhaps he would see her again one day. One evening as they sat around the fire, Sue brought up the fact that the only way to increase their gene pool was for Gary to sleep with Jungsuk and Neville with herself. Everyone was silent for a bit gazing into the fire. Jungsuk agreed. There was not the tension in this decision that had been there when Mandy arrived because Jungsuk and Sue trusted and loved one another.

After a time it became obvious that both women were once again pregnant. After which they settled back into their normal routine- Sue and Gary, Neville and Jungsuk. The pregnancies proceeded and in a very strange way the episode of exchanging partners although initially difficult and awkward had somehow made more firm their allegiance to one another.

Gary and Neville could rarely be found apart and had become linked in a way that they could not understand. It was year five now and both women came through their pregnancies without any trouble. Jungsuk gave birth first to a baby boy that she named Lee, a name that had been in her family in Korea. His skin was pale and he had almond shaped eyes and black hair. He was handsome from the day he was born.

Sue gave birth a few weeks later to a little baby girl that she named Anna, a name that had been in her family for many generations. Anna was also a beautiful baby. Her olive skin glowed with an inner light and her eyes sparkled with energy. Acoba and Caleb, who were now 4 and 3, were fascinated by these newcomers.

After the birth of Anna, they decided that this would be the last time they shared partners. It was easier to keep those boundaries in place. After they came to that decision they sat around the fire talking about Mandy. They wondered what had happened to her. And always, they wondered, were their other survivors? Or were they alone on this earth?

Chapter 13
Rumblings
Year 15

It was another bright sunny day on the tropical island of Dominica. Sue walked through the jungle to the meditation place Gary had made for her in a small clearing just outside the compound. He had built a wooden gazebo to protect Sue from the rain and a small simple altar. She carried a flower to the altar each time she meditated. She loved to sit there listening to the birds and the wind in the trees.

The large sundial occupied the center of the clearing. She had asked Gary to make the sundial to keep track of time. She carefully marked the length of the shadow of the sun throughout the year at the highest point each day. In this way, she was able to determine when the solstice and equinox occurred.

She didn't keep track of months or weeks or days. But because she could determine when it was the longest day of summer and the shortest of winter and the midpoints of fall and spring, she knew roughly what month it was. She was the timekeeper of the family.

So much had changed in the 15 years since zero year and the plague that it was comforting to keep track of steady progression of the year. They still had made no contact with any other people except for Mandy. Their small community had grown and become closer and more cohesive. Though strife and troubles arose, they had always worked through them. Sue and Jungsuk had taken on leadership roles and the two of them had become very close. They spent a great deal of time talking about their community and the future.

Sue sat in front of her altar and let her body relax. She loved this peaceful place. She sighed. I wish we never had to leave, she thought. But the children were becoming older and adolescence brought to light the difficult issues of sexuality and the continuation of the human race. As the children matured, the push to find them mates grew stronger. Their gene pool was far too small for the human race to survive. They all knew that, but most resisted the idea of leaving this island of tranquility and relative safety.

She heard rustling in the trees. Wendy appeared in the bushes and waved to Sue. She was a special child. She had an insight into things that astounded the adults. She was able to predict the weather and events within the community. She came closer and stood looking at the sundial. She was 13 now and already had developed into a young woman. "Almost winter solstice," she said smiling. Sue nodded, admiring Wendy's shining hair and long graceful legs. She will need a man, Sue thought, if the race is to continue. Where will we find him?

Wendy sat next to Sue in front of the altar and they embraced. Then Wendy drew back, looking serious. "I feel like there is something different today," she said. "Something is changing on the island."

"What do you think it is? " Sue asked. Wendy shook her head, frowning. "I don't know. I just know something is going to happen. I can't tell if it's bad or good, but something is going to change. I can feel it."

Sue nodded. She respected Wendy's intuition. "Well, let's meditate a bit," Sue said. "Maybe that will make things more clear." They meditated together, their breathing becoming synchronized, bodies and minds relaxing.

***

Neville picked up his bow. He was ready to go hunting again. He loved to move through the forest silently, all his senses alert. Caleb came alongside him, holding his bow and looked into his eyes expectantly.

"Ready?" Caleb asked. The best hunter of all the children, Caleb followed Neville on almost all his hunting expeditions. Even though Gary was his biological father, Caleb and Neville were inseparable. Their favorite game was wild pig. The pigs were smart, ferocious and very good to eat. Neville nodded. "Ya mon, let's find the wild pig."

They moved silently through the forest on their moccasined feet, pausing to set traps that would snare the foot of an animal and catapult it high into the air, leaving it hanging from a tree branch.

Caleb and Neville knew every stream and trail, mountain, cliff and beach. The whole community could use a bow and hunt a little. But Caleb and Neville had naturally evolved into the community's main hunters. They had come up with their own hand signals and language to communicate silently in the forest when stalking game. Neville looked at Caleb, He was proud of this young man. He had grown tall and had a light complexion with sandy blonde hair. They moved together silently graceful, holding their weapons. They would probably only be gone for a day or two. At night they would sleep on the forest floor in a hollowed tree trunk with the frogs and fireflies creating light and sound around them. Sometimes they would build a small fire and talk of what life was like before zero year. Neville wanted Caleb to understand what Dominica had been like...its villages, his loving mother and family. Caleb tried to picture the island the way Neville described it, but it was hard. He had seen the ruins of the buildings in Roseau and the crumbled remains of the roads, which helped him to imagine the time before zero year. Neville impressed upon Caleb that he needed to remember what the island was like before the plague so he could tell his children. Caleb understood that the reason they had all been able to survive was because they all had AB type blood. Sue had taught him that. He knew that all those who had become beasts were type A or B. And those that died were type O.

They all suspected that some diabolic plan had been conceived to wipe out the human race. Neville was not sure there were any other humans and was content to stay on Dominica. But as he watched Caleb move through the forest in front of him he felt the familiar gnawing anxiety. Where would Caleb find a mate, he wondered.

***

Anna looked up and smiled at Jungsuk as they worked in the garden. Together they had created a lush, abundant garden of banana, papaya and mango, squash and beans. Tomato plants filled the air with their spicy aroma. Their garden provided far more fruit and vegetables than they could eat. Jungsuk and Anna often gardened together and each could coax abundant life from the earth. Jungsuk smiled happily in the warm sun. It was such a relaxing ritual to weed the garden. It was irrigated by bamboo pipes that traveled downhill from a nearby stream, filling the furrows with clear fresh water. As they worked, they spoke often of the days before zero year. Jungsuk wanted Anna to understand the different religions and cultures of the world. She loved telling her stories of China and her childhood in Korea.

Jungsuk looked with great pride at Anna. She was the youngest. She was very fair skinned with lovely silky blonde hair and even at 11 was showing signs of womanhood. Often she and Anna would do yoga together when done with the gardening and would talk about the religions that had existed. Anna tried to remember all the things Jungsuk told her. It seemed like their world was so simple in comparison. It was hard for her to picture this huge world that once existed beyond the shores of their small island. In Anna, Jungsuk found a willing receptacle for all her knowledge of culture and society. She hoped that through Anna, some knowledge of religious practices, the arts and culture of the world would not be lost.

Anna bent down and pulled up some weeds around one of the tomato plants. She loved the smell of the garden and she could identify each and every plant. She sometimes thought of the world the adults described and her head began to ache. Then she would come to the garden and remember what was truly important, tending these plants, nurturing them, nurturing each other. It was all so strange to her when she heard the stories and went into town and saw the old buildings that stood stark and burnt out. The jungle is stronger than the things man can make, Anna thought.

Jungsuk began to hum a Korean song from her childhood and Anna took up the cadence. It was just as natural as breathing.

***

Gary looked at Acoba and smiled as he poked his head through the porthole. He and Acoba spent enormous amounts of time at the docks refurbishing a yacht to take the Minnow's place. They had chosen a yacht of relatively good size. They had biodiesel for fuel and had been working diligently on the engine. They had installed solar panels to run lights at night. The sails had been salvaged and repaired from other ships. Gary was fixing it up to be as comfortable as possible because it was his intention to take everything they had developed and leave the island to find other humans. More than any of the others, he felt a strong desire to leave. To explore and find other humans so the race could continue. He and Acoba often sailed to neighboring islands and they found no other people. He still hoped and watched at night for lights in the darkness. He remembered vividly the signal fire that Mandy had built and hoped to see it again.

Gary had become an expert at tinkering with technological devices to make them work again. Acoba shared this mechanical skill and knowledge. Gary saw in Acoba the possibility that at least some of the world's vast technological knowledge would be kept alive.

Acoba had a keen mind and an ability to understand even the most complicated devices and the process of electricity and physics. Gary and Acoba had worked well together and together they had named the ship the Enterprise. It was their pride and joy. And although it was fit for a long journey they had been forbidden to go any farther than the neighboring islands. The rest of the family was always concerned they wouldn't make it back. The loss of any one member would have been devastating.

Gary told Acoba stories as they worked. He told him about technological devices Acoba had never seen and could only vaguely imagine. He explained to him about Canada and Wales. There was far too much knowledge for Acoba to absorb all at once so he tried to be selective.

Gary thought for a moment. Really the most important thing we need to impart to these young people is that love and caring and the nurturing of each other is far more important than creature comforts or technological advances.

But Gary had made sure they had creature comforts. It was one thing he could occupy his time with. He often found his mind racing with ideas as to how to make their lives more comfortable. And always, he thought about leaving. He tried to express to the others the urgency of finding others to continue the human race.

Acoba was anxious to leave as well. He wanted to see some of the places Gary had described, the huge cities, the machines. They all fascinated him. Acoba tossed Gary another wrench and he turned the last few cranks and declared that the engine was ready. He pushed the button. It fired up, belching diesel fumes. They had power! They now could sail or use the motor, whichever they felt was necessary. The cabins were ready. They had food stored with other equipment. They smiled and embraced one another. The engine purred and they knew they had accomplished a great thing. They went up to the deck of the ship and stood together at the railing looking out to sea. "Will we leave soon?" Acoba asked, his eyes shining with excitement.

Gary sighed. "We will tell the others tonight the ship is ready. But we may have to talk to everyone time and time again. They are frightened to leave."

Acoba nodded. "Yes, but we have to go, don't we, Papa?" Acoba asked. All the children called the adults that were not their biological parents mother or father, but Gary was always called papa.

Gary nodded. "Yes we do Acoba. Sooner or later we have to leave if the human race is to survive." Somehow I will convince them we need to go, Gary thought.

***

Lee and Jacque were doing what they almost always did—exploring. These two young men had become not just half brothers, but also the best of friends. They could hunt and scout and to the dismay of their parents often left for days at a time exploring the island. They had researched every little town. They had mapped the island. They had swum in every stream and were great fisherman. Their strong, sturdy legs were relentless in their quest to explore the entire island. They had even gone to the top of Mt. Diablotin and found the wreckage of Sue's plane. It was just as she had told them and they marveled at the plane. They had no fear of animals or of being alone. They were the ultimate explorers.

They were going now to one of their favorite places, Boiling Lake, a volcanic crater filled with water that periodically boiled from the heat below the earth. The sulphurous smell was very curious to them. They loved to watch it and wonder. As they neared the rim, they looked at each other. "Can you feel the heat? Jacque asked Lee. "It is stronger and listen to that strange popping sound."

Lee nodded. "There is something strange going on." They stopped, listening and sniffing the wind. Just then they felt a small tremor below their feet. They looked at one another, eyes large with shock. They scampered to the rim and as they got closer they could see the small spouts of lava spurting above the rim.

When they reached the top, they saw that the lake was gone. There was no longer a boiling lake of water. Deep below them in the cauldron was lava. The magma had come from deep within the earth. Another tremor shook the ground. "The volcano is waking up!" cried Jacque. The adults had explained to them what volcanoes were and that this whole island had been created from volcanic eruption. They understood the power and danger of what they were looking at. The heat was almost too much for them to stand near the rim. "We have to tell everyone right away," Lee cried and they started jogging down the trail. They traveled through the night at a slow lope they could keep for hours.

When they got to camp everyone was sleeping in the compound. "Wake up!" Lee called. "We have important news."

Everyone tumbled out of their houses. "What is it?" Wendy asked. She had been expecting something and so was completely awake.

"The volcano is waking up," Jacque said.

"What do you mean? Gary asked. Just as he finished speaking, the earth shook.

Jacque and Lee quickly told their story. When they were finished, Gary said. "We have to leave this island now. We cannot be safe here."

For once, the family did not object. Concern showed in all their eyes and faces. They knew he was right. The time had come to leave. They all decided to go back to sleep and to continue the discussion in the morning as to what they needed to do.

Everyone embraced Jacque and Lee and thanked them for coming back so rapidly with their news. They lay silent in their beds that night, listening to the distant rumble and feeling the tremor of the earth. Would there be enough time to leave? Had they waited too long?

Chapter 14
Landfall
Year 15

Everyone worked together to load the schooner that Gary and Acoba had named the Enterprise. With the volcano rumbling and spewing smoke, they worked quickly and for once silently. On the morning of the second day after the volcano had come alive they were ready to leave. They had loaded chickens, coconuts, grains, canned goods and fruit, as much food as they felt they could carry. Sue and Jungsuk supervised what they were to bring and everyone gathered medicines, weapons and tools.

When Neville and the boys returned, running down the beach, it was obvious from their faces that it was time to leave. "The mountain," Neville panted. "She is ready to blow."

"There is red hot lave flowing down the mountain side," Jacque said, his eyes alive with excitement. Jungsuk and Sue looked at one another and nodded. It was time to go.

Everyone boarded the Enterprise. The children were excited about the journey and the idea of living on a boat. All of them had sailed with Gary before, but this was a whole new adventure. The adults were more somber, particularly Neville, knowing that they may never return to the place they had come to think of as home.

Gary and Acoba had spent a great deal of time getting the schooner ready. They had worked on the small pony engine that ran with biodiesel fuel until it ran smooth and efficiently. They had new sails that they had sewn together from other deserted boats in the harbor. They had collected everything they needed from other ships to make the Enterprise a seaworthy vessel, one that could take them on a long journey if need be. Caleb untied the bow line from the dock and threw the line onboard to Acoba and jumped on. They cast off, motoring away from the dock and their home.

Neville leaned against the rail of the ship watching his beloved Dominica recede into the distance. Hot tears ran down his face. He bowed his head, hoping his long dreadlocks would hide his distress. He knew he may never again see the place of his birth, the place where his mother was buried. He had been the person most resistant to leaving. He was a Rasta, and a Rasta loved the place of his birth. Only the imminent danger that could not be denied had finally forced him to leave. They all could hear the rumbling of the volcano even above the engine and even now and again loud explosions. Ash and pumice rained down on the deck and Sue and Jungsuk made the children go down into the cabin below. When they left the bay, the wind freshened and they set sail, cutting the engine off.

It's like Noah's Ark, Gary thought. "We are carrying all we have and may be the only people on earth."

They all hoped that they would find other humans. They had not seen anyone on their previous sailing trips. Gary and Acoba had even gone within sight of Cuba on one trip and had not seen any lights, but now they were going farther than before. They had agreed the night before to sail to Cuba and set anchor in Havana Bay. Perhaps they would find someone on shore and supplies that they had not been able to scavenge on Dominica.

Gary sailed straight west to get away from the falling debris of the volcano and then gradually began to turn north. The charts he had gathered from various places were more than sufficient. In his heart, Gary wanted to sail to North America, but this had not been agreed upon. So for now, his sights were set on Cuba. He felt an intensity to go back to North America that was hard not to express, but he wanted it to be a group decision. It had to be a consensus.

As they sailed farther from the island, the children were allowed to come back up on deck and were soon playing and running around the ship. Suddenly, there was an especially loud explosion and in the distance they saw a huge cloud rise over Dominica. Neville hid his face in his hands. The children shrieked in excitement. The adults gave thanks they had escaped. This small family, perhaps the last vestige of civilization, stood and watched as Dominica disappeared into a cloud of grey smoke, lit from within with a red light from the lava spewing down the sides of the volcano. They gathered together and held each other and watched in amazement as the volcano created a new island.

Gary steered the ship effortlessly. The breeze was fresh and steady, the seas calm, a perfect day for sailing. He caught a glimpse of himself in polished chrome of the cabin. He was startled, surprised as always by his long hair streaked with grey and full beard. He didn't look at himself often these days and in his mind he still looked like the young man that had first come to Dominica, devastated by the loss of Amy.

Gary was proud of the Enterprise. He had named the ship Enterprise because like Star Trek, they were travelling into unknown worlds. He was proud of the fact that he and Acoba had the foresight and skill to prepare for such a journey and knew that he had saved his family by being ready. And more than anything, he was proud of his family. He knew it had been very difficult for some, especially Neville, to leave, but they had all faced facts and pulled together to make the journey possible. He was proud of the way they cared for each other and shared whatever resources they had. He was especially proud of the way they loved one another.

Gary felt content and peaceful surrounded by his family, even though they were all starting on a new journey. It was as if there was nothing they couldn't handle if they were together. He considered all the children his own, even though they weren't related to him by blood and thought of Neville and Jungsuk as his brother and sister.

What a strange world my children live in, he thought. He knew they were excited about this journey and he shared their feeling of anticipation. He did not know where they would go or what they might find in the days ahead, but in that uncertainty the dance of the universe, there was an excitement. He knew Jungsuk and Sue were less excited and more apprehensive and that Neville was bereft. He hoped it would become a good journey for everyone.

Jungsuk and Sue had become true Rastas in the process of caring for this tiny family. They were always looking out for everyone's needs. In a sense, they had become a matriarchal society. Not that the women commanded the others or had authority over everyone. But everyone, including the men, looked at them for advice and counsel. Both Jungsuk and Sue had grown in beauty and grace in the years they had spent on the island. Both Neville and Gary saw it and they all felt it. Their beauty was deep and their bearing regal. They both wore their hair long and flowing. They took good care of their physical appearance and of the children's appearance as well.

Sue looked down at her feet. Like everyone, her feet were bare. She loved the feeling of wiggling her toes on the warm deck, feeling the breeze off the ocean water on her legs. It was midday and the sun was hot and the water was calm. And despite the uncertainty of their future, she felt at peace and was filled with affection for Gary and all the other members of this family. As she gazed at the children playing on the deck her eyes stopped at Anna and Acoba. They leaned against the railing, heads close together, hair intertwined in the breeze. Sue knew their hormones were deepening the already close friendship they had. The adults had talked into the night about the inevitable attraction that would occur between the adolescents as they grew older and hormones flooded their bodies and minds. They knew sexual activity between the teenagers must be actively discouraged, but not with hysterics and taboos, but rather facts about inbreeding and genetics.

Anna and Acoba were brother and sister and it would be genetically detrimental for them to pair up. This was explained to them often by all the adults. Nevertheless, Anna and Acoba spent a lot of time together and when they looked at each other you could see the attraction and longing in their eyes.

Sue sighed. There had been no sexual contact among the children that she knew of. But she knew they could not watch them constantly and it was hard to know. They had all grown up in honesty and openness about their bodies and nudity. Nothing was hidden in this family. Nothing needed to be hidden. But there had to be rules to protect the human race and to ensure that it would survive upon the earth.

"Look!" Anna suddenly cried with amazement. She pointed out to sea where grey and blue porpoises were leaping into the air. Everyone except Gary ran to the rail to watch the porpoise playing in the wake of the ship. Anna nestled close to Acoba, his arm around her shoulders. She looked up at him. "I want Acoba as my husband," she said to herself. But that cannot be. But still she loved to touch him and be close to him and he always responded warmly. They had often shared back rubs the way Sue had taught them. Sue had taught all of them how to give therapeutic massage but for Anna and Acoba the massage was more than therapeutic. It was getting harder and harder to resist going further.

Anna looked out to sea, still watching the porpoises, but now with a solemn expression. "Who will be my mate," she wondered. "And when will I start my own family?" She wanted so badly for her children's father to be Acoba.

Acoba had felt these same feelings. Often when he and Anna swam naked together in the warm water of the bay his member became rigid with desire. He had to turn his eyes from Anna and think of the Enterprise or some other task to distract him until he softened and could get out of the water without embarrassment. Although he loved his father very much, he found it difficult to talk to Neville about his feelings for Anna. Instead he talked to Gary as they worked on the boat. Acoba sighed. "I'll talk to Gary soon, he thought. Maybe there is some way Anna and I could be together."

Caleb and Neville sat in the hold of the ship, going over the many bows, arrows and spears that they had accumulated to make sure that they were in good repair and ready. The bows and arrows were for hunting and protection. They also had brought the old .45 but this was saved for emergencies. Both Caleb and Neville were experts with the bow and spear. They were excellent marksmen and knew how to the keep the equipment in good repair. They had trained everyone else as well as they could. The whole family agreed that everyone should know at least something about survival. Caleb ran his hand over the smooth arrow and blew on the feathers at its end. "I already miss hunting," he said to Neville. "And our island."

"Ya mon," Neville answered. "Me too," and his eyes were sad.

Caleb too struggled with adolescence. He and Neville spoke of his new feelings and impulses often. Neville taught him about genetics and the importance of not inbreeding. Neville was not judgmental and they had not talked about right or wrong in terms of sexuality, but only about the blatant facts of pregnancy and its repercussions. Caleb enjoyed talking to Neville. He knew that he was honest and straightforward and trusted him.

Caleb's closet companion besides Neville was Acoba. They had grown up together and were inseparable. They told each other everything. Caleb was concerned about Acoba and Anna and wondered when he would meet a woman he could start his own family with.

Neville looked at Caleb, admiring his long almost blonde hair pulled back in a ponytail and his soft pubescent beard. The young man looks so serious, though. Maybe I can cheer him up. He is catching my sadness. "Your beard is growing like your father's," he said, smiling.

Caleb stroked his beard. "Yeah. I am a man now. "

Neville shook his head, smiling. It was hard for him to imagine that these children had not known the world that had preceded zero year. He and Caleb had talked many times of the time before, but Caleb found it hard to imagine something he had never experienced. "Maybe it was better that they don't know what the world was like before," Neville thought. "They can start fresh." He felt better than he had ever since he had known he was going to have to leave his home. "But we must find Caleb a woman," he thought, "so maybe it is good we left." He started to tell him this, when he was interrupted by the sounds of vomiting.

The seas had become rougher as evening approached. They came up on deck and saw Sue and Jacque leaning over the railing, retching. Lee was teasing Jacque and laughing. Anna and Acoba looked concerned. Gary had talked to them about sea sickness that they might experience. Neville and Caleb turned away, not wanting to be sick themselves.

The sun was sinking toward the water in a glow of red and gold. Guadeloupe was clearly visible to the starboard and Dominica was just a speck with a plume of smoke on the horizon to the south. As they grew close to Guadeloupe they decided to take shelter in the bay for the night and drop anchor.

Sue and Jungsuk called the family together. It was time to discuss what their final destination was and they knew this decision would be a difficult one. Neville and Caleb wanted to make their new home on Guadeloupe and return to Dominica someday if the volcano became dormant once again. Neville's desire to do this was confused by his competing desire for the older children to find mates.

Gary and Acoba wanted to keep going until they found other humans, cities and some form of civilization. Gary wanted to see the states again, maybe even Canada. Jacque and Lee sided with Gary and Acoba. They were the explorers. To go on meant everything to them. Wendy and Anna tended to want to stay in the islands and sided with Neville and Caleb although neither one felt very strongly about the issue.

Sue and Jungsuk listened intently, withholding comment. It was decided that they would sleep in the protected bay and in the morning decide what to do. The children slept on the deck in the warm quiet evening with the stars bright overhead. Gary and Sue slept below and Neville and Jungsuk made a pallet on deck.

They awoke in the morning when the sun rose and Jacque and Lee immediately dove off the deck into the warm water. Jacque had spotted a turtle and they wanted to catch it. It was comforting to Sue and Jungsuk to know that the kids were as home in the water as they were on land. The adults met again over coffee and discussed the matter again. Jacque climbed back on board dripping wet. "Can we go explore the island?" he asked.

Sue and Jungsuk looked at one another and Sue nodded her head. "Yes," Jungsuk said, "You can go."

"But stay close enough to hear the ship's bell," Sue said.

Gary smiled at Jacque and Lee. "You heard Sue, no further than the ship's bell." They jumped off the boat laughing. Anna, Wendy, Caleb and Acoba sat with their parents. Everyone was silent. No one wanted to start the discussion in which they knew they would disagree. The atmosphere felt heavy and grim. Neville sighed, "Mon, I am bushed. Maybe we should just spend the day on shore, enjoying ourselves." The teenagers looked relieved.

"That's a good idea Neville," Gary said. "We had to leave in such hurry and have been working hard. We need a day of rest."

Sue and Jungsuk nodded. "I could use a day to do some yoga," Jungsuk said, smiling happily.

So it was decided they would all go to shore. Gary and Acoba would explore the ruins and swim while Neville and Caleb decided to explore the jungle and took their bows and arrows. Sue and Jungsuk swam to shore together and planned to laze around the beach watching Anna and Wendy swim and play, keeping an eye on Jacque and Lee. Sue and Jungsuk lay in the shade of a palm tree on the white sand beach. "You know," Sue said. "The last time I went to the sun post I saw it was the solstice. There was no time to celebrate. But it is the start of a new year."

Jungsuk nodded. "A new beginning," she said.

Sue put her hand on her friend's arm. "That's not all. I had a vision."

Jungsuk sat up looking at her expectantly. "I saw a bay," Sue went on. "It was large and shallow and the water was warm. But it wasn't anywhere near the islands. It looked familiar like it might be the States." She shook her head. "But I'm not sure. I remember the shape of it though." She described the bay of her vision in detail.

Jungsuk's eyes grew wider. "I saw that bay too!" she cried.

"What?" Sue asked. "How...."

"I dreamt it," Jungsuk said. "Just last night. I was going to tell you about it."

This was not the first time this had happened to Sue and Jungsuk. Before, in times of crisis they would have dreams or visions together. They trusted these visions and knew they were important.

"We'll tell the others," Jungsuk said. "I don't think we can stay here knowing we both saw the same bay. It couldn't be on this island, could it?" she asked Sue.

Sue shook her head. "I don't think so. It was a place not as tropical as this. I don't even think it could be Cuba."

When the ship's bell rang in the evening, all the family members gathered and they had a meal together. After they had eaten Jungsuk and Sue explained their vision and dream. When they finished, it was silent except for the gentle flapping of the sails in the breeze.

Finally, Neville nodded his shaggy dreadlocks. "We gotta keep going. Even though I don't want to. We gotta see if we can find that bay."

Gary sighed with relief. "I agree!" The others nodded.

"But what if we never find it?" Caleb asked in a worried voice.

Sue and Jungsuk looked at one another. They had already discussed this possibility. "Here's what we were thinking," Sue said. "We'll look for this bay and other people until spring and if we haven't found the bay or any others by then we'll return to Guadeloupe."

Neville grinned and thumped his heart with his fist. "Ya mon! Good idea." Gary agreed as well and everyone seemed satisfied. They went to bed that night feeling at peace. Once again they had all worked together and found a solution to their differences.

As they approached Havana and its bay on a quiet full moon night, Gary and Neville were the only ones awake. They were disappointed that they saw no lights, no signs of other people. Gary woke Sue up. "Is this the bay you saw?" he asked.

"No," Sue shook her head and yawned sleepily. "It's not it."

"Are you sure?" Gary asked. "It's dark."

"I am sure it's not it, but ask Jungsuk too." They woke Jungsuk and she agreed with Sue that it was not the bay she had seen but they decided to anchor there and explore in the morning.

As they came on shore at first light, they saw that very little was left of Havana. Most of the buildings had been destroyed by fire or overrun by the jungle. The beasts had left nothing but havoc and desolation, and nature's return took care of the rest. They soon returned to the bay for swimming. So far their trip had been more like a vacation than an epic adventure. The weather had been good and the winds favorable. Everyone seemed to get over their sea sickness.

The next day they skirted the western edge of Cuba and Gary set a heading straight north northwest, hoping to hit the southern coast of the United States. His charts showed him a large bay called

Mobile Bay in what had once been southern Alabama. He decided it would be a good place to put down anchor and see what was there.

The sailing across the warm Gulf of Mexico was pleasant. They had been sailing for a month and a half now. It was close to the two-month time limit that the family had decided on before turning back. Neville and Caleb were feeling certain after all this time that they would not find the bay of Sue and Jungsuk's dream or any other people. They were anxious to turn back and head for the islands. But on the seventh week they came in sight of the southern coast of what had been the United States. As evening approached, they watched for lights on the shore. They put a light high up in the mast of the Enterprise, as a beacon, hoping someone on shore would see it and reply with a similar signal. Gary could barely contain his excitement. He felt like something momentous was going to happen. It was late at night and he lay sleepless in his bunk, occasionally getting up to make sure they were still on course.

Lee was on watch, when he saw the small blink of a light along the coast. He rang the ship's bell and yelled, "I see a light! I see a light!" Immediately everyone was awake and gathered at the bow, straining their eyes into the darkness. But no light appeared. "Are you sure?" Gary asked. "Could it just have been your imagination?"

"I saw it," Lee said firmly.

But no light appeared and everyone went back to bed. Gary knew he would not be able to sleep and so took over the controls at the helm, steering the Enterprise in the direction Lee had seen the light. When the morning sun broke they were in clear view of the coast. Jungsuk and Sue stumbled on deck wiping the sleep from their eyes. Sue's voice stuck in her throat when she saw the shore. "It's our bay," Jungsuk whispered and then more loudly, "This is it! This is the bay we saw!"

They looked at each other and eyes alight with excitement. Everyone hugged each other. There was still no indication there was civilization on the shore. But this certainly was the fulfillment of the vision and dream. They lowered the sails and motored into the harbor once known as Mobile Bay. When they got close enough to row to shore with the dinghy they dropped anchor. They decided that

Gary and Neville should go to shore first armed with the .45 and see what they find before the rest of the family would follow.

Upon Neville's request they decided to come ashore away from the obvious ruins of what had been a prosperous port at one time. They made landfall and pulled the dinghy up on shore. In front of them was a monument. They walked up to it cautiously. Gary read the inscription, "This is a place where Modoc, a Welsh prince, made landfall in 1160 AD."

Gary and Neville looked at each other. Gary chuckled and said, "One small Welshman in 1160 and another small Welshman in 15.What a coincidence."

They laughed and continued on cautiously, making sure it was safe for the Enterprise to dock and the family to come to shore.

Chapter 15
A Tale of Two Cities

Neville and Gary walked through the ruined city of Mobile, Alabama, until they found the outlet of a sizeable river. It appeared to flow into the bay in which they were moored. They slowly made their way up the west bank of the river into the city. They were surrounded by the remains of gutted and burned-out buildings that now were heavily overgrown with vegetation. The streets were littered with the hulks of rusting and burned-out automobiles. They saw no sign of other humans and an eerie silence lay heavy on their ears. The day was overcast. Heavy clouds, dark on the bottom, moved slowly like a blanket across the sky. It felt like it could rain at any moment. Both Gary and Neville felt that they were being watched.

"Mon, "Neville said uneasily. "I don't like this place. It feels haunted."

Gary nodded. "Yeah. We seem to be alone, but it sure doesn't feel like it."

They came to a bridge across the river and decided to cross it. They had to climb over debris and broken, uplifted asphalt. Parts of the bridge had fallen into the river and the muddy water swirled around the pieces of concrete and rusted metal. In the middle of the bridge there was a barricade they had to climb over.

"Damn." Gary muttered as he cut his hand on the strand of barb wire intertwined through the sharp pieces of sheet metal.

"Somebody don want us to cross over here," Neville said.

They began to tear the barricade apart, working slowly and methodically, so as not to cut their hands. A shot rang out, pinging off one of the metal struts over their heads. Both Neville and Gary dropped to the ground.

"Hey brother!" a deep voice yelled. "What are you doing with that white piece of shit?"

Neville and Gary looked at each other, both afraid and excited. Another human being had just spoken to them for the first time in fifteen years.

"He is my brother!" Neville called.

"He ain't no brother of yours," the man yelled back.

"We don't come from here. We come from Dominica," Neville replied. "We've come in peace, mon. To find other survivors."

"Well you found 'em," the voice replied. "You can come over here, but you leave that white honky mother fucker there."

Neville and Gary looked at each other, not sure what to do. They had to come up with a plan. They quickly decided that Neville would proceed.

"We'll meet back at the boat at sunset, "Gary said, "and if one of us doesn't show up we will go looking for the other."

Neville nodded. "Be careful, mon. "We have the family to think of back there."

Gary clasped Neville on the shoulder and smiled grimly.

Neville raised his hands and turned slowly to show that he carried no weapons. He climbed through the barricade and made his way toward the sound of the voice.

Gary stayed hunkered down, watching Neville. He was glad he had the .45 tucked in his pants and at the same time desperately hoped he would not have to use it.

When Neville reached the east bank of the river, Gary saw a band of about ten black men with weapons emerge from the bushes and gather around Neville. Gary could hear their voices but not their words. They did not sound angry or violent and he relaxed somewhat.

They gently nudged Neville with the muzzles of their rifles and began to walk upstream in a group with Neville in the middle. They were soon out of sight. Gary waited a bit and heard nothing but the sound of the water gurgling past the bridge abutments. Thankful that he heard no shots, he slowly made his way back across the bridge. I'll go back to the boat, he thought. And tell everyone what happened.

When Gary reached the west bank several white men with rifles appeared from behind a building. They yelled at him to halt. Immediately he put his hands up, not wanting them to know that he had the .45 tucked in the back of his pants. He faced them as they approached.

"What are you doin' with that nigger," a large man with a chiseled face growled at him.

"He's my brother, he's my friend," Gary answered hesitantly. "We're not from around here; we came from an island looking for other survivors"

"Well...he found his people you found yours," the man said.

"I have a lot of questions," Gary said.

Another man, short and wiry and extremely strong with only one good eye, stepped forward. His one good eye shone with hatred. "We've got questions too," he said. "Is that your boat out there in the bay? "

"Yes, it is," Gary replied. "My name is Gary, Gary Llewellyn. I come from Canada." He stuck his hand out, hoping to make friendly contact.

"My name is George Wallace," the man said. "I am the leader of the people and there are no countries anymore. I am not sure if we have answers but come with us. We want to find out what you know and who you are." He put his hand out slowly. Gary and George shook hands.

Gary looked around at the other men, feeling somewhat safer. They were of various ages and were all white. They were dressed in handmade clothing.

What a strange world, Gary thought to himself.

George motioned his gun toward Gary, signaling him to walk. They started slowly walking away from the river. The others followed with their guns still pointed at his back. When George saw the .45 stuck in Gary's pants he grabbed it. 'Just for safety," he said. "We can't allow you to hurt anybody." He smiled with a toothless grin.

This man has lived a hard life, Gary thought.

They proceeded into the ruined city. "We've come in peace looking for other survivors," Gary said conversationally.

"I understand that," George said. "But we have to be careful. You were with a nigger."

Gary thought for a moment. "I obviously don't know what is going on here," he replied. "But I'd like to know. Are there many people left? What has happened to the United States?"

"All in good time," George replied.

They walked for a long time. As they walked, everyone became more relaxed and they carried their weapons easily at their sides. Each man introduced himself to Gary. They've decided I'm not a threat, Gary thought.

In the distance, Gary could see a large stadium. "Is that where we are headed?" Gary asked, pointing.

"Yep," George nodded. "That's home."

They came to a huge wooden gate and George pounded upon it and called out a sequence of words Gary guessed must be some sort of password. A guard opened the gates and they walked through. There were houses built of wood and cinder blocks with metal roofing all along the inside perimeter of the stadium and up into the stands. In the stadium field were well tilled garden plots and fenced in livestock—cows, sheep, horses, mules and pigs. There was a large chicken coop as well and the chickens pecked in the dirt yard. The men directed Gary to a large cinderblock room. The floor was dirt and the walls were bare. It wasn't long before it filled up with all the other members of the community. About a hundred white men, women and children gradually filed in, talking in hushed voices, staring at Gary curiously. They were dressed in homespun garments and seemed healthy. Gary was afraid but tried to appear at ease. It can't end here, he kept telling himself.

Across town, Neville joked and talked with his captors trying to put them at ease. They finally lowered their weapons and began to converse with him.

"I am Neville Lincoln," he introduced himself.

They all laughed when they heard the name Lincoln. The leader, a man about Neville's age, sporting a large afro and a broad, flat nose, claimed his name was Malcolm X.

They came to a large fort-like structure and entered through a wooden gate. Wooden houses painted in many colors stood in a circle. There were apartment buildings as well built of stone with corrugated tin roofs. There were garden plots at each home and a communal garden in the center of the stockade. People came out of their houses, laid their hoes and shovels down and swarmed around Neville. He guessed there to be about a 150 men, women and children of various ages. They were all black. When they were all gathered around, Malcolm told them to sit down and Neville was asked to explain who he was and where he came from. He was pelted with questions from people of all ages.

He told his story and the people listened intently. When he was finished, the people were silent. Malcolm X motioned for Neville to follow him. They entered a small house painted bright blue and sat in comfortable armchairs.

Women brought in food for him to eat. They giggled and smiled at Neville, obviously attracted to this fine Rastafarian. They pointed at his dreadlocks, which hung down to his waist. Malcolm rolled a cigarette and told Neville about the horrible plague that had hit them as well. He recounted the war with the beasts and the continuing hatred between the whites and the blacks. He asked Neville how he could stand the stink of being with a white man.

Neville explained that in his family race did not matter. They all lived and worked together and loved one another. It was the Rasta way.

His explanation was met with cynical laughter and taunts. But Malcolm did not seem threatened by Neville.

"Can I go home now?" he asked. "Back to the ship? The children and women will be worried."

Malcolm nodded. 'You can go. And you can come back anytime. Maybe make us some new little ones," he said and the women laughed. "But don't bring any white son of a bitches with you," Malcolm said sternly

"I'll come back after I talk to the family, " Neville said.

Likewise, Gary told his story to the crowd in the cinderblock room, then George took him to a house built high in the stands of the stadium. He began asking him questions. After a while he appeared satisfied that Gary was telling the truth. He told Gary about their lives...the beasts, the struggle, the constant worry of attack from the blacks, the worry that inbreeding would ruin them.

Gary asked if they had made contact with any other people. "Yeah," George nodded. "At first we contacted others with the short-wave. But then the radio broke and we never fixed it. It seemed like most of the contact came from the big cities."

But George seemed uncertain of how many people were actually left. He was sure there were people in New Orleans. They had sent two men to New Orleans in the past year and only one had returned. He had been badly beaten and his story was a violent one. A tyrant called Caesar who had a faithful following of a small army ruled New Orleans with an iron hand. According to George, he was an evil man and he had questioned the two men from Mobile. He assumed they were spies out to steal their women and supplies. When the two scouts did not give Caesar the information he wanted, he killed one man and beat the other. He forced the survivor to work in the fields. The man Caesar had enslaved eventually escaped and made his way back to Mobile. But his wounds and his treatment had been so severe that he did not live very long afterward. The story that he told, and the evil that he witnessed, made the people suspicious of anyone outside their community.

Eventually, Gary asked if he could go. George nodded and waved his hand. "But you can only come back alone. Don't bring that nigger with you. Or any half breeds either. " He handed Gary his .45 back. "Every white man needs a weapon," he said.

Gary was disheartened as he left. This was not the kind of message he wanted to bring back to his family, a message of hate. He was concerned about the safety of Neville. As he left the stadium, he observed that these people had regressed to the time before electricity and machines. They had not harnessed the energy of the wind and sun and apparently did not know how to make biodiesel. There is much these people could learn from us, Gary thought. But do I want to teach them?

When Gary returned to the bay at sunset he could see Sue and Jungsuk and the children waving from the boat. He was relieved when he saw Neville's great shaggy head appear from below and his long black arm waving. Caleb jumped in the dinghy and motored out to get Gary.

It was so good to come aboard. He was smothered with kisses and hugs by all the women and children. They ate a meal together and then had a family meeting to discuss everything they had learned. It was a long meeting. Neville and Gary took turns explaining. Everyone listened with eager attentiveness. They were all glad to solve at least a piece of the mystery....what had happened to them had happened in the states as well and probably the whole world.

Just like on Dominica, those that had survived the plague had either become beasts or like themselves, survivors. "Their leaders' real names are not Malcolm X and George Wallace," Gary explained. "Malcolm X and George Wallace were two leaders who believed in keeping the races separate and each hated and distrusted the other."

"They made the river the dividing line," Neville said and shook his head sadly.

The children looked confused. This was a completely foreign idea to them and they had many questions as to why a man would hate another just because of skin color. Sue explained the best she could with a heavy heart.

Like on Dominica, the beasts had pretty much annihilated themselves and although there were probably some that existed, they were no longer a threat to these people. The whites and blacks had salvaged all the weapons and ammunition they could find and lived lives of fear. The white population had been struck a few years early by some kind of flu and they felt that their hold on life was tenuous, Gary explained.

The blacks were more numerous than the whites, but not by much. There was little or no communication between the groups. Over the last 15 years, they had settled to the task of survival, raising animals and crops and keeping away from each other and the beasts.

"It seems like they didn't explore much," Jacque said, shaking his head.

Neville nodded. "They are too afraid."

"We don't belong here,' Jungsuk said sadly. "Even though this is the bay we saw in our dream we cannot live here among these people."

"They would tear us apart," Sue agreed. "I don't want our children to learn their ways of hatred."

Gary looked out over his small family and felt pride in the acceptance and love they had developed. We are starting a new way of being, he thought. A new civilization. He knew they had to find a larger, more evolved group of people.

The family was not sure what their next move should be. Should they stay and resupply and then move on? Would the people here even let them leave? Should they leave right away in the cover of darkness?

"Maybe we should just go home," Neville said slowly. "Back to the islands."

They decided to sleep and have a meeting in the morning to try to come to a decision then. Jungsuk and Sue both had dreams that night. Over breakfast they discussed them with each other and realized that they had seen the same thing. They saw the family with horses, mules and donkeys travelling over a great sea of grass. Sue recognized the grassland as the great plains of her ancestors. In their dreams, their journey ended at a small valley with a stone church. They were amazed and thankful that once again they had dreamed together. They kept the dream to themselves initially. When the family gathered for the meeting after breakfast, the children were anxious to get off the boat. As Jungsuk and Sue told their dream, they became still, listening.

"I don't think we can go back to the islands," Gary said. "I think the dreams are telling us to go inland."

Neville sighed and nodded his head, feeling farther than ever from Dominica."What will it be like to be away from the sea," he wondered.

The rest of the family seemed energized by the prospect of another journey. "Somewhere there must be more evolved people," Jungsuk said excitedly.

"These people have very little technology," Gary said. "I wonder if they would trade biodiesel and the knowledge of how to make it for horses and supplies."

"I bet they would!" Acoba cried. "Let's ask them."

Neville and Gary decided to return to the two settlements and propose a trade. After much bargaining a trade was agreed upon. The greatest fear for both the white and black communities was that one community would learn something more or better than the other and therefore have the upper hand for survival.

Gary and Neville agreed to present the information together to both communities so both would know they were getting the same information. This was a huge obstacle at first because neither trusted the other race, but eventually it was settled. The settlements agreed to trade biodiesel, and the knowledge of how to make it for livestock. Caleb accompanied Gary to the white community, as he looked the most white. Acoba went with Neville to the black community as his curly hair and dark skin allowed him to fit in with the blacks. Both Acoba and Caleb thought it very strange that skin color was such an issue.

During this time of bargaining, Sue and Jungsuk had set up a makeshift home on the shore of the bay. It was an uneasy time, this mixing of white and black and two very different cultures. But the communities reluctantly came to accept the strangers in return for their knowledge. The women and girls spent their time fishing and making a temporary home and the little ones played. Jacque and Lee were a constant challenge to keep at home and at times they did sneak off.

On one of his visits to the black community, Acoba learned they called themselves the Panthers. Two twin girls about his age explained this to him. The girls followed him through the village asking him questions and laughing shyly. Their names were Heather and Nicole. Acoba flattered them with attention and smiles. He liked both of them and was attracted to their young beauty. Nicole and Heather had a younger brother and a father. Their mother had died in childbirth giving birth to their young brother, Fredrick. Their father, Marcus, learned how to make biodiesel easily and explained it well to the other members of his community. Fredrick watched his father and Acoba work on the biodiesel with fascination.

At the end, of the day after the work was over, Acoba often snuck away with Heather and Nicole and shared his ganja with them. The girls loved the herb, but loved spending time with Acoba just as much. Acoba began to dream of having two lovely wives. But how can that be, he thought. They cannot leave here.

One evening as the family sat together eating dinner. Marcus, his girls and the little boy Fredrick came into camp. The family was surprised as this was the first time anyone had come to visit. The leaders had forbidden the people to come to their camp, fearing the minds of the people would be polluted by seeing whites and blacks and half breeds living happily together.

Marcus was nervous and the girls shy. Fredrick immediately began to play with Jacque and Lee. Sue and Jungsuk offered Marcus and the girls food and tried to make them feel more at ease.

After they ate, Marcus quietly explained how he had lost his wife Shawna and had not been able to find another mate. Marcus was a man of medium build and light brown complexion. His alert brown eyes revealed great intelligence with a withdrawn, secretive air. Before zero year he had been an aerospace engineer with NASA. Living with the Panthers had been a choice made out of survival. He disliked the whole concept of segregation and especially the seething hatred. Marcus purposely withheld many of his skills and knowledge to keep the playing field level between the two groups. It was a difficult choice but he knew any advantage on either side would fuel bloodshed. With the Maroons' arrival, he saw his chance to leave the whole situation behind.

The girls began to come to camp regularly and sometimes Marcus as well. They were all taking a risk they knew. Finally, one evening Marcus asked if he and his children could accompany them inland. The family agreed happily. And Acoba jumped in the air whooping. This was too good to be true!

But Gary was not enthused. "This means we will have to sneak away," he said. "Malcolm X will not let these people go willingly."

"But we have no choice," Sue said. "It is the Rasta way to take them with us so that they can be free. We'll leave first, and they can follow. " Gary reluctantly agreed.

Caleb had met a beautiful blonde-haired, blue-eyed girl about his age named Lori. She told him that her community was called the Clan. When Gary explained to Caleb the history behind this name, Caleb was horrified. But he liked Lori and shared ganja with her. The sexual tension between the two of them was so great you could feel it. She had to sneak away from the community at night to smoke with Caleb as, like the others, she was forbidden to have anything to do with the strangers. She sometimes brought her younger brother, Abel, along with her to visit the family on the shore of the bay and both were welcomed and loved. One night, Lori explained that it was her father that had gone to New Orleans and had died from his beatings shortly after he returned. She said her mother, Cyndra Dietz, had remarried a man who beat them. She left him but he constantly bothered them, breaking into their home at night, demanding that Cyndra be his wife. Sue and Jungsuk looked at each other firmly.

"Tell her to come to us," Jungsuk said.

"Ah...that is bad juju," Neville said. "This man is a bad one and he will come after her." He shrugged. "But she gotta come if she want to."

Cyndra began coming at night to the camp with her children. She immediately attached to Gary. She was apprehensive of Neville and the children she could see were mixed blood, but she did her best to be friendly.

Gary was able to talk with Cyndra about their community, the life they hoped to build in this new world and their plans to move on and find others. Cyndra was definitely interested in leaving. She was constantly tormented by a man she did not want. She was attracted to Gary and came on to him strongly in a sexual way a few times. She was about 35 years old, much younger than Gary. But Gary pushed aside her affections; Gary had learned to keep his loyalty to Sue, whom he loved very much.

The day came when both communities understood how to make biodiesel and understood the rudiments of restoring the old engines that lay in the city. Malcolm X and George sent parties of men separately to the family with horses, mules and provisions, weapons and ammunition. The trade was complete.

At this point, by Sue's calculations, it was midspring. It was hot and humid. Both Marcus and Cyndra and their children had decided to go with the family. They would leave at night with the new moon so that they would not be seen and try to catch the family. They would be faster than the family on foot with few possessions. They wanted to leave and make a new beginning.

On the last day before the family was to leave they powered up the Enterprise, stored the dinghy and secured the hatches. Gary ran the ship aground. It would be there in case things didn't work out and they had to return. It was sad to leave the Enterprise. It had been their home and their sanctuary for the past three months. They packed up their mules, donkeys and horses. Keeping all the pigs, chickens and sheep together was a difficult task but slowly they made their way north. Gary had located maps of what would have been the road system. Lee and Jacque had studied it constantly and had made explorations to the north to size up the lay of the land.

No one from the Clan or the Panther camps said farewell. As they passed under the bridge Neville began to dance and sing, "Is this love, is this love, is this love that I'm feeling!" he sang loudly. The others laughed and joined in. It felt good to leave this place of hatred and tension

They followed an old interstate, heavily rutted and overgrown. There was no way they could have taken a cart or vehicles. The pack animals found their way through the debris. The mules were especially sure footed. Caleb and Neville roamed ahead with their arrows, always hunting. Game was surprisingly plentiful...deer, rabbit and birds. They had enough horses to ride but they all preferred to walk, sometimes hand in hand. They hugged, kissed and sang songs. The children laughed and played. Lee and Jacque were the assigned scouts and each day they would move forward, exploring, checking out the way ahead. They reveled in this. They came back at evening with news of what was ahead. There seemed to be little sign of other humans. Occasionally they would find an old beast sleeping, which they would not awaken. They were experts at what they did and they loved it.

The family had taken to calling themselves the Maroons and this kept them in touch with Dominica and made Neville especially happy. They had made some canvas tents to sleep in. The tents were hot and stifling, but kept the rain off at night. They moved slowly and steadily. One dark night, about a week after they had left, Marcus, Cyndra and their children showed up in camp exhausted and hungry. Sue and Jungsuk fed them and made them comfortable. Everyone welcomed them, but also felt a bit uneasy. Gary asked them if they thought they had been followed and both said they thought not.

Sue, the timekeeper of the group, knew that they needed to find some stable situation before winter arrived, which left them with only about 6 months to travel, locate and prepare for winter. They constantly talked as they walked along of what they had learned and seen. They talked about the Panthers and the Clan. They talked about where they should go and where this sea of grass was and the stone church that appeared in the dreams of Sue and Jungsuk.

Nicole and Heather spent all of their time with Acoba, much to Anna's chagrin. And Lori was inseparable from Caleb. The boys Abel and Frederick seemed to circulate quite easily among the adults and the other children. It was good to have these new additions.

One morning as they were packing up, Brian Whitehead, Cyndra's abusive husband, walked into camp. He was wild-eyed and waving a .38 special.

"I come to get my woman," he yelled. "She doesn't belong with niggers and nigger lovers."

"I don't want to go back," Cyndra said, cowering behind Gary.

Gary moved forward with his hands up. "Put the gun down and let's talk about this," he said.

Almost instantaneously, Marcus struck Brian's gun from his hand. The gun went off and Heather crumpled to the ground. The gun rolled to Abel, who picked it up. Brian turned on Marcus and pummeled him senseless. Abel came around and shot Brian through the back. The bullet passed through his heart and he crumpled on top of Marcus. Neville grabbed Abel and pulled the gun from him. Gary rolled Brian off Marcus to reveal that the bullet had passed through Brian into Marcus's lung. Heather lay dead, hit in the forehead by the stray bullet. Sue tended to Marcus, attempting to stop the flow of blood from his right lung. Nicole and Frederick cried hysterically, holding their sister. It had all happened so fast it was hard to believe what had just transpired.

It was a sad day for the Maroon clan.

Chapter 16
Trackers
Summer 015

Marcus looked up from his bed and as his eyes came into to focus he beheld the same thing as each preceding day. The face of Cyndra as she watched over him. It had been touch and go for at least a week since the incident. The Maroons had chosen not to proceed with Marcus on the brink of death. Guards had been posted and there was great concern that others from Mobile would follow and cause trouble but so far no one came. Lee and Jacque had even ventured all the way back and observed the two encampments from a distance.

"You're like an angel to me," Marcus whispered.

Cyndra smiled at his first words and they could not have been more pleasing. "I am so glad you are getting better; we almost lost you a couple of times," she said softly, touching his cheek.

At 35, Cyndra was a striking woman with a slim build and platinum blond hair. Her face was lined, however, with worry and abuse at the hands of Brian. So unlike her first partner, Alan, a gentle and loving mate. She had been young when the world fell apart, just entering adulthood.

The Clan had been her only chance for survival in the devastation and panic. The acceptance of the prejudice was an agreement that was foisted on her and never felt good. She gazed with her green eyes at this black man who had almost laid down his life for her freedom. That old agreement was now broken and she was dedicated to helping Marcus recover. Cyndra cradled his head and helped him sip some warm broth. He seemed to respond more to human touch than to the broth and gave a weak smile.

"How is he doing?" Cyndra heard Sue say from behind.

"Much better" was her reply. "He spoke and smiled for the first time today." Sue had been instrumental in Marcus' recovery with her skills as a nurse in the military. The Maroons lacked many crucial medical supplies but they had made do. Sue tilted her head and watched the interaction between Cyndra and Marcus with amazement. Here very different people at one time opposed had become entwined by a tragic event. Marcus still did not know about his daughter Heather, now buried a short distance away. They decided to wait until he had recovered to break this awful news. Brian's body had been left into the forest as far as they could take it. The bad feelings were hard to remove from the group. Each night around the fire Jungsuk carefully guided the Maroons in discussion, helping each member voice feelings about the event. There was a great deal of weeping by Nicole and Frederick and everyone took turns holding and consoling them. Lori and Abel had shown the most remarkable compassion and the four children were becoming inseparable.

Gary and Neville had walked some distance from the camp into the thick Mississippi woods. It was hard to believe that civilization had ever existed here. The foliage was intense and even the once-broad Interstate 20 was being retaken by the vegetation. They had followed the old Highway 45 north to the interstate that they intended to follow west. The occasional sign helped them determine where they were. The nearby town of Meridan had provided some needed medical supplies but the ravages of the initial years, the beasts, the decay and climate had made what was left mostly unusable. The other side of that coin was the forest was teeming with wildlife and to date they had no need to use any of their domesticated animals for food.

Gary and Neville looked at each other. Communication between them was as natural as breathing and sometimes words were never even spoken. The striking difference between the color of their skin and Neville's dreadlocks and Gary's ponytail now streaked with gray was so opposed to their obvious affection for each other. It had been a long road from that first meeting on the road to Calibishie.

The intent was to head northwest to the place of the Rasta dream of grassland and a stone church, although no one knew where this was. No one had known the bay to which the Rasta dream had brought them. The two-week delay at this point was of some concern and it was hard to suppress Gary's desire for a definitive plan that they made happen as opposed to the intent and allowing things to happen. Neville was more relaxed in attitude and this had a calming effect on Gary. The long discussions with Cyndra of what she had learned from her first mate Alan after returning from New Orleans had made up their minds not to head that direction. The stories of the Caesar-type of individual who ruled by violence and force were enough. His authoritarian rule with the use of slaves and sadistic games in the Superdome was reason to avoid at all costs.

"I think it's time to proceed on our journey," Gary spoke first. "Summer is upon us and if we make a travois like Sue has mentioned we can transport Marcus with relative comfort."

Neville nodded, "Ya mon, I have the need to move as well. I want to find a place to settle down." They discussed the logistics and got up to leave. "We will discuss this with the family at the fire to-night." They lit up a cone and smoked it in silence.

The next day everyone dove into the activity of packing with much laughing. It would be good to move from this place physically and get some mental distance from the tragedy. The most difficult task was gathering and herding all the domesticated animals so precious to their future. All the children took part and it was a constant occupation of their energy and time. It was also a great team-building lesson and there was so much to be learned.

Lee and Jacque, however, continued their exploring. They had already ventured as far as the great river called the Mississippi and reported that there was a bridge across it intact. These two half brothers had made scouting second nature. They moved silently, communicated by hand and observed flawlessly everything around them. The eyes and ears of the Maroons, they were not to be stopped although Sue and Jungsuk often voiced concern for their safety when they were gone for days at a time. Off they went again to make sure the way was safe.

Caleb and Acoba, the oldest sons, had taken it upon themselves to provide food for the family. Their skills as hunters had now far surpassed anyone else's and rarely did they come back empty handed. Gary and Neville concentrated on the security of the family, often taking turns standing guard at night. Already there had been close calls with a pack of wild dogs on the chickens and there was evidence of mountain lions and bears prowling the perimeter. This left the younger children to help Sue and Jungsuk with the domestic chores and the search for vegetables and herbs to balance their diet. It was a regimen that seemed to fall into place naturally. The evenings were spent telling stories of the past, discussing the future and openly talking about the deeper issues of life, which held even the youngest child spellbound. The adults occasionally would imbibe in the ganja and its loving ways, laughing and loving. In some ways life was idyllic.

As they began the journey to the Rasta dream, the two scouts breathlessly caught up with the slowly moving convoy of horses, livestock and people. Lee found Neville first and began to tell him excitedly about what he and Jacque had found. "There are other humans ahead in the city of Shreveport many miles ahead," he panted. Neville called for the advance to stop and put his hands on Lee and Jacque's heaving shoulders to calm them down. "Wait, my fine scouts to tell the story to the family as a whole," he quietly spoke.

Slowly in the humid heat the column halted and the family of Maroons began to gather around. Only Caleb and Acoba were missing, out hunting for the night's dinner. The journey, though slow, had been uneventful except for the awe-inspiring crossing of the river. Watching the muddy waters of the Mississippi churn and flow far beneath the bridge at Vicksburg left the children in wonder at the accomplishments of the generation and civilization they had never known. Now there was excitement in the air again as Neville calmly asked everyone to be quiet and listen to Lee and Jacque.

Neville motioned for the two to begin. Between the two, they recounted what they had seen: A small encampment in the town of Shreveport off the interstate. Three wagons pulled by mules. The wagons carried cages. In two cages were beasts slumbering in the broad daylight. In the other cage were five young girls. There was a driver for each wagon and one man who rode a large bay horse. All the drivers were male and armed with rifles. Neville thanked them for this factual information and then allowed the family to ask questions. Lee and Jacque were inundated with questions that they could not answer about the cages, why were there beasts, what kind of men these were. Their only response was their feeling that contacting them was not a good idea. They both simply observed and felt these men were not friendly.

Once again, Neville commended them for doing such a good job for the family and everyone lavished them with praise and affection. The family was strong and cohesive. Jungsuk and Sue, in particular, took them aside. These two had become very courageous young men but the women could not disguise their deep concern for their safety when they would strike out alone. This was not Dominica of which they knew every inch. They were strangers in a strange land full of unknowns and they were so young.

When Caleb and Acoba returned from the day's hunt, another meeting was called to decide what should be done. It was a difficult meeting with the adults discussing all the possibilities while the children listened and watched. Marcus, who now could walk, was adamant that these men should be avoided at all costs; he was sure they were connected with the community in New Orleans. Cyndra also urged great caution. The fear in her eyes was intense after the loss of her first husband. They were 16 in number and the loss of even one person would be disastrous.

Shreveport was 10 miles away. It was finally decided to hold the camp here in a safe hidden location and well guarded. The .45 would remain in camp for defense. A party consisting of Gary, Neville, Caleb, Acoba, Lee and Jacque would go to Shreveport and only one would make contact with this group. Gary was firm that it should be him as the oldest. They would leave tonight, observe this other group and make a decision how to proceed with the safety of family paramount. Gary collected his finest clothes and everyone carried their best bows and arrows, food and Neville his father's cutlass. The family could hardly let them go from their embraces and many tears were shed. Gary hated to leave Sue's strong embrace, her brown eyes burning into his own with concern and strength. It was time to go.

The journey to Shreveport was somber and silent. Gary was amazed at Lee and Jacque's ability to move silently and remember each detail of their previous journey. When they reached the place where the campsite had been, it was well after dawn but it took little time to see that the group had moved south on Interstate 45, heading for New Orleans. This made everyone feel safer for the Maroons in hiding to the east. It did not take long to catch up to the caravan as it slowly moved down the overgrown road working its way around the many obstacles of old vehicles and downed trees. The Maroon party followed them and when they stopped at noon they decided to make contact. Only Gary would move forward, dressed in his finest clothes fashioned by Sue of soft skin and beautiful beadwork.

He presented a unique appearance with his graying ponytail and day's growth of whiskers. He walked unarmed with slow confidence toward the circle of men eating and chatting. His appearance startled them and they jumped to their feet, reaching for their weapons. Gary recognized the M-16 military weapon of the former United States Army. Their shaggy bearded faces and matted greasy hair could not contain their alarm. Gary stopped and held up his arms and called out "don't shoot; I come in peace." They did not lower their weapons but the man who had been riding the bay horse stepped forward to meet Gary.

"Senor, you startled us, it is not often we find someone alone, come forward". Gary moved cautiously forward, knowing in his heart that he had made a bad decision. He glanced at the hairy beasts sleeping in their cages and then at the young women who were looking anxiously in his direction.

"My name is Gary Llewellyn; I am from Canada," he spoke as the apparent leader and he came face to face.

"You are well dressed for one who has come so far senor, my name is Jose," and just when Gary let his arms down to extend his hand he felt the butt of the weapon against his skull and blacked out.

Gary awoke instantly after they doused him with water. He was tied to the wheel of one of the carts. His head was throbbing but he could see they had made camp and all four of the men were looking at him. Jose knelt in front of him and spoke. "Gary, it is time for you to tell Jose everything and do not lie. Tell me where you come from and where are your people? My brothers and I are trackers for Caesar; we will find out anyway. So make it easy on yourself and perhaps I will let you live to perform in the games."

"What games?" Gary replied, "I told you I come in peace. I am from Canada, I am looking for other survivors."

"Senor, you lie," and Jose punched him in the face. breaking his nose. "It has been 15 years since the disaster and no one survives alone; where are your people?" he again questioned.

"What do you mean Caesar? And why do you have these beasts and these women in cages?" Gary replied. The sun was at its highest and the heat oppressive; Gary was desperate for water.

Jose's reaction was another pummeling and kicking and he almost lost consciousness again. "Caesar rules the world now and if I let you live you will get to see these beasts again in the Superdome before they tear you apart in the Games. The women are new breeding stock. Now if you cooperate I may let you live, my friend, and spare you this future. I am a merciful man." With that he poured some water from his canteen onto Gary's lips.

Gary was delirious but struggled to say "I have no people, I am the last of my family and have come searching for others," he lied. With this, Jose became furious and began beating Gary again, yelling and screaming in Spanish words of obvious hatred.

They came with a whisper, almost silent, the arrows simultaneously striking each man. Two were fatal but Jose and one other were able to pull up their weapons and began firing on automatic in the direction the arrows came from. More arrows came and only Jose stood, stunned. He dropped his weapon when he expended his clip of rounds and drew his large knife. He turned and began moving toward Gary. Just before he reached him, he heard the yell and turned to see Neville running from his hiding place with his machete raised. Jose turned with fire in his eyes to finish Gary off with his knife. Just before he reached him the machete came down on his neck and Gary groggily witnessed Neville hacking again and again long after Josc was down and dead.

When Gary opened his eyes again he was laid out on the ground and Neville was looking down on him. Tears were falling onto his face and Neville was saying over and over, "You must live, I love you. I cannot make it without you." Gary managed a wry smile, "I had to lie, brother." Neville grinned with satisfaction that his friend was not dead and replied, "I had to kill, and now we are going to steal" as Gary slipped into the blackness of unconsciousness.

Chapter 17
Light on a Hill
015-016

Rising slowly, Neville surveyed the carnage. Acoba, Caleb, Jacque and Lee stood motionless, their eyes flitting from him to Gary, lying unconscious on the ground. The young men had never witnessed this side of their role model. They waited as Neville looked from face to face, his own streaked with tears.

With a sweep of his large muscled arms covered in blood, he signaled them to come to him. Still weeping, he gathered them in his arms and held them, no one speaking but all sobbing. Neville finally spoke in his deep voice. "My sons, there is much to be said but now is not the time. We must do what needs to be done while it is still light. My heart is very sad but very proud of all of you and I love you. Let us work quickly."

"Please help us," one of the girls in the cage yelled. The four of them looked toward the cage on the wagon that held the girls. They were all young, and their eyes were full of fear as they held onto the cage stiles and watched the small group of Maroons. Neville snapped into motion and began to issue orders. "Acoba set those women free. Caleb, prepare the wagons to travel. Lee, take the saddle horse and leave now back to the family. Be careful but move quickly, tell them to meet us in Shreveport at the camp where these trackers came from. We will meet you there; go now." Neville never left Gary and immediately bent down to adjust his position to make him comfortable. "Jacque, gather the weapons and anything useful from these trackers and put it in one of the wagons." Everyone moved purposely and no one spoke.

After Acoba found the keys to the girls' cage, he unlocked it and let them out. They were young and very scared. They all wore the same white robe-type garment now soiled by dirt and sweat. They moved cautiously from the cage, not sure whether to run or stay. Acoba saw their eyes and spoke calmly to them, "We will not harm you, don't be afraid. Are you hungry or thirsty?" They stood completely traumatized. Acoba produced his water container and began to offer it to each one and they drank rapidly.

"My name is Acoba, what are your names?" Each one after drinking their fill gave a name shyly. There was Sarah, Mariza, Joan, Peggy and Nile. "You are safe now, this is my family," Acoba motioned to his brothers and father. "Please rest while we prepare to leave," Acoba spoke quietly. He looked toward his father. Neville had not once left Gary's side but was constantly issuing commands and answering questions.

"Father, what should we do with the beasts?" Caleb asked as he approached Neville.

"Shoot them with one of the trackers' weapons, son, I know they are living creatures but we cannot allow them to escape and harm any of our people." Caleb located one of the automatic weapons from Jacque and searched for ammunition to replace the empty clip. Jacque worked with Caleb to figure out how to reload and between the two of them they decided how the weapon worked, never having used such a thing before.

The beasts were awake and ferocious, snarling and grabbing at the bars on the cages. It had been a long time since either of them had seen a beast yet they were very aware of the great strength and vicious nature of these seemingly human beings covered with hair. Even now they approached with extreme caution. At the first cage Caleb pointed the rifle at the head of the beast baring its canine teeth and staring with its piercing eyes. It seemed like a lifetime before he was able to pull the trigger only to find the safety still engaged.

The shot surprised everyone and the beast slumped to the floor of the cage. Caleb felt relief and remorse but not as intensely as when he had let loose the arrow that killed the tracker attacking his father. He stood for a moment watching the beast twitch then turned and repeated the action on the beast in the other cage. He then dropped the weapon and sat down, clenching his teeth.

This was not the same as hunting and his stomach did not feel good. Jacque sat beside him and Caleb reached out and put his arm around his brother. They would never be the same again, he knew, after killing other humans, beast or not. He wanted to run away but knew his father was near death and that is where he needed to be right now. Caleb helped Jacque up and the two began to unlock the doors of the cages and drag out the bodies of the beasts. The horses were nervous so they guided the wagons some distance away and began to clean out the cages and prepare a bed for Gary.

Neville carried Gary to the wagon as tenderly as he would a child. He climbed in next to him, stroking his head softly and reassuring him that he was safe even though he was unconscious.

Acoba did his best to make the girls less frightened. Given the option to ride in the wagons or walk, all five girls chose to walk. The five miles back north to Shreveport went slowly so Gary would not be disturbed. When they arrived Sue was waiting with her medical herbs, supplies and some water, having demanded that Lee ride ahead with her. The saddle horse was lathered and lay in the shade barely moving. It may take another day for the Maroons to reach this site but Sue wanted to be ready to take care of Gary and the others.

In her characteristic way she carefully looked to every detail of Gary's injuries and bathed and dressed his wounds. He had not regained consciousness and appeared to have broken ribs beyond his battered face and bruised body. She was concerned that he may have a concussion but was not sure if she should awaken him. She decided to and, after several attempts, he opened his eyes slowly and even managed a small smile at the concerned faces of Sue and Neville. She told him not to speak but try to stay awake as long as he could and he nodded. Neville and Sue wept in each other's arms.

Sue then began to attend to the others, going from son to son with hugs and choked-back words of praise. When she came to the young girls she embraced them too, all of them weeping now that they were safe. She brought them to the fire she had prepared as the evening shadows fell. She asked no questions but waited for them to speak.

Joan spoke first, saying her name was Joan Hannum and that she was 12 years old. Her long black hair and narrow face bespoke an Irish background. She explained that they had been taken captive from their home in Dallas. Mariza spoke next, "I am Mariza Vasquez and I am 11 years old." She had dark, reddish hair and large brown eyes, now very sad.

Sarah Smith, 9 years old, chirped in, "I want to go home." Sue looked at her and assured her they would do the best they could to take them home. Peggy King, now 11, and Nile Fukazawa, 10 years, finally opened up and expressed the same.

That night Sue decided to let Neville sleep with Gary and not far away she gathered the frightened girls next to her. Their nightmares woke them all several times but Sue just lovingly held them tighter. She could only imagine how traumatized they had been. Caleb and Acoba took turns standing guard with their newly acquired weapons. Sue could hear them from time to time talking about what had happened. They were so close these two. Sue slept very little thinking about this life that had become theirs so far from the little paradise of Dominica.

***

The next evening brought the rest of the Maroons to the encampment with all the animals and baggage. It was decided to stay a day or two until Gary was in better shape and a course of action could be made. Gary would survive but at age 46 the beating that he suffered would take its toll. It was now late July and very hot in Louisiana but food was plentiful and time was taken to introduce the new members to the Maroons, to recount what had happened and discuss what to do next. Marcus, now in better shape, would share one wagon with Gary. The other wagons would be better suited to hauling the possessions accumulating every day. This left the mules and donkeys to be available for riding.

From the girls it was learned that they came from a large community in Dallas now called Light on a Hill. The girls were very young but they conveyed that there was a very wise man who led this community named Joshua and that his wisdom directed all the actions and his word was law. The girls explained that everyone dressed in the robes that they wore and each person was given a duty as part of the body. Dallas was directly west on the old interstate according to the old maps, perhaps 200 miles. This would take them up to a month at the rate of travel that they were used to.

Neville wanted to return to the islands; he had had enough of the brutality of this country. Sue and Jungsuk still had the recurring dream of the sea of grass and the small stone church, and now even Wendy was having the dream. Sue had also promised the girls they would take them home. Gary, Neville and Marcus would sit together discussing what facts they knew. The disturbing reality of the community in New Orleans, the divided community in Mobile and now this strange community in Dallas. Neville and Gary both had come to have faith in the dreams of Sue and Jungsuk though Marcus was unconvinced.

A family meeting was called and even included the young girls from Dallas, who maintained their desire to go home. The other children, given the opportunity to speak, chose to listen as the adults debated courses of action. Finally Cyndra made the point that fall was around the corner and after that winter, when unlike Dominica you had to prepare or die. "Perhaps we should go to this community in Dallas and they will reward us for returning their children with sanctuary for the winter and then make a decision of where to go in the spring from there."

After a long silence, everyone consented to Cyndra's suggestion, even Neville. The adults passed around the pipe and everyone danced around the fire except Gary and Marcus and the girls from Dallas. The girls watched, fascinated by the revelry and joy and despite a desire to participate they held back. Dancing was forbidden among their people.

The days progressed slowly as the Maroons followed the old interstate toward Dallas. Gary and Marcus spent many hours in the wagon and sometimes walking and talking about their lives and the new world they now lived in. Cyndra and Marcus had become a pair, a signal of hope from such a different beginning. It was awkward at first but even their children had adapted to this new group and the different way everyone related. The events with the trackers weighed heavily on Gary's mind. He contemplated not only the huge difference between the Maroons and the people they had met so far but the tremendous possibilities for civilization in this new world that had been foisted upon them. Was it possible for this small group to make meaningful change for the future? He must talk to the other adults, he decided.

The landscape slowly changed from the dense forest to the open sky and sea of grass as the plains opened up to the Maroons. Neville liked the big sky that reminded him of the ocean around his blessed Dominica. Sue also was visited by memories of her childhood when she would visit the reservations of her people. The most amazing thing, however, was the almost total lack of evidence of the civilized world that had inhabited this area a scant 15 years ago. It was obvious that successive fires had burned anything combustible. No trees had survived, or houses, only the occasional metal hulk of some burned-out vehicle or a lone metal fence post and on occasion the tall concrete grain elevators that stood where communities once flourished. The massive interstate itself was cracked and overgrown with grass. The air was fresh and everywhere the abundance of wildlife was astonishing.

The greatest concern was for the wild bovines and packs of dogs that they encountered. There were many close calls and the domestic animals and the children were kept in the circle of adults, now armed with the automatic weapons. The weapon of choice for the scouts and hunters were the bow and arrow. Food was very plentiful and seemingly unalarmed by this small group of humans traversing the plains. Jungsuk and Sue still fretted about the forays of Lee and Jacque. These intrepid scouts had become amazing in their ability to see and not be seen. Using hides and grass camouflage, they would even come into camp and surprise everyone. When they would stay out overnight their mothers did not sleep well.

Days were spent slowly herding the livestock, laughing and playing with the children. Acoba and Caleb did most of the hunting and started to make use of the horses, slowly learning about them and mastering the art of riding. Marcus and Gary rapidly recovered at least to the point that they could walk instead of riding in the wagon. Evenings were spent around the fire of grass and cow chips gathered during the day's walk. Once in a while in a hidden bend of a creek or river they would find a tree protected from the grass fires and this was always a preferred camp spot.

The five new arrivals also had warmed up to this family and joined in the talk and duties, sharing what they knew about this land and their people. They were attracted to the open affection of the Maroons and as their comfort grew began to open themselves up to the hugs and touch of this strange group.

The adults sat often as a group and Gary shared his ideas of a new world that they could imagine of their own making. The old simple rules that had guided them for so long of always telling the truth, never stealing and never killing had all been broken. This new world had to be based on something that was simple and versatile and could be modeled from generation to generation.

They had all come from different cultures and religions and they needed something generic. They had all read many books in the days before the zero year and it was agreed that to have a vibrant healthy society there had to be some base beliefs that could guide the coming generations to hopefully not make the mistakes of the past. They also discussed the issue of propagation that would be easy and healthy to ensure a viable future. These discussions went long into the night and there was no easy answer.

When the time was right Gary, Neville and Marcus gathered Lee, Jacque, Acoba and Caleb to a meeting and discussed what had happened with the trackers. Lee and Jacque, especially had been having nightmares of having to kill these men. Each boy was encouraged to talk about how they felt. Neville stood up and went from boy to boy, touching them on the head as he bent to kiss them and saying, "You were very brave in what you did and though it is not good to take the life of another human I tell you there is a time for everything under the sun."

Gary spoke next regarding the breaking of the simple rules they had been taught all their lives. "My sons we know it is not good to lie or kill or steal, but even these things have a place. In the future we will only expect you to do things out of love. What does this mean? It means that when you are presented with a situation where you're not sure if it is good or not you must ask yourself if you're doing it out of love and your heart will tell you the truth, that is what you must follow."

This then would be the paramount rule, the only rule, that would guide the Maroons. "You must love all things but first of all you must love yourself." To this Marcus nodded and said "If you love yourself it will overflow to everyone and everything around you, if you love you will never fear because perfect love drives out fear." The meeting ended in silence but the smiles on their faces spoke more than words.

Sue and Jungsuk had spent many an hour discussing a strategy for the healthy continuation of the human species. The concepts of marriage and lifelong partnerships were hot topics. So many cultures and religions of the past had dealt with this in different ways with ceremonies, taboos and commitments. They needed something for this new time that would give guidelines but not confinement to the many possibilities. The closeness of the group and the lessons learned on Dominica were good references for them. The pairing of two people to create new life must be done with serious considerations. No viable form of birth control existed and they both felt the family unit was the foundation. The two Rastas agreed that sex was a wholesome and pleasurable healthy outlet, but the lack of birth control made the need for guidelines all that more important. They had to start somewhere. Last names or surnames could be effectively used to determine if propagation was safe. "Perhaps, if each person carried the surname of the mother and father we could use that," Sue remarked. "Yes, if any of the surnames were the same you would be forbidden to mate." Jungsuk replied. Then to keep the surnames from getting far too long the child of a union would take on the two surnames of their grandmothers. This then would hopefully achieve the goal of warding off inbreeding. They smiled at each other. "You know this will be difficult at best, given the hormones of youth." Jungsuk laughed. "It's a start and will take a very open discussion to work." Sue said. They both agreed to bring it to the other adults to consider.

These two had become so close in the last 15 years it was almost as if they knew each other's thoughts. The fact that they shared the same dreams in the night was something they often talked about in wonder. Sue reached down and grabbed Jungsuk's hand and they walked in silence gazing out over the sea of grass that surrounded them.

A large thunderhead was off in the northern sky tonight and they would watch the lightning flashes as the darkness fell. Sue was so much at home remembering her youth when she would visit her relatives on the reservation in Montana. She gave a long peaceful sigh. It was good to be here, she thought to herself.

It was pushing September as far as Sue could tell despite that she had no way of knowing the actual day with no tracking of the solstice. The grass was turning brown and the heat of the day was noticeably changing. Neville was sure that they were getting close to Dallas and asked for a family meeting that night. The young girls had told them that the "Body" as they referred to the community in Dallas had a standing army and patrols were always on the lookout for strangers. Ever since the great war, as they called it, Joshua had been the uncontested savior of the Body. They were too young to give accurate details of these events but their reverence for Joshua was evident.

"We cannot risk a confrontation in which more blood is shed." Gary spoke up. Everyone agreed. Lee and Jacque, the intrepid scouts, both gave accounts of what was ahead as far as they had explored. They also concurred that they had seen what appeared to be a large flame in the far horizon. "That's Dallas," Marisa exclaimed, adding that Joshua had decreed that the community would be a light to all survivors and he had built a huge tower on top of the great sanctuary that had a flame burning day and night for all to see.

"Maybe the best thing to do would be to send a messenger with one of the girls ahead and let them know we are coming," Marcus remarked. This seemed to be the best plan but who would be the messenger. The Maroons could ill afford the loss of anyone should something not go right. The country was a hostile environment to anything but a large group with all the large herds of animals and the predators that followed them. Acoba and Caleb both volunteered to make the journey. They had become good horseman and already excellent hunters. It seemed to the family a tremendous risk and both could not be sent. In the end lots were drawn to see which one would go and which one would stay. They used two sticks, one short and one long, hidden in Jungsuk's hand. She held it out first to Acoba and then to Caleb, her face deeply serious. Caleb drew the short stick which it had been determined would be the one to go. Caleb's response was one of joy but he contained his reaction since he loved Acoba. Acoba showed marked disappointment but he quickly offered his brother his assistance and asked that he be allowed to go at least part of the way and watch what would occur. The family agreed that this would be ok. They chose Joan, the oldest of the girls, to accompany Caleb on his horse. Joan Hannum was tall for her age of 12, outgoing and sharp with dark hair and a long Irish face, her pale blue eyes alert. She readily accepted the task. The rest of the evening was spent preparing the two for this important mission.

In the morning the family gathered around Caleb, Acoba and Joan. Caleb had selected his favorite horse, a black and white paint mare he called Morning Star from the white marking on her forehead. The horse blew through her lips comfortingly as Caleb stroked her neck. He had made a strap that wrapped around the blanket on her back. It kept the blanket in place but also had attached loops for stirrups so he could rise up if he needed too. Caleb dressed in his finest buckskin and tied his hair back in a ponytail. His mother Sue had braided one part on the right side of his head and in the end put a meadowlark feather. His sandy brown hair reflected the light of the Texas sun and he put lines of black charcoal below his eyes to stop the reflection off is face. Joan washed her white robe as clean as she could, combed her black hair and Sue gave her some new moccasins she had been working on. Acoba selected the palomino gelding to ride. He had started to wear his long hair in dreadlocks like his father. His dark skin and white teeth made a stunning contrast when he smiled, which was often. Caleb was given one of the M-16s taken from the trackers for protection since they would be alone on the prairie. This he slung diagonally across his back. They had also been given a flag of truce, white in color, in hopes that if seen from a distance they would come to no harm. Acoba was instructed to stay with them until the city was sighted and then hold back out of site and watch what occurred. Everyone gave them a hug and then watched them mount and slowly move toward the horizon. The Maroons would wait here for their return.

Acoba, Caleb and Joan rode slowly along the old interstate now almost covered with the native grass resistant to prairie fires. Fortunately, the Maroons had not had any close encounters with fire despite seeing them in the distance and crossing the black patches of recent ones. A meadowlark sang its blissful tune to their right. Caleb smiled, knowing this was sdasdona, his mother's middle name carried down for generations with the Tststa or Cheyenne. He had a strange affinity for this bird with a yellow breast and the song spoke to him. Sue would tell him it was his spirit guide and to listen to the song and take strength from it. he whistled its tune loud and clear. Joan asked him about it while riding behind. Caleb explained the story passed down by his mother Sue while Acoba rode alongside.

Joan was fascinated by the many cultural facets of the Maroons and how they seemed to comingle into one. She especially loved Sue since the first night she gathered the girls in her arms. The capture by the trackers had been a horrible experience, not just the forcible capture but the successive rapes and abuse. Sue, Jungsuk and Cyndra had spent many hours with the girls, helping them talk about the events and consoling them.

It was the affection most of all that had helped them pull through their trauma. Her people had such taboo about sex and never spoke much about the subject, hugging and touching was not a common act. In fact, Joan was not sure how they would be received back into the body being tainted in this fashion. She hugged Caleb closer despite the weapon between them.

Acoba glanced over at her. From the beginning he had taken on a protective role. The whole family had adopted these five young girls and the thought of them leaving made him sad. He was deeply concerned about Caleb's safety and wished it was him that would be taking this risk of making contact.

Late in the afternoon they caught glimpses of the flame on the horizon. Caleb and Acoba decided to continue into the night and get as close as possible under cover of darkness. They had bedrolls and jerked meat for food and, if they could find fuel, the ability to make fire with flint and steel. Being on their own carried excitement along with the realistic concern of the dangers.

On top of this, in the distance a large ominous thunderhead was making its way toward them. As the daylight diminished they could see the flashes of light and hear the distant thunder. They had limited experience on the open plain but knew enough that this was something to watch. They had never witnessed a tornado but the adults had explained what they were and pointed out the destructive aftermath when they had seen it. Joan told them that they should find shelter soon. She had experienced several devastating storms in her 12 years. She explained to them the best place to be would be a low depressed area or old basement if they could find one.

"What makes this flame that burns so brightly that we see?" Caleb asked. "It is a gas that comes from the ground," Joan replied. "We use it to also heat our homes in the winter and cook our food and even to power machines, but I do not know where it comes from." The darkness of the setting sun and the approaching thunderhead only accented the glow in the distance. The air had become strangely still and Joan remarked that shelter should be found soon.

An old grain elevator—what Gary often referred to a skyscraper of the plains—was not too far in the distance so they made their way at a canter toward it. Like most hamlets that once surrounded such structures, only masonry and steel, now rusted, remained. They made their way to the concrete elevator and Acoba dismounted. "Let me make sure it's clear first," he said as he slipped the weapon from his back. He slowly approached the entrance of one of the silos, stooping to pick up a stone. Standing to one side, he threw the stone into the dark opening and listened to it bounce off the far wall. There was a flutter of wings as birds escaped through the entrance. He repeated the exercise several times until he felt certain all wildlife had escaped. Acoba carefully entered into the darkness, letting his eyes adapt and listening for movement. It was dusky smelling but he could not detect the odor of death or decay of flesh. He made his way around the circumference, feeling with his moccasined feet for any obstruction.

Emerging from the entrance again, he smiled at Caleb and Joan. "It is clear, I think it will work for tonight, we should make a fire so we can see better, we will have to collect some dry grass and chips." "I will do it," Joan said. She slid off of the paint and quickly began to search for fuel. Caleb began to gather their things and hobble the horses. The sky was dark now and the smell of rain was in the air. The thunderhead was almost a constant glow from its internal display of lightning. "I think we should bring the horses in with us," Caleb commented. Acoba shook his head yes and helped him guide them into the silo. They were nervous, the confinement, the storm, maybe both.

***

Once all inside and a fire going they could see how cavernous it was. The numerous mud dauber and swallow nests that hung off the walls put out eerie shadows created by the fire. This along with the echo of their voices only made the horses more nervous. It began to rain, slowly at first and increasing with the wind that howled past the opening. The rain became a torrent and if the silo had not been on a small rise it surely would have entered the opening. The three cuddled together with Joan between them listening to the storm increase in fury. Lightning was flashing all around, illuminating the entire area both inside and outside of the silo accompanied by thunder so loud they had to cover their ears. Then the hail started pounding the sides of the silo and bouncing thru the opening. Some were as large as apples.

"How could any living thing survive this, what will happen to our people?" Caleb whispered. "Sue will know what to do, she has lived here before," Acoba whispered back. They held each other tighter and after a short time the storm began to subside. Acoba got up and picked up a large hailstone. It was cold; he had never seen anything like it. He brought it over for Caleb to touch. "It's ice," Joan explained, "frozen water. In the winter you will see much of this." Caleb and Acoba looked at each other in amazement. The three sat up and discussed this strange world compared to their island home of Dominica. The rumblings of the storm faded in the distance as the fire died and they finally drifted off to sleep.

The morning broke clear and bright and all evidence of the hailstones was gone. There was, however, a silence like they had never experienced before. They led the horses out onto the open plain now wet from the storm. The silence was understood when they began seeing the bodies of birds, small mammals and even a snake of two pummeled to death by the hailstones. The swath was defined by the grass laid down along the path of the storm. "Does this happen often?" Caleb spoke, looking at Joan. "Not like this, but sometimes there are tornadoes as well and it is far worse," Joan said.

The flame in the distance was burning and they went over their plan. They would ride together until they were in sight of city where Acoba would hide and watch with the wonderful device they had retrieved from the trackers called binoculars. Caleb and Joan would ride in full view with the white flag hoping to attract attention. When they encountered people from the Body, Caleb would signal with the flag. If he kept the flag things would be going well; if he dropped the flag they were in trouble. After the horses had a moment to feed, they mounted and headed toward the light.

The city in the distance was a great city with very tall buildings, the tallest one having the flame burning on its summit. When it was obvious that they were close, they chose a small hill for Acoba to watch from. Acoba and Caleb embraced and Acoba whispered into Caleb's ear, "remember what our fathers said, perfect love casts out fear. I love you." Caleb's deep green eyes met the brown eyes of Acoba. "Watch over us. I will be back."

Caleb and Joan raised the white flag and rode slowly toward the city. Joan was excited to be back in many ways but was unsure what would happen. She did not want anything to happen to Caleb or Acoba. She knew the army of the Lord would come, but what would they do? As Joan expected they appeared, approximately 40 horsemen all dressed in the same tunic of white with the red cross on front and back. They were all armed with weapons and approached at breakneck speed.

Within moments they had surrounded Caleb and Joan with weapons pointed. "Don't shoot, I am of the Body," Joan yelled. A large white man with short hair but a well-grown beard answered, "Who is this heathen that has you captive? Give me your weapon, heathen," the man replied. Caleb sat motionless, looking at the speaker. Something in this young man's gaze unnerved the apparent leader; he did not see fear but could not detect what it was he felt.

There was an awkward moment of silence until another younger man spoke up. He moved his horse closer to Caleb and came between the two locked in a stare. "Elder Levi, Joshua has kept the flame burning to bring all who need salvation to us, let us not shed blood before we know why this pilgrim comes."

His reddish blonde hair moved slowly in the breeze as he looked back and forth between Caleb and Levi. "Very well, deacon Nathan. Speak, heathen," Levi barked.

Without breaking eye contact Caleb spoke slowly. "My name is Caleb, my people are called the Maroons and we come in peace, we are returning your children whom we captured from the trackers and seek a place of refuge for the winter."

"If you come in peace give me your weapon. I promise you no harm, we will take you into the city." With that Nathan smiled and nodded toward Caleb. Caleb felt an immediate trust for this man and smiled in return and slowly removed the M-16 from his back and handed it to Nathan, who handed it to Levi. "I will ride beside you Caleb," Nathan said. They turned and with the flag still raised high moved toward the light on the hill.

Chapter 18
Joshua
015-16

Acoba watched the encirclement of Caleb, wondering what was happening. The distance for the binoculars was barely within range for him to see the white flag. As the group moved out toward the great city, the flag was still upright, giving him comfort that things were going well.

"I must wait here for Caleb's return," he said to himself. He settled down in the warm sun, reflecting on the storm and all the wondrous and not-so- wondrous things that had happened since leaving their island home. He wished that they were all back on blessed Dominica while at the same time enjoying this great adventure. His horse Honey blew through her lips and he turned to give her some attention. There was nothing like this beautiful animal on Dominica. She represented so much strength and freedom to him. He gave her a few strokes on her neck with the back of his hand. Slowly he moved to a place in the sun and sat down cross legged and fell into the meditation that Jungsuk had taught everyone to empty the mind and live in the now, the moment he was in and not the past or the future. Acoba felt the warmth on his skin and the meadowlark sang in the distance.

The Maroons had not been in the direct path of the great storm of the night before but close enough to get the rain and wind. Jungsuk and Neville came out of their shelter blinking in the bright morning sun. They looked at each other with the affection of those who are truly intimate. Neville gathered her up in his arms and whispered, "I hope Acoba, Caleb and Joan are all right; maybe we should go and search for them?"

"I, too, am concerned but my senses tell me that they are fine; we should wait here as we agreed for thcir return, we must meditate and send them love and strength," she whispered back.

The rest of the camp was coming alive and Jungsuk pulled Neville's face close to her own and kissed him hard before heading toward the campfire to cook breakfast for the hungry Maroons. Gary and Marcus, relieved from the night's watch by Jacque and Lee, came in smiling and talking about the great storm. Sue and Cyndra met them with a hearty hug; their buckskin cloths were wet and stuck to them like chamois. The camp was alive now with the hubbub of life as the children gathered the domestic animals and helped prepare the day's first meal. The talk was all about the storm and what might have happened with the three emissaries. It had been a lot to ask of ones so young but these were different times.

Back at Light on the Hill, Nathan rode alongside Caleb and Joan, looking at this young man who was young and self assured. He must be around 15 or so, he thought, but projected a maturity far beyond that. His olive skin and light hair spoke of mixed blood. He rode erect on his paint horse with Joan hugging him from behind. Nathan already felt a kind of kinship and wanted to start a conversation. Nathan, now 21, had been 6 years old when the world turned upside down. His parents had hidden him when the beasts had discovered them in their cellar. He had heard the struggle but had kept quiet as he had been told. He did not remember how long he had stayed hidden before his hunger and thirst made him come out to find what was left of his parents. He quickly blocked that scene from his mind. It was Joshua who had found him and taken him to safety and raised him along with the many other survivors. Joshua was more than a savior to him, he was closest thing to a parent he had ever known. He felt he owed him his love and allegiance, his very life. It was the same for everyone in the Body. But this one beside him was different even in the way he held himself and he was drawn to that. The other outsiders who had made their way to the Light on the Hill had come searching for refuge or in conquest like Caesar had done, but this was different.

"My name is Nathan Pierce," he spoke. "We will take you to see Joshua the savior; do not be afraid."

Caleb turned his head and locked his green eyes with Nathan's blue. "I am not afraid, Nathan, there is no fear in love," Caleb said slowly. "My name is Caleb Llewellyn Pratt of the Maroons," and he reached out his hand. Nathan grasped it with a strong shake and they both smiled.

"I am Joan Hannum, I have heard of you, Deacon Nathan," Joan chirped in.

Nathan looked at her, "Shhhh Joan, you know you must not speak until spoken to in the company of men, remember the teachings of Joshua." Caleb looked puzzled but kept silent. They rode toward the great flame working through the ruins of what was once a great city. There was still a long way to go and Caleb wondered at the size of such a city and how many people had once lived here. It was by far the largest he had seen in the months since they had landed on the great land. The adults in the many lessons and stories had explained what the world had been like before zero year as they called it, the year that everything had changed but now to witness these things made Caleb all the more curious about the vanished civilization.

"How did you know we were coming to you?" Caleb questioned Nathan, who gazed over at the one called elder Levi for approval to answer the question. Levi nodded.

"We constantly survey from the great tower and other points for pilgrims seeking refuge or enemies seeking to do us harm. We have many soldiers of the cross as you see at many points," Nathan spoke.

"No more questions for now, pilgrim," Levi gruffly interrupted. "You will soon have an audience with the savior Joshua and you will learn more then." They all proceeded in silence from then on, Caleb taking in every detail as they rode.

***

The city that once was vast stretched far to the left and right of the overgrown road that the soldiers of light, Caleb and Joan now followed. Everywhere were the rusted, burnt-out hulks of automobiles and the remains of hundreds upon hundreds of buildings burnt and collapsed, and everything was covered with vegetation. Here and there were still some trees that survived the inferno that had happened. Ahead lay the flame burning brighter and brighter. It was atop a very large building, taller than anything Caleb had ever seen. He was in awe of the massive city. When they were close to the flame, they came upon the wall of automobiles stacked like bricks three high. It was a continuous wall as far as he could discern. In front of them was a formidable gate of iron grates manned by more soldiers of the cross. On approach the gates swung open and the group passed through. The gates closed and Caleb turned and stopped. The feather in the braid of his hair blew lightly as he watched the gates close. Nathan, seeing his concern, reached out and grasped Caleb's shoulder. He smiled, "I give you my word, you may leave whenever you wish." Caleb smiled back and turned Morning Star toward the center of the most amazing collection of tall buildings. Inside the compound, trees were growing and flowers were everywhere. He could see people everywhere all clothed in the same robe as Joan wore, white and flowing to the ground. There was much activity with people going here and there, open areas being farmed. He heard the sound of various livestock coming from different directions. Whenever they came in close proximity, people would stop and wave and greet them with the same "peace be to you brother." And the Soldiers would return the same greeting. It was late afternoon and the group came to a halt in front of a large auditorium. Everyone dismounted and tied their horses to the hitching posts by the entrance. Caleb helped Joan slide off the horse and then dismounted himself. The soldiers of the cross quickly swept Joan away, leaving Caleb with Nathan. "She will be well taken care of, Caleb," Nathan spoke and ushered him toward the entrance.

Caleb had never seen anything like this cavernous building filled with seats facing the front podium. The late afternoon sun filtered through the large stained glass windows depicting scenes strange to him. Nathan watched Caleb gazing in wonder around him. "Caleb, please feel free to walk around, I will return to get you when Joshua is ready to receive you. Are you hungry or thirsty?" Caleb reached into his satchel and brought out a piece of jerked meat and held it up. "No," he replied. Nathan vanished to the rear of the building, leaving Caleb alone in its vast space. His attention became directed to the front as he walked down the low sloping floor. Before him on the back wall was a huge effigy of a man nearly naked suspended on the same cross drawn on the tunics of the soldiers. He appeared to be nailed to it and on his head was a crown of thorns. From his side and his head and hands blood was flowing. This must be Jesus of whom his father had spoken on occasion. Caleb walked up close and looked up at the man on the cross. This must have tremendous meaning to these people, he thought. He had the peculiar feeling that he was being watched and felt some anxiety being left alone here in this strange place. Slowly he sat down in his familiar cross-legged position and closed his eyes, focusing on his breath to bring himself into the now of being conscience and aware. By facing his fear in the form of anxiety it diminished and the comforting peace that replaced it made him feel connected to his family somewhere out on the plains.

Caleb did not know how long he had meditated when he opened his eyes to see Nathan standing over him. "Are you all right, Caleb?" he asked.

Caleb smiled and replied, "I was only meditating, Nathan. I am fine."

Nathan held up a robe and said, "You will have an audience with Joshua soon, you must be clean and wear this robe, come with me and I will help prepare you."

Caleb got up from the floor and looked quizzically at the robe and Nathan. "Follow me," Nathan said with a smile and turned to lead Caleb out of the auditorium to one of the large high- rise buildings. They entered and walked directly to a small room after which the two doors closed together on their own. Nathan pushed a button with the numeral 12 on it and Caleb felt them move. He reached for something to hold onto and Nathan laughed. "It's an elevator to take us to my home. I will try to explain." Nathan told Caleb that the Body, as these people called themselves, used the same gas that kept the great flame going to produce not only heat but electricity. Caleb understood electricity from the photovoltaic cells that his father used back on Dominica. When the elevator stopped and the doors came open, he was still in wonder. Nathan led him to a door in the hallway, which he opened and welcomed Caleb in. Nathan's wife, Gretchen, welcomed Caleb warmly. She showed him what she called the bathroom and explained to his delight the toilet and the sink and shower that gave cold and hot water simply by turning the knobs. She showed him the soap to use and left him to clean himself and put on the robe.

Caleb had so many questions for these people. He did not feel threatened in any way and trusted Nathan and Gretchen despite their short relationship. He did not know where to begin. Nathan tried to anticipate his questions and explain as well as ask him about where he came from with great interest. They shared a meal of vegetables and meat that they called beef. Enjoying the moment was short lived as Nathan said, "It's time to go meet Joshua. We will have time to talk more in the future." They headed for the door. Gretchen did not follow and Caleb looked at Nathan. "Women are not allowed to come or speak before Joshua without invitation. Women are only allowed to speak to each other or in the privacy of their own home." Caleb glanced back at Gretchen. She smiled and then reached down and picked up the beautiful feather that Sue had put in his hair when he left. She placed it back in his braid and closed the door.

The robe Caleb wore did not feel normal to him and the fact that he had no garments underneath made him feel vulnerable. Nathan explained as best he could what they would be doing and how to act in Joshua's presence. It was all so foreign to Caleb but he said he would try to comply. He hoped to see Joan again to make sure she was all right. He missed his family and wondered how Acoba was doing waiting for him alone. He wanted to know what had become of Morning Star. All these musings faded when he and Nathan entered the audience chamber. Before him in the room was seated on a small throne a man much older than he had seen before. He was distinguished and sat proudly erect, dressed in a purple robe drastically different from the white ones he had seen until now. The man had a large hawkish nose with faded blue eyes. His grey hair was cut short on his balding head. His complexion was pale and had not seen the light of the sun in a long time. Clean shaven, his skin was wrinkled with dark spots here and there. Along the platform to his left and right sat six more men on each side in white robes with a purple sash. "I am Joshua, come forward pilgrim." The man gestured to him. Caleb walked slowly forward and stopped in front of the man. "You are so young to carry so much responsibility, tell me the message you bring from your people the Maroons." Joshua boomed in a thick low voice.

"Our people bring back your people and ask safe haven for the winter until we can leave and find our own place in the spring." Caleb recited with a shaky voice. He felt unsure about this person in front of him and his feelings were unclear what to think.

Joshua looked straight at Caleb, unflinching with no betrayal of his own emotions. The seconds seemed like hours to Caleb doing his best to keep his own composure in the withering stare. Caleb wanted badly to turn and look at Nathan for some assurance but instinctively knew not to break eye contact. Finally Joshua drew in a deep breath and released it slowly. "I have spoken to Joan and know much about your people and what has happened. We will give you sanctuary for the winter. We will prepare a place for the Maroons outside the City of Light. You will return and bring your people there. Nathan will go with you and escort your people back. You will leave in the morning. Nathan, I will give you direction before you leave." Joshua spoke and then folded his hands as if to bring closure.

Without thinking Caleb blurted out, "What has happened to Joan? Is she all right?" The look on the faces of the twelve men surrounding Joshua was startled. Joshua's face showed no change in composure but only sat silently staring at Caleb.

Nathan stepped forward and touched Caleb on the shoulder and beckoned him to withdraw from the chamber. They retraced their steps and the door closed behind them. "You may only respond to Joshua when he speaks to you, I will find out what I can and try to answer your questions, Caleb. Stay here while I return and get my instructions. I won't be long," Nathan said quietly. He turned and re-entered the audience chamber.

Caleb felt unsettled by this experience. He felt comfortable with Nathan but could not quite place what he felt about Joshua. On their walk back to Nathan's abode, Nathan assured Caleb that Joan was all right and being taken care of—that is all he knew. He pointed out the stalls where Morning Star was being kept and they went over there to visit her. Everywhere they were greeted by "peace be unto you brother" and Caleb learned to respond with the same phrase. The evening was spent in Nathan and Gretchen's apartment talking and discussing so many things. The high point, however, was when Gretchen brought out a device that, when she flipped a toggle, played music. Caleb was entranced by the device and the wonderful sounds by instruments he had never heard before. His sleep was filled with dreams of the many happenings of the day but especially the music. In the morning Nathan woke him. "We must leave soon, come eat and prepare yourself, here are your clothes." It was not long before they were leaving the City of Light through the large iron gates. It felt good to Caleb to be back on Morning Star. They had returned his weapon as promised. Nathan rode alongside on a crisp fall morning. Caleb was anxious to meet up with Acoba and tell him of all the strange things he had seen and learned. They rode mostly in silence through the once-great city but when they reached the outskirts Caleb felt much more at home with the open plain. There was a herd of buffalo in the distance and the meadowlark was singing. Caleb nudged Morning Star into a canter; his brother was out there waiting for him and he could not wait to see him.

Acoba watched them from a long way off through the binoculars. His heart was racing when he saw it was Caleb. When he could see that Caleb had his weapon and was in no trouble he quickly mounted Honey and raced at a gallop to meet him. Their horses nearly collided they approached each other so fast. Both were on the ground in a strong embrace. Acoba could hardly let go he was so elated that Caleb was all right. Nathan watched them curiously; he had not ever experienced this kind of affection between two men. Finally Caleb pushed him away and said, "This is my brother Acoba. Acoba, this is Nathan of the Body." Acoba approached Nathan and cautiously put out his hand. His shoulder-length dreadlocks and dark skin were a huge contrast to this ruddy, short-haired soldier of the cross. Nathan took his hand and gave it a hardy shake. "I am happy to meet you, Nathan," Acoba said. Nathan's becoming smile was his reply. "We must hurry back to the family. I am sure they are very concerned about us. It will be another day and night, so we can talk on the way," Acoba said. They mounted and headed east, a constant barrage of questions and answers between them.

They spent the night by a single tree in the shelter of a small bluff. There was little sleep around the fire. Although Nathan was somewhat reserved in his answers to the myriad questions, he found himself delighted in the presence of these two younger men. His allegiance to Joshua was obvious but his curiosity about the tremendous difference in the Maroons made him far more open. What was most odd about this group was the lack of hierarchy and regiment he was used to. He found himself laughing and joking as if he had known them all his life.

Lee was the first to spot the trio the next afternoon. He sent Jacque to go to them while he sped back to camp to alert everyone of their arrival. When Jacque reached the three it was a repeat of the reunion that Caleb and Acoba had. By the time they reached camp everyone was waiting and the two messengers vanished in a sea of hugs and kisses. Nathan waited separately, observing. Finally, a small man with a ponytail with wisps of grey approached him. His smile was one of the most welcoming Nathan had ever seen. "My name is Gary Llewellyn; welcome to our camp," he reached out his hand. "Please dismount and come join us, we have food to eat, water to drink and many, many questions," Gary said. Nathan responded with his own name and dismounted. He handed Gary his weapon, surprised that he had never been asked for it. "Keep it, young man, we have plenty," Gary laughed. He threw his arm around his shoulder in a fatherly way and guided him towards the raucous crowd. As they approached, Nathan noticed that the four young women in tainted robes were watching and they slowly moved away from the other well wishers. He looked at them and at the rest of the people and felt their separateness.

One by one each of the Maroons hugged Nathan, which he stiffly received. Around a large fire, the Maroons brought out instruments and drums to make music; the adults passed around a pipe of something Nathan had never smelled. He was offered the pipe but politely refused. There was dancing and singing and an endless barrage of questions while everyone, even the smallest child, listened to the answers that he gave. The experience was unlike any he'd had. The laughing and dancing was fascinating to Nathan. The revelry lasted long into the night. When Nathan finally retired he spent a long time looking up at the stars in a state of peace. He wished Gretchen could be here with him now to observe what he had. Tomorrow they would begin the journey back to the City of Light.

Chapter 19
Winter
016

The crisp chill of fall made its presence known early in the morning, but quickly turned back to the comforting warmth of the end of summer. Of all of the Maroons, Gary could relate to it best from his many years in Canada. It had been 16 years now since he had felt this change in seasons. His mind filled with memories triggered by the simple change in temperature. Sue had made him a small cup of coffee this morning from their meager store brought from Dominica; it was a precious thing to be savored, knowing that this once common item of trade when gone probably would never be tasted again. He had risen early and went out onto the plain by himself to watch the sunrise and listen while the earth woke from its slumber of the night. The act of silence and stillness in meditation was a common practice now among the Maroons and he relished each and every moment. Despite the concerns of this life and the unfolding of events he found himself in a state of peace and contentment he had never experienced before zero year. The last of the coffee and its wonderful aroma drifted up to his nostrils as he sipped it slowly.

Watching the rest of the Maroons come to life, he was overwhelmed with affection for each and every soul in the camp below. When his eyes came to Sue, his body vibrated with energy. Even from this distance he could see her long dark hair now with a line of grey. The bond between them had become so richly entangled he often wondered if they were in each other's minds thinking the same thoughts, feeling the same feelings. They communicated more often without words but by gazing into each other's eyes. He shook himself to come into the moment.

This new earth had so much strangeness, he thought. Sue, Jungsuk and now Wendy were dreaming the same dreams often. The dream of the small stone church in the grove of trees had recurred over and over and now the dream of an older man had also taken place. When Caleb described the one called Joshua, the three of them all looked at each other in wonder. There was no explaining this and Gary felt no need to. It had become accepted by everyone as natural. Gary caught sight of Nathan and fixed his gaze on him. This young man was truly genuine but he was holding back in some way that Gary could not pinpoint. Most of the time Nathan was at ease and conversed without reservation about everything he was asked but it was obvious that some of his responses were guarded. In a few days they would reach the City of Light, Nathan called it. Gary wanted to know as much as possible about the Body, as Nathan referred to their people and the man called Joshua before they got there. It was time to head back into camp and he made his way back, feeling the earth under his moccasined feet.

Marcus held the reins of the dismounted horses, smiling. He would have never dreamed what he was witnessing before him. Growing up in the deep south, he had slowly climbed the corporate ladder and carefully maneuvered through the obstacles and prejudice of society. He had taken advantage of the opportunities afforded by the pendulum swing of guilt by the opulent white majority. The collective pain, hatred and anger of his own black culture seethed below the surface. There was always a barrier between the races even in the most polite circumstances. When the world as he knew it came to an end, these walls stood firm, even when they needed each other more than ever.

Now here he was on the plains of Texas watching these young men all of mixed blood except for the escort from the City of Light wrestling and challenging each other, testing their strength and agility, all the while laughing and cajoling. They had no idea of any difference between them, had never been taught to look for it. Jacque tackled Acoba and immediately Caleb entered to pull him off, to which Lee pounced atop them all. Fredrick and Abel climbed on. Nathan, despite the awkward robe, joined in and it became a pile of arms and legs that ended up all lying on their backs out of breath and laughing.

Marcus thought about his new wife, Cyndra, how tender and lovingly she had nursed him back to health and now was expecting their new child in a new world. He looked up toward the midday sun in thankfulness, closed his eyes and felt the breeze blow the dreadlocks that he had started to grow. It seemed so natural to grow his hair out though he remained clean shaven to keep from scratching Cyndra's soft skin. Is there any man as lucky as I, he thought. A yell from the young men snapped him back to the moment. "Father, come tell us a story of the world before," Abel called. Marcus' heart beat rapidly; this was the first time his stepson Abel had referred to him this way. He led the horses forward and passed the reins to each owner and they sat in a circle, each holding their own horse. He sat down next to Abel trying not to show his intense emotion. "What story would you like to hear?" he addressed Abel with pride. "Is it true that a man has walked on the moon that we see in the sky at night? Tell us that one," Abel said, and the others nodded in agreement. This was a favorite subject for Marcus, having been an engineer in the aerospace field. The young men sat quietly as he began looking intently at Abel. He smiled, "This could be a very long story," he said softly.

***

Reaching down, Cyndra picked another berry sun ripened and sweet. It was hard not to pop it into her mouth instead of her bladder pouch for use later making pemmican, as Sue called it. She was always concerned about the large diet of meat (which seemed to be in limitless supply). Sue's knowledge of edible plants and berries learned from her grandmother and younger days on the reservation was now invaluable. They were on one of the women's many forays collecting the plants Sue had taught them. It was more than a gathering of food but a wonderful time of socializing and bonding among the women. Cyndra had been transformed in the few months with the Maroons. Her deep-seated unhappiness from youth had vanished. She had always been victimized, be it by her father molesting her to one failed relationship to another. Even after zero year she had chosen men that mistreated her in some fashion. At many times she had considered suicide to end the cycle of sadness. Now she could not imagine such an option with the way she felt about life.

One of the braids in her long blonde hair fell across her face as she bent over. Jungsuk had carefully taught Marcus how to braid hair and it had become a loving ritual for him to braid her hair after he carefully combed it. The love between them was so foreign to what she had experienced in the past. She reached down and touched her abdomen where the child they had made together was growing. No other pregnancy had felt this way. She caught a glimpse of Lori and Nicole together. It had been so hard for Nicole losing her twin sister but her grief was like a catalyst to snap Lori out of her shell of shyness to console her. They were like sisters now.

To Cyndra, each moment of this new life was a wonder and she found herself relishing each with delight. The one exception was the dream she had the night before. Jungsuk, Sue and Wendy had dreamed the same dream on many occasions and now she had dreamed the same one about the man they now called Joshua, only this time it was different. Different in that after visualizing him in his purple robe, she saw him turn around in a military uniform with a sinister and angry countenance. This was very troubling, especially when she spoke to the other three about it and found they had had the same experience. They had decided to tell the family about it to-night after they had made camp.

The four young girls worked their way off together from the main group. How long had it been since being taken in by the Ma-roons, a month? The transformation in all of them was hard to be-lieve. The acceptance and love from the Maroons, in particular Jung-suk, Sue and Cyndra, had opened them all up to a different world. They spoke freely to everyone, even the males. There was time to play and daydream. They had even learned to dance. Then Deacon Nathan had arrived and it was hard to be who they had become in his presence. They all wanted to know what had become of Joan but were afraid to ask. The prospect of return to the Body held so many unknowns and the dark secret they could not share. On top of that, Mariza had missed her period and could be pregnant with a child of one of the trackers.

"I don't want to go back," Sarah spoke up when they were beyond hearing of the other women.

"I don't either," Nile, Peggy and Mariza chimed in.

"What can we do, does Deacon Nathan know about us?" Peggy asked.

"We should tell Sue, she will help us," Nile responded.

" In a day or two we will be back to the City of Light, we must tell her soon or it will be too late," Sarah replied.

"We will never be accepted as whole in the body and we have failed in the mission that Joshua has given us; I want to stay with these people. I say we tell the truth tonight," Peggy spoke, her dark red hair shining in the midday sun. The girls all nodded agreement and decided that Peggy would speak for them all.

Slowly they worked their way back among the other women, selecting berries and herbs as they went. The time for rejoining the others to continue the slow march to the City of Light was at hand. Everyone took up their jobs herding the domestic animals, driving the carts with all their belongings. It was a noisy parade with much laughing and talking. The intrepid scouts Lee and Jacque headed out to the front as always. Caleb and Acoba took Fredrick and Abel out with them to hunt the evening's meal. You could tell they were happy by the smiles on their faces. They too had become adept horseman riding straight and tall on their two buckskin mares.

The flame of the City of Light could be made out in the far distance, in the darkness of night. It was perhaps another two-day travel for the methodical pace of the Maroons' caravan. The pace was slow so the animals could forage and not get tired. Lee and Jacque had chosen a fine campsite along a small stream with small hills surrounding. The foundations of what had once been a farmhouse and other outbuildings remained in the tall grass, a perfect place to build a fire and gather around for the evening meal.

Sue had called the Rastas together for a meeting. As always all the children gathered around to listen to what was being said and decided. Nathan watched, fascinated by the way the Maroons conducted business and especially how the women seemed to take such a predominant leadership role. Cyndra spoke about her dream of the one called Joshua and the addition of the reverse side with the sinister look and military dress. Jungsuk, Sue and Wendy agreed that they had had the same dream. Gary, Neville and Marcus contemplated this new disclosure. They had come to accept and trust this extraordinary phenomenon. After a long silence Gary looked directly at Nathan. "Deacon Nathan, can you shed some light on what this might mean?" he inquired. Nathan was dumbstruck: How could these women know? Did the girls tell them anything? He sat still trying to decide what he should tell. Slowly he nodded his head in affirmation.

"I will tell you the story of Joshua and what I know" Nathan said. He began with his own story, of the loss of his parents to the beasts and his rescue by Joshua. "I know that before zero year, as you call it, Joshua had a different name and had been a man of high rank in the military of those times but what the name was and what his position had been is not known. What I do know is that he had marshaled the survivors of the plague as they had called it, gathering them together, rescuing whomever they could find from the beasts, storing food and weapons, keeping order in a world gone mad. The people looked to him for leadership and he gave it to them. They had known that there were other survivors in other cities because he had established radio contact and was in communication. Mostly in other large cities across the country. Most places were in chaos but Joshua brought order and security to the people in what was once called Dallas, Texas. He put up the flame as a guide for anyone searching for refuge and organized the talents of the survivors to rebuild civilization."

All eyes were on Nathan as he told the story of Joshua. "It was not the end of the madness, however. Radio contact with other cities would abruptly end, sometimes there were calls for help before they would end, speaking of a large force that would appear and pillage, kill and enslave the survivors. Some would escape and had made their way to the City of Light for refuge. From them, it was learned about the one called Caesar of New Orleans. This man had created his own fiefdom of conquest and equipped an entire army. Some suspected he too was a military man with designs on control of the new earth that had emerged from the plague. Slowly, radio contact with other cities stopped. Either they had been vanquished by Caesar or were afraid he would come should they make their existence known."

The Maroons gathered closer, spellbound by the story. "Joshua began to gather as much information as he could from refugees and then sent out spies. He put together a small fighting force with what people he had and trained them in what weapons they could find. It was a small army mostly on horseback but highly mobile and dedicated. They became the soldiers of the cross. By espionage Joshua now knew that Caesar was aware of the City of Light and had mobilized his entire army to subjugate the City of Light. Joshua knew that Caesar's army consisted of many vehicles and tanks with fuel trucks to help move his army long distances. Joshua, however, with the help of God through him would save his people."

The Rastas all glanced at each other with a questioning look when Nathan made this statement. Nathan continued to explain how Joshua had carefully located a place to meet Caesar and his army before he made it to the City of Light. "He had chosen an area of heavy overgrown plain and in a brilliant move they surprised Caesar's army on a windy night by torching the grass blowing toward Caesar's camp, the inferno swept through their camp, igniting the fuel tankers and burning the vehicles to leave the army running with little more than what they could carry. On their horses they terrorized and killed as many as they could for days, chasing them back towards New Orleans. It was said that Caesar himself had been badly burned in the conflict. Joshua had become the savior of our people and we follow him without question. His brilliance is our salvation, a gift of God." Nathan beamed with pride as he told the story. "You will find sanctuary with the Body and Joshua's love." He concluded.

There was silence as everyone absorbed this amazing story. Then Peggy slowly rose up and walked toward Sue. Standing next to her, she began to speak with hesitation. "Nile, Sarah, Mariza and I do not want to go back and be part of the Body." The smile vanished from Nathan's face. He rose to approach Peggy and she moved closer to Sue. "Peggy, please tell us why?" Neville spoke as he rose to stop Nathan from approaching Peggy. In a low voice she began, "Joshua has saved our people but we (pointing to the other girls) have failed in the mission he has given us. To go back will either be shame or something else, we want to stay with the Maroons."

"What mission, what do you mean," Marcus barked.

Sue put her arms around Peggy and bent over and whispered "It is all right, you are safe with us, go ahead and tell us what the mission is that you are on."

Peggy straightened herself and began to explain how the five girls had been chosen for a sacred mission to preserve their people. Joshua knew that Caesar would return and this time with a vengeance. Joshua had trained them in reading a compass and had them study maps and then they had been put out purposely to be caught by the trackers. They were to gather individually as much information of when, where, and how Caesar would return. Being young girls they would not be expected to be spies and the hope was that at least one of them would return with information the Body could use to defend itself. "Mariza is pregnant by one of the trackers and none of us want to continue our mission, we do not know what awaits us with Joshua and the body, we want to stay with the Maroons."

Nathan broke away from Neville. "Liar., he yelled. "Joshua would never ask such a thing." Neville jumped forward and restrained him.

"Joan is with them now," Caleb screamed. Pandemonium broke out with everyone talking and Nathan fighting to get to Peggy.

Jungsuk and Gary both jumped up on the old foundation wall calling for silence. When there was silence, Jungsuk spoke. "We must take our time now and sort this out; we must gather all the information we can. Can you be patient, Deacon Nathan?" she looked at him directly. Nathan stopped struggling against Neville, glaring at Peggy and then at Jungsuk. "Do you promise to open yourself up to truth and not react?" Jungsuk directed it at Nathan. He slowly nodded. "Neville, let him go," she said. "We should stay in this camp until we have a full understanding of what has and what will be." Everyone nodded. The girls of the Body were all weeping, their secret finally in the light. "First we should all sit down and find stillness in the moment, please," Jungsuk spoke with calmness. Everyone sat down and there was a long silence as they closed their eyes. Almost in unison the eyes of each person opened, ready to hear. Jungsuk spoke, "Deacon Nathan, you have told us an amazing story of your leader Joshua, we the Maroons are grateful for the offer to spend the winter with the Body. It is apparent your allegiance to this man for what he has done for you and the survivors of the plague. We come from a different place with a different perspective. We do not hold secrets here, you have called Peggy a liar, do you truly know that what she has said is not true?" Everyone sat silently and waited for Nathan to speak.

Nathan sat with his head bowed for a very long time and then raised his head slowly. "I do not know if they are true or not but I do not believe them. My orders from Joshua were to bring them directly to him and speak with them as little as possible. You must understand that we are in danger of attack by Caesar and Joshua wants only our health and safety."

Jungsuk then asked each of the young women to tell their story. One at a time they spoke of how their fathers had been killed in the great battle against Caesar, how they had been taught to sacrifice as their fathers had done. That Joshua selecting them was an honor and they had sworn to secrecy and only Joshua and the twelve apostles knew of their mission. Each one spoke of the cruel treatment by the trackers and what would await them in New Orleans. They agreed that now they wanted to stay with the Maroons because they did not know what their fate would be with Joshua and they certainly would not be accepted in the Body because they were tainted; no one would want them for wives now. Without judgment, Jungsuk stated that no more should be said tonight, that everyone should sleep and the answers would come to them. Sue took the girls with her and stayed with them.

Gary spent a good part of the night talking with Nathan about what kind of man Joshua was, trying to understand his motives and his sense of fairness. In the process of answering Gary's many questions Nathan was becoming more aware of his own blindness in his allegiance to Joshua. He knew in his heart that the story the girls had given was true and reconciling the goodness that he knew in

Joshua and this awful use of his own people was disturbing. Gary, it seemed in all his questions, was without judgment. His concern for the Maroons and the girls of the Body was obvious. Nathan thought of Gretchen as he passed into fitful sleep.

The morning fire was burning with Cyndra, Jungsuk, Sue and Wendy alone sitting around it. The dream of Joshua had returned with more to each one of them. Almost simultaneously they had gotten up before dawn and found each other at the fire in the chill of the autumn air. Wendy was most perplexed with the image that had appeared, she had never seen this thing and did not know what name to give it. When she described it to the other women they smiled, knowing that Wendy could never have seen such a thing in her life. It only amazed them more about this strange phenomena of dreams that they all shared. Now the image of Joshua kindly and loving in the purple robe with the reverse of the stern military image was joined by the image of a black airplane. They tried to explain to Wendy how there was a time when man had built machines they could fly like birds in the sky.

"What does it mean?" Wendy asked the older women.

"I have no way of knowing its significance but my feelings when I saw it were not good," Jungsuk responded. The others agreed.

"We must decide soon whether we should proceed to the City of Light or find shelter for the winter somewhere else soon," Cyndra commented.

"Let's meditate together, watch the sunrise, I am sure the answer will come," Sue said. They gathered close together near the warmth of the fire, putting their backs together and closing their eyes. When they opened them next, they found Gary, Neville and Marcus standing side by side watching them and smiling. The rest of the camp was still asleep and the group of Rastas walked together discussing the dream and the situation. They agreed to proceed to the City of Light and to keep the new image of the black plane between them. They would try to find Joan and if the Body would not give them refuge make their way somewhere quickly and prepare for winter as best they could.

Everyone was anxious to know what they would do. Gary spoke for the Rastas, explaining that they would proceed to the City of Light and find Joan. He assured the other girls they had a home with the Maroons. He explained that if there was no refuge there they would travel on and find another place as soon as possible. They must move quickly now as the seasons were changing.

Nathan felt ill at ease and looked over at Peggy, Sarah, Mariza and Nile. Their eyes showed fear and he wanted to go over and tell them everything would be all right but he did not know it to be so.

Caleb came over to Nathan and said, "You told me Joan was all right, do you still think that?"

Nathan stood in silence for a long time looking at Caleb. "I don't know; I want to believe that. I will do what I can to help her and the Maroons. Please believe me." He replied.

Caleb embraced Nathan. "Let us help prepare to go, I will get the horses," and off he trotted towards the herd. The camp was alive with everyone doing chores and moving with purpose. They would reach the City of Light in a couple of days and the anticipation was thick in the air.

***

"They're coming fast." Lee and Jacque yelled as they rode at a full gallop into camp, scattering the chickens and pigs and making Lori and Anna yell back with frustration as they tried to keep them together. The moving camp came to a halt and gathered around the two intrepid scouts, anxious to learn what they meant.

When there was some semblance of quiet, Neville beckoned them to speak. Lee spoke first, "There are many men on horses coming this way, they wear the red cross like Nathan."

Jacque continued, "They are armed and riding fast, they should be here in less than an hour."

It was almost midday and time for the camp to stop and rest. "Let us stop here and prepare for them," Neville spoke. There was no disagreement among the rest.

"They have probably come to escort us into the city," Nathan spoke up. "Maybe I should go out to meet them."

"NO!" Everyone turned to Jungsuk "You must not speak to them Nathan, not yet. The Rastas will go out and meet them before they come to our camp, we should go unarmed."

There was a look of confusion on everyone's faces with complete silence. Then Cyndra broke the silence, "Jungsuk is right, with what we all know now we must be very careful how things are handled."

"So be it then,." Marcus said. "Let us prepare." There was communal nodding and the Maroons prepared for the noon stop. The hunters were called in and the Rastas dressed in their best clothes and saddled their horses. It was a grand sight as the Maroons watched the six adults riding together out of camp to meet the Soldiers of the Cross.

Nathan wondered about the meaning of all this; he felt conflicted about what to do. Looking over at the young girls of the Body, he could see they were afraid. He wanted to comfort them but could not.

The six Rastas sat on their horses abreast on the small rise, watching the approach of the Soldiers of the Cross. It appeared to be a very large group in the area of 50 or more riders. A group far too large for just a messenger party. They sat in silence each contemplating the meaning of this.

Gary finally broke the silence. "Am I dreaming or is this for real?" and began to laugh.

"It's all a dream, let's hope this is a good one," Sue responded.

"Whatever happens, let us live or die in love and not fear like we have been talking about, not reactive but accepting and responding," Marcus said.

"Easier said than done," Neville chuckled and dismounted. The others followed suit and they stood side by side as the dust from the approaching horses drifted into them. When the dust cleared, they were surrounded by the small army of men on horses lathered by the recent ride and blowing hard. There was a long pause as the dust settled and the horses settled down.

A large bearded man dismounted and approached Gary, who was obviously the oldest of the small group, "I am Elder Levi with a message from Joshua to be delivered to the Maroons."

Gary looked around at the other Rastas seeking nonverbal permission to speak for them all. After a nod from each, he looked back at Levi. "I am Gary Llewellyn, a Rasta of the Maroons and we are pleased to meet you," as he tried to look into Levi's stern eyes.

Levi was visibly taken back. "Rastafarians?" he replied.

Gary smiled, "Rasta is a term of endearment we use for those that truly love and care for all the people, you see before you the Rastas of the Maroons."

Levi blinked and with a small shake of his head brought himself into his mission. "Joshua will meet with a single representative of your people here tomorrow at this time; he will come alone."

Gary looked around at the many armed Soldiers of the Cross of all ages listening to the exchange. "Does it take so many to deliver so simple a message to so few?" he slowly spoke.

"This is a show of force and the orders of Joshua not to be questioned," Levi barked.

" What a fine job you have done Levi, someone will be here and peace be unto you," Gary responded, realizing the sarcasm in his voice and feeling sorry for speaking it immediately as he forced himself not to laugh.

Levi mounted with a huff and led the small army off at a gallop.

The Rastas stood in silence, each pondering what had just taken place. The sun was high but a cool breeze was blowing. "Well, who wants to meet Joshua?" Cyndra said with a laugh.

"It is sure to be an experience," Marcus replied.

"Let's draw straws for the lucky one," Gary said, still laughing. It was agreed and six stems of grass of various lengths were selected. Jungsuk held them in her hand evenly matched on the top. Each Rasta drew one, leaving Jungsuk with one.

They each compared and the shortest blade belonged to Sue. "Lucky?" she said.

"You don't have to do this if you don't want to." Neville said.

"I will," Sue responded. "I need time to prepare." Sue mounted her sorrel. "Let's go."

Sue wanted to perform a sweat lodge as her Grandmother had taught her in her youth. She explained what she needed and what it was about and everyone was anxious to help her. She also explained that this would be for her alone and in the future she would do sweat lodges for anyone who wanted to experience it. All the materials were put together as per her instructions and she took off her clothes and entered the lodge. Everyone curiously waited outside and wondered what was happening. They could hear her sing songs in Cheyenne and occasionally the flap of the small wickiup would open and she would call for more stones heating up on the fire outside. The smell of the herbs she was throwing on the hot stones along with the water produced a wonderful smelling steam that would escape from time to time. After some time Sue came out glistening with sweat but smiling.

"I will be ready tomorrow for the meeting with Joshua," she said. Everyone clapped though they did not know why. Gary followed her to their shelter to take care of her needs. He wanted to know what she had experienced in the sweat lodge but did not ask. He knew that for Sue it was her own personal power and she would share it when she felt like it. What an amazing woman he had for a partner, he thought.

In the morning Caleb came to Sue and Gary's shelter. He asked his father to leave so he could speak with his mother alone. Sue waved him in with a smile, always happy to see her son. She had picked out her finest doeskin garment beaded with her own designs. Caleb reached up and took the comb from her hand and began to comb his mother's hair. Carefully he began to braid her hair as she had done for him so many times before. Sue contentedly accepted this wonderful gesture of love.

Then he slowly took the meadowlark feather from his own braid and placed it in his mother's hair. "This man you go to meet is very powerful and I feel not truthful, mother, please take this feather to protect you, and I want you to ride Morning Star, she is gentle but will carry you back safely." Sue gazed into Caleb's eyes, a combination of his father's and hers. Tears came down her face as she bathed in the love they shared.

"Thank you, son, I know that it will be all right and I accept your gifts. You have become a fine young man, a good hunter and warrior, I am so proud of you," Sue whispered. "You will need to find a partner soon to go through life and produce children. Have you thought of anyone?" Sue said, despite knowing the answer.

"Yes Mother, I would like to have Joan as my partner but she is with Joshua," Caleb whispered back.

"One can never know the future, Caleb, there is always hope." Sue smiled and embraced her son. "Now please tell your father I am almost ready and bring Morning Star." Sue kissed him on the lips and sent him away.

The entire clan of Maroons watched in silence as Sue rode the paint toward the hill in the distance. The flame of the City of Light could be seen in the overcast darkness of the fall day. When she was out of earshot, Gary called the others together, "Bring all the weapons and the horses and let's be ready in case there is trouble. Where are the binoculars, Acoba?" Everyone scrambled to prepare and then watched the hill in the distance for the arrival of Joshua.

Sue arrived first at the place of meeting. The ground still showed the marks of the many horses that had passed there yesterday. She hobbled Morning Star and sat down in her familiar cross-legged fashion and began to meditate. She was calm and centered when she felt the vibration in the earth of the coming horse. Morning Star whinnied at the white gelding approaching. She knew Joshua from the dreams immediately. He was wearing the military uniform from the dream with a large purple sash across the front. His stern face was accentuated when he recognized that it was a woman who awaited him. Sue could feel the burning of his eyes as he dismounted and stood before her. She slowly got up and stood facing him.

"I did not expect the Maroons to be led by a woman," Joshua huffed.

"The Maroons are not led by any one person, Joshua, I am the representative you asked for," Sue replied. She extended her hand and smiled. "I am Sue Pratt."

Joshua eyed her hand but did not take it. "Are you an American, Sue?" Joshua demanded.

"I was born in what was the United States of America, my race is Cheyenne, but I am a Maroon now on this very new earth and we do not consider such things like that anymore," Sue calmly spoke.

"I am Joshua, savior of the Body and commander of the Soldiers of the Cross, I have given my word of honor to give refuge to your people but I have some stipulations which must be obeyed."

Sue waited a moment then said, "I know who you are and I know what it is you want."

"Do tell, woman" was Joshua's sarcastic reply.

Sue engaged his fierce eyes with her own. "You want the other girls before they can reveal your hideous mission you sent them on so no one will know the kind of person you really are."

Joshua trembled with rage, his face red with explosive anger. "Who are you to judge me, you contentious woman, I have brought salvation to the Body, I have brought safety to the Body, I have brought order to what was chaos. What I do is for the protection and safety of the Body as a whole. The good of the many outweighs the good of the few."

Sue allowed a few more moments to calm the mood. "Joshua, what kind of building can survive with a foundation of lies? What you resist will persist if even in your own self."

Joshua clenched his fists, "Enough of your new age bullshit; it did not help before the plague and it will not help now. Caesar and the cesspool of iniquity in New Orleans must be stopped and you fight fire with fire. But you would not know anything about that. Wake up, we know what he is like and we even know he is working on weapons of mass destruction, sacrifices have got to be made." His lip curled up slightly at the edge and Sue remembered immediately where she had seen it before. It was on TV when the then-president George Bush would give his speeches. She was sickened by the thought.

"And the black plane, Joshua?" Sue replied. Joshua was taken aback "How do you know of the black plane? Did Nathan tell you? He cannot have known." His face showed perplexity. "The Caesar problem may involve more than waiting for his return."

Sue realized in that brief moment the truth. "You cannot possibly be thinking of nuclear weapons, Joshua. Haven't we learned our lesson of preemptive strikes;, no good can come from this."

Joshua bent lower to stare at Sue. "Does Nathan know any of these things?"

Sue straightened. "We have no secrets and certainly do not lie to one another, Joshua,"

Joshua stood for a moment, stroking his chin. He turned to Sue, "There is a small town we have been preparing for future settlement when the Body grows, it is fifty miles north of the City of Light, it has gas and electricity and water and sewer all ready. We call it the land of Goshen, Nathan knows it well. You will have him take you there and find refuge for the winter but you must be gone in the spring. Your people must never enter the City of Light or have contact with the Body. Do you understand?" Joshua said with disdain.

Sue thought for a moment, "And what of Nathan, what of Joan?"

Joshua took another moment. "I will send Joan with Gretchen to you; she is tainted and knows too much, she may be carrying the child of that swine of New Orleans. Nathan must never return, you tell him that."

Sue looked up at the sky, now clearing of the overcast clouds. "And how will you explain all this to the Body Joshua, more lies?"

Joshua exploded, "You vex me woman, now do what you're told and I don't want to ever see you or your people again. You are lucky I let you live." With that he mounted his horse and rode away at a gallop.

Sue took the hobble off of Morning Star and stroked her mane. She took her time and walked back leading the horse, pondering what had just happened.

***

Nathan watched his breath come out in clouds of white mist that the gently falling snow passed through. He sat in his favorite place of contemplation under the large cottonwood tree, its bare branches reaching out in perfect grace. A loner, a relic of the past able to withstand the many prairie fires because it was so old. This winter in Goshen had brought so many changes to his once very structured life. Now all was so new and open. Gary had told him once in their many talks, "Uncertainty is the dance of the universe." Nathan was enjoying the dance once he had learned it.

The thought of his newborn son quickly filled him with joy. Despite the crushing news that he could never return to the City of Light and the uncertainty of the future with the Maroons and a pregnant wife, he had become grateful for the change. So they named the child Joshua. Gretchen adapted and even thrived in the new community. Their bond only became stronger. The acceptance into this new family amazing. Joan and Mariza were almost due as well, the result of their brief encounter with the trackers. You would never know it with the way they were doted over and the anticipation of new life. Nathan did not even think of going back now.

He thought about the coming end of winter and the search for a home for the Maroons. The four women had been dreaming again about the small stone building in the grove of trees but it had the new image of the Big Dipper and the North Star. Everyone took it to mean they would head north after the spring solstice. The biggest concern was for the newborns. His thoughts fell back again to the last contact with the Body. Elder Levi had escorted Joan and Gretchen to Goshen. His meeting with Nathan had been curt . Elder Levi had mentored him through the ranks in the *cursus honorum*, as Joshua called it. The ladder of honor, the regiment that had kept him blind and uninformed. It had been so difficult at first to accept that he had lived under the cloak of lies in total allegiance to the Body. It was painful that Levi did not know what he knew and did not want to know. For a moment he had seen in Levi's eyes the pain and sorrow of never seeing Nathan again, then the return to duty as a true Soldier of the Cross. Nathan had wept that night, a combination of sorrow for the separation and joy in the reunion with Gretchen. His blonde hair was much longer now and the small breeze that came from the south blew it across his forehead. He remembered the first night he had danced around the fire to the beat of the drums, taking his tunic with the large red cross on it and throwing it into the fire. He felt so free.

Chapter 20
North Star
016

Gretchen was constantly in wonder at the newborn son she cradled in her arms. Like most newborns, it was hard to tell the hair or eye color, but he definitely had the pale white skin of his father, Nathan. They had named him Joshua after the only father they had known.

She thought back to the late fall when Levi had come for her and told her to gather what she could carry and be ready to leave that night. The three-day ride north to Goshen with Levi and Joan was awkward without her husband present. The reunion with Nathan was warm and worth the trip, though.

The rest was all such a surprise—the new people, the new ways, the new home. Not only did the lifestyle of the Maroons seem somewhat primitive but the familiarity between them was so foreign. Now 22, Gretchen had lost her parents in the plague; she barely remembered even the way they looked. Nathan was her closest friend and eventually became her husband.

Watching and experiencing the bond among the Maroons was new. She enjoyed it and easily forgot the life of the Body. Gretchen immersed herself in the new things about survival in nature, open speech and the sharing of feelings and opinions. She especially enjoyed learning how to meditate and dance. Sue would often take her to the sundial that Gary had set up to mark the length of the shadow at high noon. It was a ritual for them. When it was the shortest, Sue announced it was the solstice and that in 90 days they would head north to their new home.

All spare time went into preparation for that day. They prepared hides, gathered things of use and stored provisions. The weird thing was they had no idea where they were going. Only north. It had been difficult to comprehend why Joshua did not want them back. This talk of flying in the sky, powerful weapons and lies did not seem like the Joshua she had worshiped all her life.

But that was the past, and the future lay ahead as the Maroons were once again on the move. They had been on the march for several days now, following the remnants of the old Interstate 35 north. The weather—sometimes warm, sometimes still cold—was hard on them but the excitement of going somewhere to settle down was electric.

She looked at Mariza and Joan, both due anytime, and was thankful for her own easy delivery just a few weeks ago. They seemed so uncomfortable on the plodding horses. The Maroons, however, doted over them and the lives they carried within them. Caleb especially fawned over Joan, looking out for her every need. Gretchen could tell he loved her and Joan returned it equally. Nathan, when he was not with her, spent his time with the younger men learning about hunting and scouting. His black stud was the fastest horse in the herd and he was very proud of that. A brisk spring breeze caught her brown hair, Joshua cried for food and she put him to her breast beneath a blanket.

***

Mariza looked over at Joan. "I think I am bigger than you," she said, pointing at her pregnant form. "That may be but I will deliver first," Joan laughed. Their dual pregnancy had made coping easier. They spent most of their time together. That is, when the other women were not constantly giving them attention. They were so young to be mothers and, despite the sad circumstances of their conception and fear of what was to come, they had come to love the lives within them. Watching Gretchen go through childbirth helped remove some of the uncertainty. They were both the center of attention among the Maroons. It was hard to imagine what life would have been in the realm of Caesar.

Joan was so glad that Joshua had told her to live with these people and never return. I never got to see my mother who had given me up for the mission although she did not know what it was, Joan thought sadly. She was happy now and patted the tummy. The other girls all felt the same way. This was their family now. She thought of Caleb, he had asked her to be his partner. Joan was not sure how to respond, she needed more time to deal with all the events, including this new child. Caleb was good in his reaction and made every effort to make her comfortable. It was always her that he wanted to dance with.

***

Anna dismounted the small black mare she'd named Midnight for its coal black coat and the early morning hours she spent with this beautiful animal. Sue had told her that Midnight was pregnant so she was very careful not to ride her too hard. At 12 years old, Anna was strikingly beautiful with jet black hair, almond eyes and creamy white skin. She looked out across the broad prairie from the small hill she had ridden to. It was nice to be alone for a few moments. Anna stroked Midnight and the horse seemed to respond, pressing its head up against her. She thought about this last winter and how different it had been, especially the white stuff called snow! Neville and the children born on Dominica had never seen such a thing and the others laughed when they watched them experience it.

The Maroons had grown to 25 souls and soon three more births would make it 28. She enjoyed helping the expectant mothers, Cyndra, Mariza and Joan. Vicariously she experienced the joy of new life and looked forward to bringing new life into this world herself. It was difficult though; her thoughts flashed to Acoba. She had been gently cautioned to see Acoba only as her brother but her feelings went deeper. They had grown up together but there was definitely an attraction between them. Anna's introspective nature made her far less assertive than she could have been.

She slowly got into the cross-legged position she knew so well. Her mother had taught her how to calm her mind and bring stillness in meditation. She loved these moments and with her face toward the south and the warmth of the sun she began to concentrate on her breath. After finding that familiar space her mother called nowness she completely relaxed. Suddenly there was a wash of anxiety within her that she could not resist. Unable to find her way back to stillness, she slowly opened her eyes.

In the far distance was a cloud unlike any she had seen before—like a mushroom growing out of the landscape. It was unnatural and anxiety prompted her to reach for Midnight. She mounted and rode quickly despite the horse's condition. When she reached the slowly moving band, she alerted them to what she had seen. They called a halt and the Rastas all formed around her. The knowing on their faces was evident. They each mounted the most available horse and headed to the hill where Anna had been.

The six adults stood silently gazing at the mushroom cloud on the horizon. No one spoke for what seemed like an eternity. Several faces were streaked with tears. Jungsuk was deep in the sadness that all were feeling. She tried to allow herself to feel this emotion and face it. To her it was difficult to imagine after all the human race had gone through and how few were left that such a thing was possible. The brightness of a new world and the possibilities that it presented seemed to be dashed on the rocks of unconsciousness. She reached over and took Neville's hand and in turn they all joined hands.

The thought came to her mind like a shock and she could not put it aside. "We must make a large fire on this hill and burn it through the night, "If there are survivors it will be a beacon for them," she said to the others. They all looked at her quizzically. "OK" was Neville's response. "There was a small grove a little ways back, I will take a wagon and gather wood." The other men agreed and mounted their horses, leaving the women to watch the strange cloud get larger. "We must explain this all to the family somehow," Jungsuk spoke to the others. Sue and Cyndra both agreed and suggested that Jungsuk be the one to explain. They also mounted and headed to the family to make camp and prepare for the night ahead.

The concept of a weapon so massively powerful was hard to grasp for the children of the new world. The concept that one would use it was even harder. The questions of why could not be answered except that it was madness and the result of great fear, the root of all negative emotions. Their naive minds could only accept the words of those who were older.

Everyone who was not taking care of the animals helped build the huge bonfire on top of the hill. It became a great game and with the evening being bright and clear they looked forward to the large fire as they looked out over the vast plains that surrounded them. After the fire was ignited, their thoughts of the large mushroom cloud vanished in the darkness and one by one the Rastas sang their favorite songs, always a special treat for the children. This night they did not smoke the sacred herb and they did not dance. They chose sad songs. Jungsuk sang *Arriyong* in her native Korean tongue; Gary sang one of the few Celtic songs that he knew in Welsh. Sue sang a Cheyenne healing chant. Cyndra and Marcus sang *Amazing Grace* together in beautiful harmony, and in the end Neville sang from his favorite Bob Marley: *Every little thing is gonna be all right*. The songs mesmerized the children, who begged for repeat performances so they could learn them.

After another round they heard the sound. It was faint in the distance, so everyone sat silently as the fire crackled and sparks rose into the air. Gary tried to explain to the children that it was the sound of an airplane. His explanation of a machine that could fly like a bird only made this moment more magical to the children. As the sound became stronger, they all knew that it was heading for their light on a hill.

Gary could tell that the plane was going to try to land near the fire. The only possibility was the old interstate they had been following north, now broken and covered with grass. In the darkness he feared the plane would not know where to land and might hit the animals or even people. He called for everyone to gather by the fire and bring the horses and mules. The other animals would have to take their chances. From the sounds, it had to be a prop plane and very large. Everyone watched in the darkness as the sound became louder. When the plane flew low and directly over the fire, it was deafening and the children crouched down and covered their ears. The animals went crazy and many of them could not be restrained and ran off into the night.

Jacque held onto his bay mare and Acoba mounted it with him and headed toward the landing direction. Gary directed everyone to be still as the sound of the plane crashing into the not-too-distant north took place. He was thankful none of the Maroons was hurt. The resulting sparks and flames did not bode well for survivors. There was a sliver of moon so Acoba and Jacque moved slowly toward the flames. Acoba squeezed his brother tight, feeling the bond between them. As they approached the wreckage he could see from the flames the shape of this thing called an airplane.

They dismounted and as Jacque held his horse Acoba carefully approached the plane. He yelled out, "Is anyone there?" He heard a moan and in the light of the flames he found a man lying on the ground. His clothes still smoked. Acoba bent over him and could see his eyes were open. "Are there others?" Acoba said.

"I don't know, it was a tough landing and I was in the body of the plane and barely got out. There are two pilots but they may not have survived the crash." Acoba looked at the mangled remains of the plane and found it hard to believe anyone in the front could have survived. He decided to drag the man away from the flames, so with all his strength he grabbed the clothes under the man's head and pulled him away from the wreckage. When he felt they were safely away, he stopped and tried to make the man comfortable.

"Where are you hurt?" Acoba spoke.

The man seemed coherent and alert. "I am sure I have some broken bones and I am burned slightly but I don't seem to be bleeding," he responded.

"Rest easy, the others will be here to help soon. I will stay with you," Acoba reassured him. "Jacque, I will stay with this man, go get more help and a wagon to carry him, my brother." Acoba yelled. Jacque mounted and rode off immediately.

The morning brought a cold spring rain with clouds but no wind. It had been a hard night after the crash, locating the animals and making sure the shelters were up. Sue and Jungsuk had hardly slept, watching over the survivor. He had been in and out of consciousness and the only thing they had learned was his name, John McCain of the Body. He was an older man with balding grey hair. His chances for survival were good but he would not be able to travel for a few days. Despite the cold rain, many could not resist the urge to inspect the wreckage. The front of the plane was completely smashed with no sign of survivors. The charred remains of this aircraft fascinated the young ones. Marcus tried to explain how it worked and their eyes were full of wonder. In any case it did not fit in on the grassy plain. There seemed little that could be salvaged from it.

John McCain watched as the two skin-clad women brought him water and food; he was comfortable in the small shelter. "Tell me who you are?" he said, looking at Jungsuk. She explained they were called the Maroons and John listened with fascination to her story of where they had come from and especially of how they had spent the winter in Goshen. He was amazed and in unbelief until Nathan came to visit him with Gretchen. They knew each other, though not well. It was then that he decided to explain how he had come to this place. Nathan asked him to wait until all were present to hear the story as there were no secrets among the Maroons.

The weather changed to bright blue sky with warm sun the next day and they brought John out into the sun. Everyone gathered around him to hear what he had to say. At first John hesitated, looking at the tribe of people around him. He recognized the young girls of the Body and his eyes fell upon the two pregnant ones. Neville stepped forward and bent down to look into his faded blue eyes with his own dark brown ones. "We have no secrets here, there is no need for any, please tell us what you know. You are safe here and no one will harm you or judge you." There was silence. Then John began.

"You are right, there is no need for secrets anymore. As you know the Body has been in conflict with the forces of Caesar for a long time. Joshua kept so many things secret. Your whole existence for one, Nate and Gretchen's reason for leaving was a lie. The sending of these young girls to be spies I did not know about. Now it all makes sense to me. I was part of a secret plan to annihilate the threat of Caesar with a preemptive strike using an atomic weapon we had found. Joshua was well acquainted with their locations and it had taken us a long time to prepare it and a plane to deliver it. We were sure that it would be the end of our troubles. Joshua had sent many spies to New Orleans to make sure we knew their plans.

"What we did not know is Caesar had sent his own spies. Despite all attempts to keep this strike a secret it failed. Elder Levi was a spy and when he was given access to this knowledge he vanished. All plans were accelerated. It is amazing that in flight to New Orleans we encountered a plane heading for Dallas. We radioed this to Joshua but even in the best of situations immediate evacuation would have given them time to get perhaps 30 miles away. We dropped our bomb and New Orleans is no more, if any survived there it would be a miracle. When we returned to Dallas, it did not exist so we flew north to Goshen and found no sign of life there. We saw the light on a hill in the vast expanse of plain to the north and headed for it. The rest you know." John nodded his head and began to weep.

"My family, my friends, everything is gone I fear, I have nothing left." he sobbed. No one asked any questions. Slowly everyone dispersed, leaving John alone with only Nathan and Gretchen to comfort him. "I must go back to see if there are any survivors." John spoke quietly to Nathan.

"You are not in very good shape to do that, my friend," Nathan replied.

"I have nothing left to lose, nothing to live for, please give me horse and a weapon, some food and water and I will go." John looked into Nathan's eyes. After a long silence Nathan spoke "I will give you my horse and my weapon and what food and water we can spare. It is the fastest horse we have. If you find anyone come find us, we are heading north and I will leave some marker if we leave the old interstate. "

John reached out and hugged Nathan and Gretchen with his good arm. "I will leave in the morning. Peace be to you, brother." he said.

"And to you John McCain, I hope you find survivors," Nathan replied. In the morning John was gone; no one questioned Nathan's decision. The Maroons resumed their pilgrimage north and the dream of Joshua and the black plane never occurred again.

Using what landmarks and signs were still readable, Gary was able to discern the progress the Maroons had made. He had gotten over the anxiety about where they were going. Like the other men, he had resigned himself to complete faith in the dreams of the women. North and a little stone church in a grove of trees, he thought. It was a wonderment they had come this far. He pacified his need to know with determining where they were and how far they had come. As far as he could figure with the old road maps, they had entered Kansas somewhere south of Wichita. They had come around 330 miles and been traveling since the spring solstice for 60 days. This would average about 6-8 miles per day with some weather and rest days. He sat on his buckskin gelding marveling at the wondrous open plains and big sky.

Amid the slow progression of the children and the animals, the sounds of talking humans and domestic livestock intermingled. Why he alone was concerned about knowing details sometimes bothered him. The others seemed completely satisfied with the cares of the day and maybe tomorrow. He smiled with the peace he felt looking at them all. The end of May had turned hot and dry after so much rain when they had started. This could be such an unforgiving land at times with little shelter from the elements. On the other hand it was incredibly bountiful, a hunting paradise.

Mariza and Joan had given birth. Mariza had a son whom she named Freedom and Joan shortly after with a daughter she named Liberty. They both were so young to be mothers but gave themselves completely to the task. Cyndra and Marcus were also overjoyed with the arrival of a daughter they named Unity. The Maroons were growing and thriving. The boys had caught some wild dog puppies and the prospect of having these as pets to warn and protect the family was a comforting thought. The blessing of so much game came with the danger of other predators. They had sighted not only packs of wild dogs but wolves as well. There had even been a sighting of a grizzly bear. They had not seen them but the signs of mountain lion were there. All the more reason to have dogs. He was looking forward to getting to Wichita in the next day or so. The prospect of finding more humans was remote since they had not found any in Oklahoma City but the possibility was there. The chance to rummage and find more salvage was always exciting to Gary.

Lee, the constant explorer, looked up and down the main street of the city called Wichita. Sue had told him it was named for the indigenous people like her own Cheyenne ancestors who inhabited the area many years ago. He reminisced about that conversation, how he had asked her who the natives of this land were and she had him look into a mirror and told him "the person you see is the native of this land now." He smiled, it was a good memory.

Like all the other towns and cities they encountered, it was a maze of rusted and burned-out vehicles and structures. The constant prairie fires had quickly turned it into a prairie with only the metal and masonry left behind. Few of the stone or brick structures could be found intact. Marcus had explained that these were mostly public buildings like schools where the children were sent to learn, or banks where the money was kept. Lee dismounted and entered what was once a bank. Like those he had seen before, the vault was open and the moldy remains of what Marcus called money lay on the floor, He picked up one and pondered it. "I would not trade one poor arrowhead or bullet for this," he said to himself. The concept of value for such a thing was beyond him; it did not even burn well. The place was now home and refuge for birds, raccoons and many other animals and the smell was oppressive.

Another favorite place he liked to visit was what Marcus called libraries. The massive amount of books was always a delight to look at with pictures and drawings. Often the roofs were gone and the books would fall apart when opened, their bloated pages many times the original size from moisture. It was at these times he came to appreciate the skill of reading and writing that his parents had taught him. It was like moving into another world to read these books.

Lee jumped on top of his faithful horse and companion, Cloud. She was a mid-size white mare. She swished her tail at flies and bent her head back for the pat that Lee always gave her. They had become so close and riding her they felt like one. They moved down the cracked and overgrown street to the large structure that drew his attention. Marcus had explained that this was a stadium where the people would come and watch games being played. As he approached the rusted metal gate there was the faded red paint of skull and crossbones. He knew this was not a good sign and stopped in front. Hanging from the latch was a cylinder on a chain. Without dismounting Lee held it up and with difficulty unscrewed the cap. Inside he found a note faded but readable, he slowly began to read it, DANGER, it started, we are all dying. Do not enter. Lee stopped and folded the message paper and stuck it into his shirt. This was important and he pointed Cloud and headed off at a gallop to tell the Maroons, who had not reached the outskirts of the city yet. Lee yelled at Jacque as he rushed past to follow and they were off.

As always when Lee and Jacque would ride at a gallop into the camp everyone knew something was up. Lee rode up to Neville and handed him the paper as everyone gathered around. Neville, not one for reading, handed it to Jungsuk who clearly read its contents after everyone quieted down. There had been a small community of survivors in Wichita but according to the note around year 10 a flu virus of some kind had swept through and decimated them. All attempts to quarantine or fight it off had failed and those that survived were so weakened that they knew they would also perish. The note was a gesture in parting for anyone who might come upon them. This was year 16 and it had been six years since the plague. The question on everyone's mind was whether the plague might still be around? Were Lee and Jacque possibly exposed? Just to be sure Jacque and Lee were to camp away from the group, especially from the babies. The Maroons could not afford such a plague to happen to them. It was also decided to skirt around the city and head north as soon as possible. Sue with her limited medical knowledge agreed that Lee and Jacque should be watched closely for a few days. Not knowing exactly what the plague consisted of except for some type of flu made it hard to determine an incubation time but it was believed a week would be enough. The sobering thought of how precarious their existence was settled in on the entire group. One thing they should be gleaning if possible from the remnants of the past civilization was medical knowledge and supplies. Neville, however, refused to leave the two alone and designated himself to be the one to take them food and supplies during their quarantine.

Wendy reflected on the past year of the voyage to land and the encounter with the different groups, the nuclear bomb and the latest scare with the plague. She was far more solitary than most and chose to spend time alone meditating and contemplating not just what happened but why. She loved the feel of the hot Kansas sun on her light brown skin, the wind in her long curly brown hair. Her green eyes were piercing and seemed to know what people were thinking. She was strikingly tall for a female with a slender frame and long dexterous fingers. Wendy had a plain look about her and moved easily among all ages of people. She made anyone she was with feel comfortable and peaceful. Having never known her real mother, she was equally attached to all the mother Rastas and always felt loved but in another way quite different. Gary doted on her and they would often take long walks and talk about the world before zero year. The peculiar thing was why she had dreamed with the other Rastas at such a young age. In some ways she felt like she had always been old. Sue had told her that she had gifts that were still to be discovered and she wondered what they might be. She watched as the four mothers shared the nursing of the children and though she helped often it did not seem a big drive for her to someday produce children.

Gary had told her they were somewhere south of a city called Salina and the June heat was oppressive. Wendy had learned to ride but preferred to walk. Feeling the earth beneath her moccasined feet energized her. She had the amazing ability to run for long periods of time without getting tired. She had done so now in the early morning hours heading west and had stopped on a rise in the plain to watch the sunrise and think. They were getting close to their destination— she felt it, as did the other dreamers.

She had been having another dream as well, but the others did not. It was of an old man with silver hair. In her dream this man would smile at her and beckon her with a wave. She had told the other women about it and no one could explain what it might mean.

She loved the sunrise and sat cross legged with her face toward the rising ball of flame and breathed. It had been a calm morning but suddenly the wind began to pick up out of the west on her back. Wendy slowly turned to face the west and in the far distance she saw the glow across the entire horizon from north to south. It took some time to realize what this was since she had never experienced it before.

She was on her feet in seconds, heart pounding; she began to run as fast as she could to camp. She covered the mile or so as if she was flying, and though out of breath she did her best to scream, waking up the camp. Gary was the first to appear and saw the urgency in her face. The animals already were nervous and everyone gathered to find out what was happening. Wendy explained that a prairie fire was heading this direction and it stretched from horizon to horizon. There was no way to outrun it to the north or south. Everyone was aware of what prairie fires had done in the past, burning entire cities but to date none had actually been seen.

The Rastas conferred with each other and made a plan. Caleb was sent west on his horse to keep an eye on the approach. Everyone else who was not watching the animals was given the duty of setting fire to the heavily overgrown grass to the east of camp in a long line. At first it was difficult to ignite the grass with the morning dew but as the wind began to pick up the flames grew more intense and it began to make a wall of flame heading east. The horses in particular were hard to hold and some ran away to the west away from the flames.

Having done this, the Maroons quickly began to make preparations to leave. Caleb returned with news that a great wall of flame was moving fast. In front of it were vast herds of animals too many to count. It was decided to wait until the last possible moment to enter the area burned by the Maroons themselves since the ground was still hot and smoldering. It was difficult not to run in fear as the approaching inferno sent billowing clouds of smoke through the camp. At times it was impossible to see even a few inches ahead and breathing in the smoke painful.

At the last possible moment the group moved into the burned area. The animals could hardly be contained and the heat could still be felt through moccasins. The lack of visibility and thick smoke furthered the chaos. Then they came, waves of stampeding buffalo, wild cows, antelope, elk, deer, turkey, coyotes, wolves, wild dogs and anything else that moved on the plains. The horses and animals that had escaped west now came back wild with fear.

The heat was incredible and the Maroons were now trapped between two walls of flames. The jumble of humans and livestock caused many injuries and cries came from many directions. The mothers and babies gathered under a makeshift shelter from one of the tents. The roar slowly subsided as the oncoming fire found no purchase in the already burned area. It took some time to calm down after the flames had passed to the north and south.

The Maroons gathered and looked at each other's blackened faces, then smiled with white teeth. Around them were the wild animals that had found refuge in the small island that they had burned. The boys all began to string their bows in preparation to take the easy prey. Wendy, however, screamed at them to stop. "No killing today," she yelled. All the men looked at her, bewildered. "Today we save them and in return they will save us in the future." Slowly the exhausted animals walked away, seeming almost tame. They had survived, a small group of humanity in the expanse of blackened, smoldering plain.

Chapter 21
Home
016-017

Lori was in awe.

The prairie fire had scorched the plains in every direction farther than the eye could see. The Maroons had traveled for two days across the blackened landscape toward the city called Salina. The animals had suffered the most, looking for nourishment, and every stream or old farm pond was a place to wash off the black ash that seemed to get everywhere. She wondered why her mother had traded the lush forest of Alabama for this.

But suddenly it all changed! An overnight storm shortly after the fire lit the night sky with a fabulous lightning show, then a pounding rain. Now the entire expanse of rolling hills was a lush carpet of green grass as if the fire had never happened. The animals voraciously devoured the tender shoots of life.

Born again the land was. Lori was in love with this dynamic place of constant change. She drew in a breath and exhaled slowly, relishing its feeling of life in her own body. She would turn 16 soon and the changes in her own body had almost put her into womanhood. Her long blonde hair brilliantly reflected the light of the morning sun as she went through the meditative acts Jungsuk had taught her. Her thoughts wandered again from the trance that started her day.

Of course she knew why Cyndra had made the dangerous decision to leave the safety of the Klan and make a new home with the Maroons. Smiling now, she recalled the foolish fear she had felt when told to pack her things, that they would leave with her brother Abel to catch up with the curious group of people that they had been forbidden to even visit on the beach in Mobile Bay. Both of them had resisted and almost stayed behind. Only the abuse that they had received at the hands of their stepfather made the prospect of being left behind with him the greater fear.

Now she could look back and know her mother made a wise choice. That world of prejudice and abuse was replaced by love and acceptance. She loved her new family. The idea of having a black father was unheard of but a more loving, caring man than Marcus you could never find. The fact he almost gave his life for her mother and the loss of his own daughter had changed everything. The sorrow she felt for Nicole and Frederick had drawn them together and Nicole was her closest friend and confidant now. She had not had the dreams that the Rasta women had. None of the young women except Wendy seemed to share this strange phenomenon.

Lori surveyed the treeless plains around her, raising her arms and dancing in circles to send her shapely five-foot-six frame spinning in the timeless cadence of life. A meadowlark. Sdasdona as Sue called it, sang in the distance. Stopping, she opened her eyes and smiled again. The Rastas had dreamed together again, this time it was not just the small stone church in a grove of woods but they had seen a large lake and a stone post. They felt they were close to their destination as well.

At Salina they had camped for a few days while the men searched for things on the dream-list, as he called it. The once-large town had no sign of life and only the things made of stone, brick or concrete were left. The enormous grain elevator was the most striking feature and some of the children led by Caleb and Acoba found their way to the top to see how far they could see. How could people who could build such a great structure have disappeared? The stories told by the Rastas around the fires at night always fascinated her but as Neville would always say at the end, "They lived, now we live."

The new dreams prompted the band to follow the river called Saline on Gary's old road map toward a large lake called Wilson. Gary did not like the idea of going across the country because the ease of water crossings provided by the old interstate bridges would be lost. The women assured him that they were close and it would be all right. He had given everyone a lesson in finding directions with the sun and the stars and the few compasses they had. Lee and Jacque were his best pupils, always in the lead and always exploring. Jacque, even his name made her tingle. Lori was hopelessly enamored with this dashing brave young man. They had spent little time together as they were both shy. She knew he had feelings towards her, as she'd sometimes catch him looking her way during meals and at the fire at night. She wanted so badly to go with him on his forays on his buckskin mare but was afraid to ask. Besides, she had other responsibilities with keeping the chickens and hogs together and, of course, helping the young mothers. She longed to be a mother herself but Cyndra had cautioned her to wait until they had settled. It was already starting to get hot being midsummer. Lori walked back to the camp by the river to help with the morning meal and pack for the travel ahead.

They were three days out of Salina following the river when they decided to camp at the remnants of a small town. Everywhere they would find the strange stone posts sticking up from the ground like the dreamers had described. The remnants of barbed wire still attached to some, badly rusted and brittle. The long lines in some places created strange shadows across the rolling hills. In the small town were some magnificent stone buildings of the same stone as the fence-posts. One such building was beautiful and somewhat intact. The words Lincoln County Courthouse could be read in the stone. Neville smiled, showing his white teeth. "This must be the right place; it has the right name," he exclaimed. Another building read Carnegie Library and to everyone's amazement it was fully intact and the precious books it held were undamaged! Gary and Marcus were in heaven. They were sure this was the place they were supposed to be, but the dreamers said no. There was no lake and no stone church in the grove of woods that had drawn them this far. They proceeded west toward the lake on the map full of excitement and awe for this beautiful country.

After a leisurely two-day march, they came to a large earthen dam that held back the waters of the Saline River to create what the map called Lake Wilson. Its tepid clear water was so inviting that everyone took off their clothes and jumped in, cooling off in the summer heat. Camp was made and everyone was in high spirits. The beauty of the country's rolling grass hills and the bounty it presented in wildlife and food was mind numbing. The dreamers all knew they were close to their destination and Wendy's dream of the old man came again. The young people all wanted to live here by this marvelous lake. Gary pointed out on the map that there was a town nearby called Lucas. "Perhaps this is where the church of the dream is," he remarked to Sue that evening.

"How far is it?" Sue replied. Gary checked the map and told her that it was maybe one day of travel for the whole group since they rarely did more than 10 miles on their best days. "Let's go there tomorrow," Sue said and gave him a big kiss. Sue was very much at home in this environment of grass and sky. This was the ancestral home of her people, the Tistista, the Cheyenne. She thought this must be how it looked before the coming of the Europeans. Now it would be the home of the Maroons.

It was evening when the Maroons came to the remains of Lucas. The characteristic foundations and grain elevator indicated it had been a settlement in the past, but little else remained. There was, however, one structure made of the same stone as the thousands of fence-posts that dotted the landscape. The stone had been carefully cut to look like the logs of a log cabin and around the perimeter was the concrete artistry of figures and words as well as a mausoleum with a glass sarcophagus inside. They made camp next to this and explored.

Marcus figured out that the figures and words were a description of the history of the world. After analyzing it thoroughly, he took great pleasure in taking the entire family around explaining what he felt it all meant. The children were fascinated by the story from Adam and Eve through the Civil War and the evils depicted of corporations and greed. They asked endless questions to which Marcus tried to explain these concepts so foreign to the children of the new world. It was all great fun for everyone and at the evening's campfire they decided to stay here until the church of the dreams could be located.

The Rastas sat down together and formulated a plan for finding it: The mothers and babies would stay with Gary and Sue while the rest of the Maroons would go out in twos in different directions to search for their home. They took great care in pairing up the teams and deciding which direction they should go. Each team would leave in the morning and return by evening to report what they had found. Caleb and Anna would go north, while Nate and Wendy would go northeast. Northwest would be the direction for Jacque and Lori. West they would send Nicole and Acoba and east Jungsuk and Abel. That left southwest to Lee and Peggy and southeast to Marcus, Fredrick and Sarah. Finally Neville and Nile would go directly south. The pairings, of course, had a double purpose in some cases to allow alone time for the budding relationships that the Rastas could see forming. It expended almost every horse available, leaving the mules and some spring foals behind. Amid great excitement, few listened to Gary and Sue's words of caution and instruction before they left and the warning to take no chances and be back before dark.

Around them stretched the wide-open rolling plains and a beautiful summer day. Though hardly needed, all the teams again heard the description of the small stone church in the grove of trees that they looking for. After they had all left Gary grabbed Sue in a rambunctious hug. His love and respect for this wonderful woman had grown through the last 16 years and he could not imagine life without her. He did not want to let her go.

The assumption that the place they were looking for was actually a town had given rise to directing people toward known points on the map. Neville and Nile rode south as instructed and found themselves back at Wilson Lake. They could not resist a dip in the clear water before heading to the town of Wilson. They had never spent much time alone together but Neville's easy manner and talkative mood gave rise to a deeper relationship. Nile was turning only 11 and her Asian descent lent her resemblance to Jungsuk with her almond eyes and dark black hair. Her experience with the trackers had made it difficult for her to feel comfortable with males, the very reason Jungsuk had paired her with Neville. His compassionate eyes took little time to begin bringing down the walls of fear that had built up. Soon they were laughing and splashing in the water and Neville's protective, fatherly way began to disarm her normally reserved nature. They reached what had been the town of Wilson and immediately knew it did not fit the description of the dreamers. They had lunch and spent some time exploring, looking for the things Gary always requested for his inventions. They headed back to camp in Lucas, taking the time to swim again and wash the horses in the lake. Nile would always reflect on this wonderful day.

Caleb and Anna had known each other all their lives and were very close. They had both wanted another partner. Caleb wanted to spend time with Joan but she had obligations to Liberty. Anna, of course, wanted to be with Acoba, which was all but forbidden. They headed through rugged, hilly country for a town called Osborne, talking the whole way. Caleb was the one person Anna could confide her true feelings about Acoba. Caleb loved his sister and Acoba was his closest friend. He understood the conflict and the reasons for it. He also knew Acoba's feelings and it was hard for him to watch and also know the reasons why. He tried to console Anna that she would find a mate but it could not be Acoba. They spent the time in Osborne noting what was there. It also did not fit the dream and the ride back to Lucas was mostly in silence, both enjoying their own thoughts and occasionally pointing out land features and animals. Caleb reached out and held Anna's hand and told her he loved her. Anna smiled back and squeezed his hand; she loved him too.

Abel was so proud to be the man of the partnership with Jung-suk and she made sure she made him feel that importance. He would carry the weapon and she allowed him to keep them on the right path. Besides, Jungsuk relished the time to get to know this shy young man of 11 years. He was bright and already taking on the muscle and stature of a teenager. They were going east to a town called Sylvan Grove, which she knew meant sacred grove. A good candidate for the oft-dreamed home, it would be the shortest distance so she purposely moseyed along to make it a full day, taking in the sights and sounds of the many animals that Abel proudly named and explained to her. She would smile and reach out to touch him, to which he responded. That people so different could now be such a close community made her heart soar. The energy of all that lived around them just seemed to flow through her very being. Sylvan Grove was not the place of the dream but Abel and Jungsuk explored the remains of the stone

buildings on what had been Main Street. At lunch they both sat together and meditated, a thing that everyone now practiced together
and alone. Then it was time to head back.

Marcus gazed at the two children riding in front of him. Fredrick, his son now 11, and Sarah, 10. They were the youngest of the
children on the trail. He now considered all the children his own,
a concept so foreign in the before time. Sarah was as white as snow
while Fredrick was black as coal. Both had suffered horribly in their
short lives. Fredrick was just now overcoming the inbred hatred of
all that was not black and Sarah had not recovered from the trauma
of the trackers. Despite it all he could see they were becoming comfortable as time went along. Marcus sang a song from his youth and
the two of them tried to learn it and join in. They asked him to sing
it over and over until he was hoarse but he sang it again. It was "Just
my imagination" and he loved to sing it. They were directed to cross
the Saline and head southeast to no point in particular but look for a
grove of trees. Marcus had no expectations with the children being
so young. It was a picnic day and he wanted it to be special, a time to
remember. It was.

Jacque and Lori were in ecstasy, alone together for an entire day.
They had been given one of the hardest routes northwest to complete
unknown and no town in particular, but a cinch for the seasoned
Jacque. He had come to love the plains and its nuances compared to
the forest of Dominica and the south. His ever watchful eye, however, was distracted today constantly looking over at Lori. They rode
in silence initially but before long they were discussing every person-
ality in the Maroon community and how they felt about things. The
electricity between them was obvious and by lunchtime they were
holding hands. Lori did not want the day to end and had no concern
at all as to whether they would find the grove of trees. Heading back
to Lucas was the hardest part of the day despite the hot sun.

Acoba and Nicole rode west to the town of Luray along the
Wolf Creek that also ran through Lucas. Acoba knew why the Rastas
had paired him with Nicole. She was the best choice for a mate for
him in age. It was not that Nicole was not pretty for she was, but it
was hard for him to imagine himself with anyone but Anna. They

spoke freely about their past. Acoba was fascinated by the strange community called the Panthers that had been Nicole's upbringing. The concept of hating others because of their race was abhorrent to him and he told her so. Nicole also loved the stories of Dominica and wanted to know if someday Acoba would take her there. "It's a long ways and we would have to sail in a boat," Acoba said. "But you never know, it could happen." They talked about the strange weapon and what it might have done to the City of Light. The day passed quickly and Luray did not fit the dream so they headed back to Lucas.

Lee and Peggy stopped on the hill and looked back at Lucas. Heading to a town called Bunker Hill to the southwest, Peggy, with her bright red hair shining in the sun, was unsure about being alone with a man. Lee, though, was a good choice; she had watched him over the last year and was comfortable with his ability. He was a very gentle, quiet young man and self assured. It was hard to find him apart from his best friend and half brother Jacque. He was in fact quite amazing for his age of 12. Peggy could remember being scared for him when he was quarantined from the group back in Wichita. His return made her happy. They talked in surface mode as they rode along. The miles, however, wore away the limited topics and gave way to deeper things. They both found themselves enjoying the other's company and before they knew it they were among the ruins of the town. They sat back to back meditating and the feeling of each other through their clothes was a wonderful sensation. Lee helped Peggy back on her small paint mare, taking care to make sure all was right with her rigging. There was not a moment of silence the whole way back to Lucas.

Nate looked over at Wendy as they rode up the small ravine to the next divide. He would have preferred to stay back with Gretchen and little Joshua but being out on the plain on this bright summer day was something he enjoyed. Being with Wendy was also a pleasure. Everyone loved Wendy; there was something about her, call it an aura or atmosphere it could not be put into words. It was not anything to do with her physical being but with the way she would interact with people and how you felt when you were around her. She was only 13 but you would think she had lived a hundred years. The differences made her attract others and at the same time set her apart. He watched her on the little mule that she had picked out and helped train to ride. Even the animal she called Moses responded to her every touch. Wendy appeared deep in thought and then as if she knew Nate was looking at her she turned and smiled.

"We should stop at the top of the rise and rest the horses; Moses is a little winded," she reached down and stroked him across the neck. The mule's large ears went up with a positive response. "OK," Nate responded as he pressed his white gelding ahead to get to the top first. He missed his black stud that he had given to John McCain to look for survivors. His mind wandered to whether John had found any and if he would be able to follow the trail of small rock cairns back to the Maroons. The City of Light and all those years seemed like a lifetime ago despite it being only a little more than a year. The others had thought him foolish to give such a prized horse to John with no assurance it would be returned. Everyone except Wendy. She had come to him and hugged him, telling him his gift would be rewarded beyond his expectations. "What does that mean?" he asked her. "Wait and see" was all she had said. He intended to ask her about it at the proper time.

Nate's hair had grown rapidly and the long reddish blonde flag bounced and flowed behind him as he sped to the top of coulee. He waited for Wendy and Moses to make their way while he looked around. This was a large divide, the term Sue used for spaces between drainages. It was relatively flat and had been farmed extensively, evidenced by the numerous stone fence posts that still stood erect in lines among the tall stand of prairie grass. In the distance a small herd of antelope looked curiously at the man on a horse. Nate started to reach around to unsling the weapon on his back. He felt Wendy's hand on his and the electricity that accompanied it.

"Not now Nate, no hunting, we have more important business to attend to, we are close," she said.

Nate smiled, "Close?"

"He is close, I can feel it," Wendy replied.

"You are something else, Wendy; you want to explain this to me?" Nate said, puzzled.

"Let's sit down and rest and I will explain." Wendy said and dismounted her mule. Nate pulled out some jerky from his satchel and they sat cross legged while the animals grazed. Wendy explained the dream that only she had been having of the old man beckoning her. Like the others of the Maroons, Nate had come to respect the dreams of the Rasta women.

"Which way should we go Wendy?" he asked.

After a long moment of silence she got to her feet. "Is that a wisp of smoke over there or a small cloud?" she pointed to the far end of the divide to the northeast. "That's where we are going." she said.

"Then let's go!" Nate shouted and was on his horse in seconds.

Roy looked up from watering the pigs from the tank below the windmill. The hot summer breeze was barely enough to push the old fins around and the water came out slowly. Its source deep in the ground ensured it to be cold and refreshing and he loved to splash a little on his face from time to time. His weathered face from years in the sun framed by his long white hair gave him a very distinguished look. He'd kept his face clean shaven since he had entered the Army in 1965 in the midst of the Vietnam War. That war had affected him greatly and despite returning to his beloved home on the plains of Kansas and the isolation of the farm he still had deep scars that made him remember his tour of duty as an infantry soldier in that hideous war. Even at 76 he had dreams that troubled his sleep.

Through the heat waves that flowed across the familiar landscape to the southwest he could see the two figures approaching. His one good eye was as good as it was in his youth when he was the best shot in the county. Roy could tell it was not elk or buffalo but horses with people on them! His old heart, strong as ever, began to beat rapidly. It had been so very long since he had seen another human being. The few that had passed through after the end of the world did not stay but moved on, looking for remnants of humanity. They had always invited him to come along but he wanted to stay here and finish his solitary life in the place he knew and loved in Lincoln County. That was what, 15 years ago? he thought. As the pair moved closer, he first thought to run to the old stone house for his rifle. NO, he thought as he dropped the bucket. He stood up, pushed back his silver hair and straightened his crude skin clothes. He was too old to run or fight; he would welcome them. His pale blue eyes began to mist over; it had been so long. As they approached his tiny oasis on the plain he walked slowly out to greet them, smiling.

Wendy and Nate were amazed to see a solitary figure walking toward them in the heat. Wendy recognized him immediately from her dream and her heart raced. She kicked Moses into a run. As the distance closed, she halted Moses and jumped off running toward the old man. With no hesitation she embraced him as if they had known each other forever. Roy, at first shocked, began to weep uncontrollably while Nate observed in amazement. What did it all mean? Nate thought. Not a word was spoken for the longest time as Roy and Wendy held onto each other. Nate finally dismounted and Roy opened his arms to bring Nate into the embrace. Roy's old body heaved with sobs of joy. When they finally disengaged, Roy grabbed both their hands and, with choked words, whispered "Welcome my friends, welcome to my home" as he pulled them along, his strong hands not letting them go. "The animals," Nate spoke and Roy let go of his hand to allow him to fetch them but continued on with Wendy toward the house.

The next hours were spent in excited conversation Roy learning about the Maroons and Wendy and Nate about Roy. His name was Roy Strecker and he blessed them in the German tongue passed down from his great grandparents that had come from the Volga of Russia as exiles and homesteaded this farm so many years ago. Time passed rapidly in the excited conversation with Roy often breaking down in tears. Wendy sat next to him and consoled him. Nate was amazed how her presence and concern for this old man flowed so naturally. The topic came around to the church in the dream and Roy's eyes lit up. "I know this place well." he said and described it perfectly. "It is the old town of Ash Grove and a beautiful little valley." He explained how it must be a natural shelter from the storms and fires since it had always been a place where trees would grow. The old stone church was all that remained of the town along with the many cellars of stone built by the pioneers to find refuge and keep perishables cool. It was a few hours ride and he would take them there. Nate pointed out that it was getting late and they should return to the family or risk worrying them.

To Nate's surprise Wendy said she would stay with Roy. "No, Wendy, your father would not understand," Nate said. Wendy thought for a moment. "Tell Papa 'Vee caree tee,'" she said and helped Nate try to roll his r. "Do you have something to write with?" Wendy asked Roy. He brought out a precious tablet of paper and pencil. Wendy wrote down *fi caru ti*. "If you forget hand him this," she said, giving it to Nate. He looked at her puzzled but knew she did not want to explain. "Now go and tell them we have found our home," Wendy smiled. "Take Moses to help carry things back." With renewed energy Nate mounted his mare and took off towards the Maroons, leaving Roy and Wendy standing hand in hand waving him off.

Nate moved rapidly across the divide. At one point he could see the same antelope that they had seen earlier in the day and they curiously approached him as antelope were prone to do. Nate slowly unslung his rifle and took aim at a nice young doe. The shot echoed across the plain as the animal dropped. Nate moved rapidly and gutted the animal thinking how excited the Maroons would be about finding their home and the news about Roy along with fresh meat. He threw the lifeless carcass onto Moses and headed down the draw toward the Maroons.

The camp was alive with conversation, everyone discussing what they had seen during the day's excursion. Only Nate and Wendy had not returned. Gary was concerned and walked out toward the northeast, the direction they had left. He was having grave misgivings about the whole thing and sat down maintaining a steady gaze while waiting for some sign of the last two explorers. When he caught sight of the two animals but only one rider, his heart skipped a beat. As they approached he could see that something was lying across the small mule. Gary screamed, "NO" and the rest of the camp came running. The little Welshman was beside himself as Nate approached with Moses in tow. Neville moved his muscled frame closer to his dearest friend. When Nate approached and it was obvious that it was a dead antelope on the back of the mule Gary went into a tirade that Neville had never seen before, his eyes red with fire and anger. Neville restrained him as best he could and Nate, taken aback, dismounted and approached them. "Wendy is all right," he tried to speak to Gary. Nate stumbled over the words he was to say but Gary was out of control. Finally he produced the paper and handed it to him. Gary stopped and read the paper with tears coming down his face. He said them aloud over and over and began to smile. Everyone looked at him and at each other puzzled. Gary finally looked up, walked forward and embraced Nate, who yelled, "We have found our home!" and a cheer went up. The confusion of everyone asking questions and Nate trying to answer finally stopped when Marcus yelled for quiet and then directed Nate to tell the story. Everyone stood motionless as Nate recounted the encounter with old Roy and the news of Ash Grove. The energy was intense with excitement and there was little sleep as everyone made preparations to move out in the morning to Ash Grove. Late that evening as Gary and Sue lay together she asked him about the words Wendy had written. They were so close it was hard for her to imagine she did not know. Gary explained that it was a phrase in Welsh that only the two of them had shared, their own special thing between father and daughter. It was "I love you." Sue smiled. She thought she knew everything about this man and did not. She pulled him close and they made delicious, soul-deepening love.

Late the next day, Wendy and Roy stood next to each other watching the large band of Maroons slowly make their way towards the shelter belt of cedars that surrounded the old stone house and outbuildings. It was an anomaly on the vast prairie. Roy had carefully back burned around the homestead each year to protect it from the fires that had eaten up the farms that had once been common across the plain. When the lone rider came at a gallop ahead of the rest Wendy knew exactly who it was. Gary flew off his horse and gathered Wendy up in his arms and kissed her on the forehead as he always did. From then on it was greetings and questions and confusion. It was decided to make camp at Roy's and in the morrow Roy would lead them to Ash Grove. Roy was overwhelmed and insisted on blessing everyone in German, especially the babies that he had to hold. The children of Dominica had never seen anyone so old and were fascinated by Roy. Roy had killed his largest hog in preparation for the arrival and it was an evening of dancing and celebration that went almost into morning.

Roy looked so stately on his old Clydesdale. The gentle giant that he used to use to plow was a massive animal. His long silver hair in the breeze atop the huge animal made a novel picture as he led the large band to the place called Ash Grove. Sue rode beside him for a while and they conversed about this beautiful land. Roy explained that before his ancestors came this was Cheyenne country and in the very valley where they headed the Cheyenne had raped and murdered many settlers. "But that was long ago and this is a new world," he winked. "Welcome home." Sue reached out and they held hands.

Ash Grove was home. The beautiful little valley with its grove of trees and the stream Roy called Bacon Creek was just as the rasta women had dreamed. It was late summer and everyone took part in the settlement of the new Maroon home. The old stone vaulted cellars were cleaned and parceled out to various family units. They were small but ideal for protection against the forces of nature. Easily heated and cool in the summer, they provided shelter from wind and rain. The many things Gary had collected with everyone's help to make their lives comfortable were stored in the old church. In the future Gary envisioned setting up solar panels for electricity and running water and all the things they'd had on Dominica. Eventually he wanted to get the shortwave radio up and monitor it for contact with other communities. There was so much to do but winter was coming and there would be time for that later. Gardens were laid out, areas prepared for all the animals. The rastas worked together to plan the community that would be their home. Neville picked out the best ground for the sacred herb and the precious seeds he carried. Wild hemp was growing here already, remnants from long ago when farmers planted it. He was in heaven! Roy was incredibly valuable with his knowledge of the area and how to live in this vast and amazingly productive land. The abundance of plants and wild life was truly amazing.

Roy visited often but preferred to stay in his stone home on the divide. To everyone's amazement Wendy decided to stay with Roy to learn everything she could about him and from him. She could not be persuaded to live in Ash Grove and Gary gave up trying. Instead he made many visits to Roy to see his daughter. When the days shortened and the snow began to fall, the Maroons snuggled together.

Chapter 22
Roy and Abel
018-022

Roy reflected on the day's events as he and Wendy rode slowly toward his house on the divide. It was a warm fall night with a huge full moon to light their way. The big Clydesdale he called Mac and Moses, the small mule, had become great companions in the last four years. The trip back and forth to Ash Grove was well marked by his and Wendy's coming and going and the animals instinctively walked it without direction from their riders.

Roy refused to leave his home on the windy divide and Wendy refused to leave him, attending to his every need and listening to his stories. She relayed to the Maroons his vast wealth of information about farming and hunting and the surrounding area.

At 80 now Roy was moving slower but he could not remember being as happy as he was. He transferred the position of the old M-1 Girande he had across his back. It was his favorite rifle and the one that had been his father's before him. His ability to make gunpowder and reload the empty casings made it the most valuable weapon among the Maroons. The accuracy of the open sights was astonishing but the weight was on the heavy side. Just touching the well-worn wooden stock made him feel safe.

Roy looked up at the orb of light in the sky and sighed. Just when he had thought he was the only one left on the planet the Maroons had come. This beautiful young maiden riding next to him had made his life in his waning years one of joy and peace. Wendy was now 18 and her physical beauty was masked by her inner beauty and grace. It was like she knew things that no one else could possibly know! She also seemed to have a concern and caring for him no one had ever given to him.

He glanced over at her riding her small mule and she instinctively knew he was looking at her and she turned to look at him. She was almost invisible with her dark skin but the moon sparkled in her eyes and when she smiled her white teeth were bright. Roy smiled back.

"That was quite the ceremony, wasn't it?" Roy spoke "I don't think I have ever participated in anything more beautiful."

"Yes it was." Wendy remarked, "The Rastas designed it to bring us all together and I believe it does." They rode in silence for a long time. Roy slipped back into reflection.

In the four years that the Maroons had been in Ash Grove so much had happened. They had quickly cleaned and made very comfortable the many old stone cellars of the old town. Working together they had made larger ones. Roy had shown them how to quarry the local limestone he called post rock. The consistent layer was ideal for building and when burned and slaked it made excellent mortar. The remnants of its use as fence posts dotted the plains.

The old stone church was the center of the community like it was today in the ceremony. The Maroons were an industrious bunch and learned to farm and care for the many animals they had brought from Mobile to augment the abundant wild game and wild plants that Sue knew to be edible. It was their ingenuity that amazed Roy. Gary and Marcus had so much scientific background and were able to make life very comfortable for the community. They had picked up the skill of blacksmithing from Roy quickly and made a handcart to ride the old railroad rails to Lincoln. There they could glean from the old library and scavenge useful things and return in a day.

Before long they were harnessing the sun and the ever-present wind to generate electricity. It amazed him how just this advance gave them means to do so many things. Roy loved to go to the old church and sit by the shortwave radio and search for other communities. There were many that they had made contact with. They were all so far away though. His delight was when they made contact with a community in Germany far across the globe. He was able to communicate in his mother tongue rusty as it was. Contact had also been made with a large community on both the coasts near New York and one near San Diego. They had also established contact with the divided group in Mobile. The remnants of the human race were many but so far away! Someone was always posted by the radio in case contact was made to a group closer and to keep track of any contact.

There was hope for the human race and it made Roy very happy. Roy however preferred to live without the modern conveniences. The simple life that had returned when the world experienced the near extermination of humans had become a satisfying thing for Roy and he wanted to finish his life this way. Gary and Marcus with the help of the others were already working on making biodiesel and putting together a tractor. Roy was happy to help but kept his thoughts of distaste to himself.

The thing that brought the most joy was the children. Roy loved to talk and play with them. He spent most of his spare time helping the young mothers. To hold the babies in his arms rocking them to sleep made him feel so peaceful and happy. There was rarely a time when the young ones would not gather around and ask him to tell them stories about the world they had never known. The world that only Roy and the Rastas could remember. Roy would take great care to tell the stories with intent to teach them lessons. Lessons that would guide them to build a better world for themselves and their descendants.

This was his purpose, he decided, and he spent many long hours thinking of how to go about this. He himself had never married and to his knowledge never had children. His great love was a Vietnamese girl he had met while on tour in Vietnam. The circumstances had been such that he could not bring her home with him and they had lost touch. It was a great sadness in his life.

The Maroons were his children now. Nate and Gretchen would visit often with little Joshua. Gretchen in particular loved to spend time with the old man and talk about his family and life on the plains. In return Roy was fascinated about the City of Light and what had happened there. Life was good, wild and sweet, as Gary would often say. The days spent doing those things that mattered to existence and the gaps filled with learning about each of these fascinating people.

This ceremony was the biggest event that had happened and Roy marveled at its simplicity and impact. The young people had begun pairing up as young people are prone to do. The Rastas in their wisdom could see that all the old taboos and societal restraints had gladly vanished and it was an opportunity to establish a new system to keep order among the Maroons. Roy was at first puzzled by the lack of unity of religion and ceremony, just a system of rules that consisted of one rule: "Do everything out of love." It seemed so simplistic. The Rastas had all come from such diverse backgrounds and had decided among themselves to withhold their own personal belief systems and allow a more generic accepting mindset to flourish to allow the individual to answer those most basic questions of who am I, where did I come from and where will I go when I die.

Leaving behind the plethora of prophets, saints, sages and attending laws and codes and regimen that would pit one against the other, they preferred to only relay concepts, ideas and, above all, choice for each young mind to make its own journey. They had asked Roy to abide by this wish as well. At first it was difficult for him to not speak the name of Jesus and the Lutheran dogma so ingrained in him but as time went by he found it easier to talk only of love and grace and forgiveness, of soul and spirit without requirement to perform ritual and ceremony of exact direction but allow each to make their own path. In return he opened himself up to meditation and awareness as he had never had before. He saw himself as consciousness with no other purpose other than to be. He had become a human BEing.

Because females outnumbered the males in the community, there were foreseeable problems. The need for unity and non-violent solutions was at the forefront of the Rastas' minds. The ceremony was designed to achieve the peace and order along with the protection and care for the innocent. The simple acknowledgment of the words delivered followed by each individual gazing without blinking into the eyes of each other member of the community one by one was profound. The words contained the duties and responsibilities of mates and parents. It did not contain any mention of lifelong commitment to any particular mate but to the community as a whole and

specifically to the protection, love and care of the children by everyone in the community. It was most gratifying that the Rastas had
asked Roy to deliver the ceremony. At the front of the small church
in Ash Grove, Wendy stood with him in his finest clothes, his long
silver hair combed and braided. He remembered looking out over
the group of couples and said all their names, often choking back
the tears of joy. They were all dressed in their finest skin clothes and
moccasined feet. Caleb and Joan with little Liberty, Gretchen and
Nate with little Joshua, Mariza and Nile with little Freedom, Marcus and Cyndra with little Unity, Acoba and Nicole, Abel and Anna,
Jacque and Lori, Fredrick and Sarah, Lee and Peggy, Sue and Gary
and Jungsuk and Neville. He finished with the now-common words
of greeting and parting among the Maroons, Fy Caru Ti, the Welsh
words for I Love You. Everyone clapped and then it was time to celebrate.

Working as always together, the Maroons lit a fire, brought out
the many different handmade instruments and launched into merri-
ment, eating, singing, dancing and, for those of the age of account-
ability partaking of the herb and its loving ways. Roy had not smoked
marijuana since his days in 'Nam. It was the only thing that got him
through that hideous war. It was legal then but when Nixon in a knee-
jerk reaction of punishment made it illegal he had been afraid to use
it. He never did understand the war on drugs, which was nothing
more than a war on the American family, incarcerating non-violent
people and destroying homes. When Neville showed him his sacred
patch started from his precious seeds from Dominica he was at first
taken back. Now he smoked it with pleasure and relished its ability
to bring him into the now of the moment and let the cares of the past
and future take a back seat. Even now as he slowly rode ole Mac home
in the dark he felt its satisfaction.

Wendy reined Moses to a stop and Mac stopped as well. "Roy,
there is something I want you to give me." Wendy said.

"Child, you can have anything you want; all I have is yours." Roy
replied and smiled. Wendy was not smiling and she reached up to
Roy and put her hand on his leg.

"I want your seed Roy, to take into the next generation and into the future," Wendy whispered. There was a long silence and even the animals sensed the need to be still.

Roy finally spoke, "Your father does not understand why you stay with me, I don't understand but you have brought such joy to my life, child. These are different times but are you sure this is what you want?"

Wendy squeezed the old man's leg, "Papa will have to understand, I have thought about this for a long time and every sense within me tells me that this is what I want and need to do. Please do this for me and for the future," Wendy said calmly and directly.

"You understand there are obstacles, child, I am an old man and it has been a long time for me," Roy said.

Wendy laughed, "You're a strong old bird I think it can be worked out." Roy reached down and took Wendy's hand and brought it to his lips and kissed it. They rode on in silence to the house on the divide.

The leaves were just beginning to come out on the trees and the prairie chickens were booming, doing their ritual mating dance to attract a mate. Wendy was large with child and Roy was so alive with anticipation of the arrival of the baby. It was as if he was young again and he spent every morning touching Wendy's abdomen and blessing the unborn child in German.

The Maroons had for the most part accepted the event and also looked forward to a new member. Gary was not so sure about the situation but with Sue's help he too accepted and encouraged Wendy. Wendy was aglow with health and she knew what no one else did that this child was special. It was appropriate that the birth of spring would accompany the birth of the child. She had asked Roy what names he would like to give. "My parents'," he had replied, "Norm for a boy and Donna for a girl." "Good names, so it shall be." Wendy told him.

When Roy did not come in that evening Wendy kept herself busy working on a wool blanket from the sheep hair sheared last winter. She knew that something was not right. She was too far along to saddle Moses and go out so she concentrated on her father, calling him in her mind. She got up and prepared a meal in anticipation of what was to come. She wept quietly.

Gary looked over at Sue and then got up and kissed her deeply on the lips. "We need to go and see Wendy," he said. "She needs us."

Sue looked at him and said "Get the horses, papa" and began to assemble a few things to go. They found Roy by Spillman Creek, where his cattle grazed. He was lying on the ground face up with a very serene look on his face, eyes open, Mac stood over him keeping vigil. It could not be determined what had caused his death, heart attack, fall from the horse, who knows. Gary and Sue carefully picked him up and put his old body on the huge horse. They made their way to the house on the divide with tears in their eyes. Wendy met them at the door, when she saw Roy's body astride Mac she broke down and wept. Sue guided her back into the house and made her comfortable. "I knew it, and it makes me sad he will never see his child," she said. Sue and Gary hugged her and stayed the night with her.

Everyone attended the burial. They planted Roy's old body next to that of his parents, a small family cemetery on a hill overlooking the vast prairie he had known as home for so long. It was explained to the children with blunt fact what was happening and the truth about death. Roy's spirit and his memory and his many stories would live in around and within them and they should never forget. Jungsuk as always carefully kept a log as always of the events and things that happened to the Maroons.

When Wendy gave birth it was fraternal twins, a boy and a girl, and she carefully noted their names Donna and Norm Strecker-Llewellyn. She put down the pen and thought how she should turn this task over to one of the younger people. She carefully opened it up to the first page and began reading about the Maroons from those first days on Dominica. Neville had been talking about Dominica a lot lately; he missed his home and was even making suggestions that they return. Carefully she put the book back into its protective cover.

The three of them walked out to the beautiful garden and place of time on the hill together. Jungsuk, Sue and Cyndra had become so close they could practically read each other's minds. This was a daily ritual for Sue walking out at midday to mark the length of the shadow created by the obelisk Gary, Neville and Marcus had erected to determine the solstice and equinox. It had become more elaborate as time went by, even to marking the days. Gary and Marcus, always thinking up innovative gadgets and things to make life easier, had come up with a timing device to tell her when the sun would be at its zenith to mark her calendar. The Maroons did not celebrate birthdays or any holidays except the solstice and equinox. It helped them know when to plant and harvest and how much longer winter would be around. The site was a wonderful place to sit and look out over the small community of Ash Grove and to all points of the horizon. It was also a Lek for the prairie chickens and Sue loved to watch them dance. The lives of the Maroons had become the dance of the seasons and the dance of nature. It was known as Sue's place and often she would take different children with her to spend special time and explain the seasons and other things in teachable moments, as she called them.

When the three had a moment such as this it was always special chatting about their men and the community at large. They talked about Wendy, who had steadily become more clairvoyant and dreaming all the time. The three of them had ceased to dream together. It was a concern that Wendy and the twins refused to leave the house on the divide and reside with the others on Bacon Creek. She seemed to be fine but her isolation especially in times of bad weather and possible emergency was troubling. Gary and Caleb would go regularly to check on her, and she would come to Ash Grove from time to time.

The topic of most concern, however, was the lack of males for partners in the community. Wendy did not seem to have a need for a mate but Nile and Mariza were in womanhood and without companionship. Contact with other remnants of humanity was far away and not much help. Sue looked at Jungsuk. "We remember the experiment on Dominica, don't we?" she smiled. Jungsuk pursed her lips and nodded. "How can I forget, it both unified us and divided us. The ability to copulate and not create the many emotions that come with it is impossible. There has to be a solution." Cyndra spoke up, "What about the possibility of multiple mates or polygamy, as they call it. Some animals do it like the buffalo and elk." The three women laughed at that. They discussed what had happened on Dominica and the current situation with the Maroons was huge and needed to be addressed. "Polygamy is not new in human culture but it must be approached with great openness and communication and tremendous sensitivity," Sue said.

"Particularly between the women that share a male mate," Jung-suk replied. The discussion went on for a long time and it was decided to bring it up with the other Rastas. Cyndra looked at her two sisters and marveled at how they had all come together. They sat down together and went into a chant and meditation as the meadowlark sang to them.

A deep voice interrupted their solitude. "What are you women up to now?" Neville grinned from his big black horse. "It's serious, I know, just looking at you." The three women looked at each other and then beckoned him to join them. Neville dismounted and sat down with them. "Joan is about to deliver and Lori is not far behind; these young ones don't waste any time," he laughed. "We will be building more homes in the ground before you know it."

"There are some that are thinking we should start thinking about building above ground," Cyndra replied as the other two women nodded in agreement. The bell rang in the old stone church. "We better go—that means the new pilgrims are arriving."

***

Abel stopped for a moment to let the breeze cool him in the late summer heat. He loved farming in all its aspects, especially walking behind the mules to guide the plow as it turned the soil in preparation for planting. Today, however, it was mowing the tall prairie grass in preparation for the winter ahead. The Maroons' herd of various animals had grown substantially and keeping them fed in the long winter months required a lot of hay. His muscles flexed in the hot sun. He had filled out from his teenage years to be a handsome well-mannered young man. His blonde hair and chiseled features gave him a very stately look. Like all the men, he wore his hair long and

Anna would braid it in the fashion that had become the way of the Maroons.

He loved Anna dearly and their life together had been affectionate and fun. Anna had hinted this morning that she might be pregnant. He had spent the entire day dreaming of this possibility. They had both agreed not to tell anyone until they were sure. In fact he was of a mind to go home early and find Anna and make love and tell her how excited he was about it.

He stroked the withers of the large mule that pulled the mower and smiled. Slowly he began to detach the mule and walked him over to the creek to drink. Yes, he thought, I will go find Anna and take her back to their small cellar home where it was cool and indulge her.

After putting the large animal back with the others, he headed home but suddenly began to sense that something did not feel right. He stopped for a moment outside the door and he could hear the muffled sounds of two people inside. Throwing open the door, he could see them together in the dim light. Acoba and Anna lying together in their bed. At first stunned, he stared at them as Anna tried to hide herself. Acoba awkwardly got up naked and stared back at Abel with a look of alarm. Abel reacted without thought, drawing his knife and lunging at Acoba. Though much larger, Acoba barely deflected the knife as both went down on the floor. Anna was screaming to stop but the two men were in a fierce struggle. Abel slashed Acoba several times, drawing blood that ran down and covered his skin with red. Acoba tried to escape but Abel pinned him up against the wall. Acoba was able to hold Abel's knife hand from delivering a killing stroke. From behind came the blow from Anna. She had picked up a cast iron skillet and struck Abel across the head. As Abel fell he pulled Acoba with him but this time the knife was turned towards him and as they landed together. Acoba could feel the blade sink deep into his chest. Abel's grip loosened and fell away. Acoba watched as the life faded from Abel's eyes and he screamed "NOOOO!"

His efforts to revive Abel were useless. Acoba looked up at Anna in horror. "What have we done?" he pleaded. Anna was crying and stepped back, her head in her hands. "I must get my father," Acoba spoke and grabbed his clothes, not bothering to even stop the bleed-ing of his own wounds. Acoba stood for a moment holding Anna's face in his strong hands. "You must never tell anyone that you had a part in Abel's death, it was all me, do you understand?" he looked at her, awaiting her response. "Swear it Anna," he said firmly. Slowly she nodded her head sobbing. Out the door he ran straight for his parents' cave.

Anna knelt down next to the body of her mate. She began to weep as she picked up his lifeless head and kissed him. She carefully closed his eyes and covered him with their finest skin blanket. The thought occurred to her to end her own life as well but she knew she was carrying another life within her. She was overwhelmed with grief and remorse for what had taken place and sat down on the bed sob-bing. A life so full of promise and joy had been shattered by lust and selfishness. At this point she could see no good solution. She did not know what to do so she did nothing. She slowly lay down next to Abel and cried herself to a numbed sleep.

Jungsuk had that strange feeling that something was not right as she prepared a meal for Neville's homecoming. He was out with Caleb doing what they loved the best, hunting. They would return as always laughing and tired with the day's kill. She loved to watch the two of them so close they communicated without noise. They were the finest hunters in the community and the bow and arrow was their weapon of choice. Today, however, there was something wrong. The door flew open and in came Acoba, the blood already soaking through his buckskin shirt. He was speaking so fast she barely under-stood. She tried to listen as she helped him get his shirt off and stop the bleeding from his wounds. She was horrified as the impact of his story began to unfold. Her heart was heavy with the future and she could not respond to Acoba's questions of what would happen. When Acoba stabilized, she told him to calm himself and she would see to Anna. As she closed the door behind her and made her way into the early evening light she had difficulty walking. She made her way first to Sue's abode and the door opened as she went to knock. Sue em-braced her and they both began to sob. Almost without a word, they made their way to Abel and Anna's home.

The ceremony of burial for Abel was so vastly different from that of the bonding a year before. It was filled with sadness and emotions that were intense. Cyndra and Marcus agreed reluctantly to put off the issue of retribution until Abel's body was put to rest. Everyone shared their precious memories and thoughts about Abel, even Acoba and Anna as Neville and Gary kept a close eye on Marcus. Wendy explained that Abel's consciousness was still with them even now and would always exist in some form. Her words of comfort and mesmerizing tone brought calmness to the body of people gathered in the old stone church. At Cyndra's request they buried the body beside Roy. It was decided to allow at least three days before making a decision on dealing with the murder. The Rastas met several times during these days to come up with some way to handle this situation. It was agreed that the one rule that everything must be done in love was violated but what should the punishment be? Cyndra and Marcus were adamant that it be severe. The other Rastas felt that Abel was at least somewhat at fault in his reaction. Everyone could see that openness and communication had broken down. In the end they decided that an unrelated and objective party would decide Acoba and Anna's fate. The only ones in this very small community were Nate and Gretchen along with Mariza and Nile.

The four met over a period of two days. They had all known the three involved and were very aware of not only what had happened but the events leading up to it. The attraction between Acoba and Anna had been obvious to all but forbidden by their close blood relation. What they did not know was Anna's part in the murder. Acoba had forbidden Anna to tell anyone that she had hit Abel over the head and also that she carried a child within her. In the end they all agreed that Acoba should not be killed in response to his act. Their decision was to banish Acoba from the community for a year with only his horse and his bow and arrows. If he survived the winter he could return and the matter would be ended. He must leave immediately and not look back. The decision drew mixed emotion. The four judges standing together before the Maroons with Nile as the speaker were somber and sad. Jungsuk and Neville were aghast while Cyndra and Marcus felt it too lenient.

Once again Wendy brought healing by her words that nature would in the end determine Acoba's fate. She stared directly at Anna with a knowing eye, hoping Anna would come forth with what she knew to be true but Anna remained silent. The judgment was accepted in the end and Acoba prepared his horse to go. Nate supervised the preparation. Everyone was given one last moment to speak to Acoba before he left. Neville could hardly let go in his deep embrace of his son. "You stay alive and come home, my son. I love you." he sobbed. Jungsuk also could hardly let go. Nicole had not spoken to Acoba since the event and did not even show for the departure. She was tortured by his deception and unfaithfulness and could not even look at the man she had loved. Fredrick, Lori and Cyndra also had a hard time taking part in the banishment. Marcus, however, stood with eyes locked and told Acoba, "If you come back before the year is up I will kill you myself."

Anna stood apart and did not stop staring as the Maroons one by one said their goodbyes. Caleb would not let go of his deepest friend and he whispered, "I will come with you" to which Acoba replied in his most serious tone, "No you will not, brother. Your place is here, take care of Joan and Liberty and make many more children." At the end came Sue and Gary. Sue whispered in his ear as they embraced. "Go north to the black hills my people called Paha Sapa. I had a dream of the faces in stone and a hot spring where you can find refuge and make it through the winter. That is all I can tell you. Follow the ladder of rivers northwest." Gary (in violation) embraced Acoba, weeping, as he did he slipped him the old .45 pistol with the remaining clip of ammunition, "Come back to us, it will be all right. Fy caru ti" and turned and walked away.

Acoba was given a chance to speak one last time to the community. He straightened himself up, choking back the emotion. First he spoke to the community asking forgiveness for dishonoring himself and barely able to look his father in the eyes. He next spoke directly to Abel's family, asking them to find forgiveness in their hearts in the days to come, that if he should live and return they would somehow accept him back. Everyone was directed to turn their backs and Nate sent Acoba on his way.

The following day it was discovered that Anna had left during the night. The first response was to send someone to bring her back but Wendy reasoned that they should let her find her fate her own way. It took many weeks for the Maroons to recover from these events. During the fall equinox celebration the mood was somber and subdued. The talk went to the fact that they had lost three very precious members of the small community and how they were missed. Everyone was taken back when Wendy made the statement that they had lost four. That Anna carried life within her. Marcus and Cyndra in particular took in this information with interest. "Was it Abel's child?" they inquired of Wendy later in private. "Yes," Wendy responded and reached out to touch Cyndra, who began to cry. This new information fermented in their minds and over the next few months they began to soften in their hatred.

During the Winter Solstice Marcus and Cyndra along with Fredrick, Lori and Nicole, who was heavy with Acoba's child came forward and told the community that maybe they had been too harsh and they should bring Acoba and Anna home. The suggestion was talked about for a long time and Caleb was the first to offer to go. Gary was against it. He looked with great pride at his son. "I know you loved them, son, but it is winter and we cannot know where they are or even if they are alive, you are far too valuable to me and to this community to risk such a search." He took Caleb in a huge bear hug. Caleb now being taller than his father returned the hug.

Wendy spoke up once again. "We must be patient; in time we will be made whole again."

Marcus stood and replied, "How is it that you know these things?"

Wendy gave her knowing smile and waited as everyone became silent with anticipation to her answer. "In the past it has been Roy that comes to me in dreams and tells me these things, but this time it was Abel who came to me. Abel who watches over them. You must send your forgiveness to them in your thoughts and meditations; they will feel it and they will return in the right time."

There was a long silence and nods of approval. This gave comfort to everyone but especially Cyndra, who began to cry tears of joy.

That night it began to snow and it was four days before it stopped. It was the deepest, coldest winter the Maroons had experienced since coming to Ash Grove.

Chapter 23
Paha Sapa
023-024

By the second night of his exile, Acoba was despondent. Traveling to the northwest, he had found shelter in what had been the town of Mankato. Little remained of the old prairie town, but the sign on an old masonry building with some pieces of roof intact told him where he was. A cold rain fell as he sat in front of his fire, gazing into the flickering flames. His long dreadlocks hung loosely to his shoulders and tears fell slowly down his cheeks.

"Miss them all," he said to himself, "even Abel." The faces of his loved ones passed before him, intensifying his loneliness. Mixed with remorse for Abel's death, it was too much to bear. How could he make it alone much less survive for a year feeling like this? There was no hunger in his belly so he had not eaten at all. The idea had occurred to him to end it all with the .45 tucked in his waistband but his mother's words would not let him. "Come back to us, we will be waiting for you, my son," Jungsuk had whispered before she released her grip on him.

Acoba looked over at Honey and their eyes met. He could tell she was lonely too; horses are social creatures and need company of their own kind. When she turned her head and looked intently toward the breach in the wall, he knew something was out there. Her nostrils flared and she raised her head to get a better whiff of what it might be. Acoba slowly reached back for the .45 and moved toward the shadows. He watched Honey's reaction and then heard the movement outside. Honey's ears pointed the direction and her mannerisms told Acoba she was not scared.

"I thought I would never find you." It was Anna's voice and her white mare made its way through the break in the wall. Acoba stuffed the gun back in his waist band and ran to greet them. Anna slid off her horse, soaked to the skin and they embraced for the longest time. When Acoba felt her shivering, he brought her quickly to the fire. "Take off your clothes and get warm quickly," he insisted and helped her cold hands untie her clothing. They spent the night holding each other and talking. Acoba could not believe she had followed him without the family coming after her. Anna explained that she could not stay with the family without him and live with the knowledge that she was to blame for Abel's death. "What shall we do now?" Anna said, looking into Acoba's deep brown eyes.

"We go north to a place Sue told me about where we might survive the winter. I know not how far it is or where exactly but we must get there before winter comes on us," Acoba replied. "It is called the Black Hills or Paha Sapa and there is a hot spring there that will keep us warm. I am sure that in one of these old towns we can find a map to help us, I only know it is north and west right now. With you with me I know we can find it," Acoba smiled for the first time in a long time. In the morning the rain ceased and they were on their way.

They carefully crossed the creeks and rivers that seemed to flow east. "This was what Sue meant by the ladder of rivers," Acoba remarked to Anna. His whole attitude changed with her appearance. He felt like he could do anything with her by his side. They found a map in what had been the town of South Platte and were able to follow the remnants of what had been a highway north to South Dakota. It was a wondrously beautiful area of rolling hills and lakes and ponds referred to on the map as the Sand Hills. They were never in want of meat as game was plentiful but the temperatures at night were falling noticeably. When they came in sight of the first conifer trees along the bluffs, they knew that something was changing. Two nights later the first frost appeared in the morning. "We must be getting close, don't you think Acoba?" Anna mentioned as they woke up together under their one blanket. "I hope so, or we better find some more blankets." Acoba replied. "But for now you keep me plenty warm!" The joy of being together made it hard to believe they were in exile but they both missed the other Maroons.

Following the Cheyenne River upstream, the pair made their way around the southern tip of Paha Sapa. Anna was starting to show in her pregnancy and had that glow that women have only when they are with child. From a distance Acoba watched her slide off the horse she called Sky and begin picking late strawberries. Her long brown hair flowed all around her since she rarely tied it back. She looked up, saw him gazing at her and smiled with delight, holding up a handful of the ripe fruit. Acoba waved back in acknowledgment, soaking in the sight with contentment. He knew they were very close to the town of Hot Springs since a sizable creek was flowing in from the west from out of the hills. An old rusted bridge marked some far gone road of the past.

At once Sky broke into a run, startling Anna. Acoba looked to his right and saw the grizzly bear heading for Anna at a run. Without thinking, Acoba readied his bow and took off at a dead gallop to cut the bear off, while yelling at the top of his lungs, "Run Anna, run!" Dropping her bounty, she was off toward the nearest bluff. Acoba and Honey intersected between Anna and the bear and with careful aim sent an arrow flying where it hit home in the bear's shoulder with no visible effect. Honey reared up and Acoba fell to the ground, scrambling to his feet just in time for the bear to send him sprawling with a blow across the face. Although blood filled his eyes, Acoba was able to reach for the .45 as the snarling bear pinned him to the ground. Before he blanked out, he sent the last six rounds into the animal's chest.

Anna screamed as she witnessed the ordeal. There was no movement except the body of the bear heaving as it breathed its last. Blood flowed onto the grass but there was no sign of Acoba. He must be beneath the carcass of the huge animal, but she knew she could not move it without help. And it suddenly arrived at a gallop, with long black hair streaming behind. The look on their faces was astonishment, first Anna and then at the bear on the ground.

"Please help me get this bear off my..."Anna was at a loss for what to call Acoba, "My husband," she blurted. The two men looked at cach other and nodded. They dismounted and the three of them pulled the heavy carcass off Acoba. "He's alive!" Anna yelled after checking his pulse. A large gash across his face gushed blood and one eyeball hung from its socket. Anna took off her top and compressed the wound, taking care to not damage the eye.

"My name is Anna, please help me, I will do anything for you," Anna beseeched them. The two men were completely spellbound by Anna and her naked breasts. "Please, I beg you," Anna screamed. This broke them out of their hypnotic stare.

"Yes," one finally spoke. "We should take him to our mother, not far." With expert dexterity they drew their knives and skinned the bear, making a makeshift travois to pull behind one of their horses. Acoba moaned as they began pulling him across the ground. "I will go get a cart and come back," one man said to the other and headed off at a gallop. It was then that Anna realized that they were identical twins.

"I must get our horses; I will catch up with you," Anna said and ran toward Honey, calmly grazing as if nothing had happened.

When they met up with the other man pulling the cart, a woman rode alongside him. Well- proportioned with long blonde hair and a kind knowing face, she smiled and handed Anna a shirt. "These two young men have never seen what you have shown them, young lady, best to cover up." Despite the trauma of the moment, the ride was filled with questions and much excitement by the three people who had rescued them. The trip into the small narrow canyon where the town of Hot Springs lay seemed like it took forever to Anna, who rode next to the cart with Acoba. Being near this woman who called herself Sharon Thompson made her feel at ease.

Cradled in the small narrow canyon was the town, now a ghostly line along the creek of beautiful stone buildings untouched by fire and surprisingly intact. Here and there along the creek small wisps of hot air rose from the many hot springs that made their escape from deep in the earth. High on the bluff overhead was a massive stone building. Sharon noticed Anna looking at it and remarked, "It is the old Veterans hospital and Old Soldiers' home." Then realizing Anna's age and her perplexed look, she added, "It was a place for soldiers in their old age to come and live." They continued to a wide area of the canyon and dismounted before a tidy little cabin adjoining a much larger masonry building.

Carefully they brought Acoba into the building and placed him on the large rectangle table in the middle of the room. Sharon began instructing the two young men whose names she had learned were Paul and Mitch. Carefully Sharon began to uncover the wound and ascertain the damage. Acoba went in and out of consciousness as Sharon cleaned the wound. Anna stood vigilantly over him, holding his hand and speaking softly to him.

"He will live," Sharon spoke in a serious tone. "But I don't have the ability to save his eye. I will have to remove it and cauterize the wound." The process was short but painful and Paul and Mitch had to help Anna hold Acoba down. After Sharon had carefully bandaged the wound, Acoba seemed to drift into a restful sleep.

It was days before Acoba became fully conscious. Anna, following Sharon's instructions, had carefully tended to his wound and rarely left his side. Sharon was constantly sending the two young men on errands to distract them from constantly staring at Anna. When Acoba finally was alert he was more interested in Anna's well being than his own. He was full of questions regarding where they were and who these people were. Because Anna had focused her attention on Acoba, she did not know the answers.

Fall was winding down and already there had been a skiff of snow that had melted on the ground. But here they were alive and snug in this small cabin with Sharon, Paul and Mitch. They took turns telling their stories and getting to know each other. Anna and Acoba explained the story of the Maroons and their epic journey from Dominica. Paul and Mitch, fascinated by the story but especially by Anna asked them to retell it endlessly. Acoba had a very hard time telling them apart as did Anna. The story of Anna and Acoba's exile and journey to Hot Springs was their favorite and they constantly quizzed Anna about the other females who lived among the Maroons. Sharon also seemed overjoyed that there were more survivors and made no secret that she wanted to go visit the Maroons when the spring came.

Acoba was amazed at the comfort and peace of Sharon's home. What she had accomplished with Paul and Mitch was amazing. Sharon explained that she had been a nurse at the Veterans Hospital and that she had a husband and a son, both of whom had died immediately when the plague came. She had been 30 at the time when her entire world had fallen apart. She described the pandemonium and the hideous killing and destruction by those that had become nothing more than beasts. The wanton killing and her own near death still haunted her. She had learned to hide and, like the Maroons, found some safety during the daylight hours. She had armed herself despite having never used a weapon before.

Sharon recounted the event in which Paul and Mitch had come into her care: "One evening I heard a vehicle slowly making its way through town. The beasts did not drive so I knew it had to be someone normal. So I waved to them and they came to a halt in front of the old stone hotel. It was a young couple from the Sioux reservation outside of town. The woman was obviously a Caucasian but the man was full blood Indian. I had them get off the street and come in to my hiding place but they had to get something from their station wagon," she recalled, tears starting to well. "It was too late and several beasts descended on them. They fought fiercely but were too badly injured before I could get a clear shot at the beasts."

"'Save my babies,' were the last words she said," Sharon continued with tears running down her cheeks."I grabbed my rifle and went to the car. There they were, these adorable twin newborns, so I grabbed 'em up and headed for my hiding place. I tried to go back out but I could see some more beasts had found the woman and were tearing her apart and then turning on each other. I bolted up the doors and tried to figure out how I was going to feed two hungry babies," she recalled. "That was one long night, let me tell you."

Sharon had devoted herself to the twin boys, naming them and protecting them in those first years. Though adept at stealth in her search for other survivors, she never found any. She did, however, find herself killing with undiscovered vengeance any and all beasts that she found sleeping during daylight, many she actually recognized as people she knew. The next few years were difficult with the taking care of the twins and surviving the seasons. She had spent numerous hours in the library researching things that she once thought out-dated. Now they were things required for survival. She had become ingenious in adapting to this new world. The natural hot springs had been invaluable to survival during the cold winters. Using the geo-thermal, she could heat the small cabin she built adjacent to the old Evans Plunge swimming pool. Her attempts at constructing a short-wave radio had met with limited success so not knowing if there were other survivors often found her depressed.

"It was watching the twins grow and become the fine young men they are that gave me purpose," she said, noting they were fine hunters and able students who "devour every book they could get their hands on."

Together they had slowly cleaned up the small town, a monu-mental task. Sharon sighed and smiled, recounting the efforts to find, and ultimately learn how to handle horses, something she had never done before. Her face, lined with care and sun, was aglow as she talk-ed with Anna and Acoba. The hope for the human race renewed. The prospect for mates for her two sons brought a smile of joy.

When Acoba was up and around, Sharon and Anna gave him a leather patch they'd made to cover his empty eye socket. At first it was hard to get used to but Acoba tried to be positive. Without his depth perception it would be hard to hit any target he was hunting. One evening as they were sitting around the fireplace Sharon nod-ded silently to Paul and Mitch. They left the room and came back with smiles on their faces, presenting Acoba with a beautiful neck-lace made from the claws and teeth of the grizzly bear he had killed. Acoba was stunned and could not speak. Anna put her arms around him. "You saved my life that day by putting yourself in danger; you are a true warrior and very brave. Paul, Mitch and I have been work-ing on this to honor you." Acoba embraced her and then the others, bonding the five together. His nickname from then on was Grizz.

As the winter drew heavy and the snows deep, Anna's pregnan-cy began to show, making her the center of attention. Paul and Mitch waited on her every need and Anna would let them touch and feel the life within her growing and sometimes kicking. Acoba and the twins spent the days together talking and hunting and discussing the Maroons and the women there. Acoba trained them in the bow and arrow. The three were inseparable. Sharon and Anna also spent the days together, readying for the day of Anna's delivery.

"You are a Rasta." Anna said once while they were working in the kitchen. At Sharon's puzzled look, she explained, "Rasta is a term we use for the people who are filled with love and concern for those around them, I do not know where the term came from but the true leaders of the Maroons are called Rastas."

As they talked about it, Sharon confided that she had dreamed of a black man with dreadlocks. "That's amazing because the Rasta women of the Maroons also have dreams that come true and actually lead us to Ash Grove!" Anna exclaimed.

"It bothers me though that you were not in the dream, but I am so happy you came to be with us," Sharon said, looking into Anna's big blue eyes and giving her a most affectionate hug.

In some ways the winter was a perfect rest. They would rise and have hot drinks and then go next door and swim in the old hot springs pool called Evans Plunge. They would practice yoga and meditate, read books to each other and make clothing and weapons. Food was stored up but often the men would hunt to bring in fresh meat. Always there was talk about the return to the Maroons. Acoba explained that the Maroons had made contact with many groups in faraway places, even across the sea. The human race had not vanished but existed in many isolated places around the globe.

Sharon would tell fantastical stories of little boxes that one could speak to others simply by pushing some numbers and machines that could look inside your body without opening it up. There was speculation as to why it had all come to an end so abruptly. Acoba told about the herb and its loving ways and Sharon just laughed. It had been a long time since she had smoked the herb, another reason to look forward to going to the Maroons!

Sharon had kept careful track of the days on a calendar for all these years and explained it to Anna and Acoba. Anna told how Sue had the job of keeping track of the solstice and the lunar periods in between but nothing as detailed as Sharon's calendar. It was May that

Sharon was sure Anna would deliver based on what Anna had told her. When the time came, everyone was excited. As Anna progressed, it became apparent that something was very wrong. She began to bleed excessively and Sharon tried to remain calm and positive.

When the baby delivered, it was a beautiful, healthy boy and Sharon carefully washed it with warm water and cut the cord and gave it to Anna. She smiled a weak smile and cuddled the child. Sharon tried everything to stop the bleeding but it only got worse. Fading quickly, Anna called Acoba over and placed the child in his strong arms, "His name is Abel and tell him that I loved him." Anna fell into unconsciousness and never woke up. Acoba could tell by the white skin that it was indeed Abel's son. Paul, Mitch and Sharon stood around him as he wept, his frame heaving with sorrow. Sharon pumped Anna's swollen breast for the vital milk to start the baby on its path of life. When Sharon finally was able to take the child from Acoba, he cried for hours holding Anna's lifeless hand.

They buried Anna the Korean way that Jungsuk had described to her daughter. They sat her cross legged on a prominent place with some food for her journey and then covered her with stones and dirt until it looked like a small mound. Acoba would visit often and it seemed his pain would never end. He was so protective of Abel that it was hard for anyone to hold or feed him. "She loved you Acoba," Sharon said to him one evening. "This child is all that is left of Anna on this physical plane but you cannot raise him alone."

Acoba turned to her with his brown eyes glazed in tears. "I miss her so much and I miss my family and friends, to take care of Abel is my mission in life now."

"I think your mission is far greater than that, young Rasta," Sharon said with a smile as she began to describe a woman she'd seen in a dream. "Who is this woman?"

"That's Wendy of the Maroons!" he exclaimed.

"She told me that soon it would be time to return, that they were waiting for you," Sharon spoke. "The time is not yet, but soon."

. From that point on Acoba was a different man, sharing Abel with his new brothers and Sharon and looking out for their needs over his own.

In midsummer Sharon convinced Acoba to go with Paul and Mitch to see the great faces. She would be fine with Abel, who was healthy and never seemed to cry. The three young men gathered food and shelters and headed north into the heart of Paha Sapa to the great faces. They followed what was left of the old highway in some place almost gone and overgrown by nature. The streams were cool and fresh and the wildlife abundant. The outing was a good one and they joked and talked of many things but the twins were very anxious to go to the Maroons. They were still saddened by the death of Anna, who had treated them as her own brothers but made them feel there was something very important they were missing.

When they came to the granite walkway with its colonnades of stone, Acoba was in awe. They camped and gazed upon the figures for a long time. "Mother says they were men just like us but they represent things," Paul said. Mitch tried to explain that the first one represented freedom from a king who owned everything and people wanted to have freedom to own land and do what they wanted to do. The second one represented freedom from oppressive government. The third one represented freedom from one person owning another person and the last one represented freedom from the greed of big business and corporations. "I really don't understand some of it but it is what mother says." Paul concluded.

"Whoever these people were, they must have been highly revered," Acoba responded. "Freedom must have been important to them. I am a free man," he yelled and it echoed down the canyon below.

"I wonder when they found the time to do all of this between hunting and caring for their families." Mitch said. "And how did they do it?" Paul chipped in.

"A Rasta told me once, 'They lived; now we live,'" Acoba replied.

"I am all for that, brother." Paul howled.

In the morning they broke camp and headed back to Hot Springs.

As summer drew toward its end, it was time to go, time to climb down the ladder of rivers back to Ash Grove and the Maroons. Mitch and Paul took little time but Acoba had to visit Anna's grave one more time. Sharon also took her time releasing the domestic animals they could not bring with them and packing as if she would never return. Abel was healthy and strong but the ride would be slow on his account, yet there was no need to rush. One last dip in the healing waters of Evans Plunge and they began the long trek down Main Street and onto the plains toward Kansas.

Chapter 24
The Center of the Earth
027

Early in the morning on a cloudless fall day, Caleb rejoiced as the earth woke up. This time of year was his favorite with its crisp air warm with a hint of winter's chill. He had decided to go west and hunt for turkey in the hills south of the town that had been Osborne. Even more dilapidated than most towns, it had been struck by a tornado a few years ago. Caleb thought about those fierce storms and how amazing nature was. A meadowlark sang in the distance and he smiled. "Is there any man as lucky as I?" he said to himself. It was a phrase his Papa said often and he had picked it up. Caleb thought about how much he loved Joan; she was the perfect mate for him. He pictured the way she smothered him with kisses whenever he returned from hunting. Little Freedom was walking and talking and he cherished her as his own. Now he had a son! Sage was healthy and always smiling, Caleb dreamed of teaching him about the world around him and spending mornings like this out hunting. Life was good, wild and sweet and Caleb loved it.

Soon, his mind drifted to Acoba's return and how happy he was to see him again. The whole community had wondered if Anna and Acoba would make it back that late summer. He remembered vividly that day at his mother's home as Sue and Wendy prepared the morning meal. Wendy had come down to spend a few days so her twins could play with the other children. "They were coming back and would be here soon," she announced at the meal. No one challenged what Wendy said, as her words had proven to be true over and over.

"I cannot wait to see Anna's baby," Jungsuk had replied. Wendy had become silent and the smile that was so often on her face evaporated.

"Anna will not be with them," she said slowly.

"Why do you say that, Wendy?" Jungsuk asked.

Wendy looked at her with sadness. "Because it was Anna who told me they are coming." There had been a moment of quiet and acceptance.

Caleb remembered asking Wendy as he wrestled playfully with the twins pulling on his long brown hair, "When Wendy? When?"

Wendy's smile had returned, "Today." Caleb let the twins down and hugged Wendy.

"I must go meet them," and he ran out the door to get Morning Star ready. The word spread rapidly and before he knew it Jacque and Lee and Nate were also getting their horses ready. They all laughed and soon were off to the north in search of Acoba.

The three had ridden to the blue hills to the north and selected the highest hill so they might watch the vast prairie for any sign of Acoba's return. It was a wonderful view and they could see all the way to the Solomon Valley. The spike of the old courthouse and huge church in Beloit could be picked out just on the horizon to the northeast. They sat in the ancient ring of stones that had been the place of vision quests for young Cheyenne warriors in the distant past. Sue had explained what they meant. Her response to Caleb's many questions regarding not only them but all the civilizations that had preceded them still resounded in his ears. "They lived, now we live."

Caleb smiled and looked at his brothers and felt a pride in their companionship and a safety in it. How he'd missed Acoba and how excited he was to see him again.

As they passed around the Maroons' one pair of binoculars, the men had laughed and told stories of Acoba from Dominica and their youth to the present. Jacque made the first sighting, his sharp eyes rarely missing the slightest movement. Even after he pointed out the direction and distance, none of the others could make it out. That was enough for Caleb, however, and he jumped onto Morning Star to gallop in the direction that Jacque pointed, with the others not far behind.

Acoba recognized Caleb and Morning Star from a distance. He'd carefully handed Sharon a soundly sleeping Abel. "My brother is coming to greet us!" he said, prodding Honey into a gallop toward Caleb. Their horses almost clashed and the raucous dismount sent both embracing on the ground. Caleb would not let go and the others soon gathered around them.

"I knew you would make it back," Caleb said, tears running down his face. Acoba smiled at him and hugged him again. When they finally stood back, Caleb pointed to the patch over Acoba's eye and asked, "What are you a pirate now?"

"I have many stories to tell," Acoba replied.

Next came the obvious question. "Where is Anna?" Caleb said excitedly. There was a period of silence while Acoba tried to keep his composure but could not. Finally Sharon spoke up, "Anna died in childbirth, but she gave us this beautiful child, his name is Abel." Acoba carefully took the child from Sharon as Lee, Jacque, Nate and Caleb gathered around, each in turn taking the child in their arms and blessing it. Nate, always with the fastest horse, decided to return quickly and ready the community while the others stayed with the newcomers talking nonstop all the way back to Ash Grove.

Caleb reflected on the most poignant memory of Acoba's return: Before any other greetings, Acoba went directly to Cyndra and Marcus and put the child in Cyndra's arms and, looking them both in the eyes, told them,. "This is your grandson, his name is Abel." Everyone watched to see what would happen. The four embraced in a group hug to the Maroons' collective sigh. Nicole then presented Acoba with his son, whom she had named Acoba and there was not a dry eye among the group.

Introductions of Sharon, Paul and Mitch followed, and the celebration was the largest the Maroons had ever had. The bonfire was huge and the food was plentiful. Dancing, singing and the herb's loving ways flowed freely. Paul and Mitch were shy at first but Nile and Mariza took little time introducing themselves, and they never left them alone. Sharon had never seen Paul and Mitch so happy. Sharon had been overwhelmed with the reception and her heart was happier than it had been in many years.

Not long after the welcoming ceremony, another ritual had taken place, this time with Mariza and Nile standing with Paul and

Mitch in the ceremony of union. Sharon read the vows to the community in place of Roy. More celebrating and the anticipation of more life and survival of the human race continued well into the night.

Yes, Caleb thought, I will treasure these memories forever. He sighed with peace and looked out at the land around him and then up at the sky. Morning Star pawed at the ground and Caleb heard an unfamiliar sound. Dismounting, he saw a round, metallic object obscured by grass and earth. It said "Geodetic center," but he still didn't know what that meant. Carefully he took some bearings on the surrounding countryside and placed several stones to help him find this place again. He would tell the rastas about this and ask them what it meant. Then Caleb headed down towards the Solomon River to look for turkey.

After Caleb informed the rastas of his find, Marcus explained that it was the point from which all surveys and maps were calibrated for the Americas, maybe even the entire globe. It must be the center of the North American continent. With the harvest in and the weather so fine, the Rastas decided to go see this place. Caleb assured them he could find it again. Sharon declined to go, instead keeping watch over the small community. "It would be a fun outing," Sue said. "Let's take some shelter and spend the night out on the prairie." It was agreed and they took their time packing and leisurely moving across the rolling plain talking and reminiscing the whole way.

Toward evening the spot was located and Caleb watched as the parents and people he had known all his life pondered its meaning.

"Whatever its purpose we know that the center of the earth lies in the people who inhabit it," Gary said.

"It is appropriate," Neville chimed in, "that this is near where the people of the earth now live." They set up their small shelters and started cooking for the evening meal. This small group of adults had become so close and the ease with which they worked together and accepted one another was profound. As darkness fell they began smoking the herb, talking and laughing. Someone posed the question, "What do you miss the most in this new world?" Caleb listened intently, not fully understanding.

"I miss driving down the highway in a convertible with the top down," Cyndra responded, shaking her blonde hair, as vibrant as it was in her youth. Everyone nodded in agreement.

"Bob Marley and reggae music," Neville said next. His dreadlocks reached all the way to his waist now.

"Yes and dancing the salsa to a live band," Sue responded. Gary reached over and stroked her long black hair in the braids he had put in that very morning.

Jungsuk spoke up, "I miss the temples and shrines of Korea." Her almond eyes pensive and perceptive turned to Neville and he gave her a smile.

The quiet pondering went on until Marcus said seriously, "It will be a long time before we return to space, so much has been lost." He turned his soft brown eyes to the sky and everyone looked up.

All eyes turned to Gary for his response. He looked around at the adults he had come to love and his characteristic smile slowly appeared, "I miss a Dairy Queen Blizzard chocolate with Reese's peanut butter cups. I want one now!" They all laughed heartily.

"Caleb, give us a beat, son," Gary said. Caleb began to beat rhythmically on a cooking pot and the rastas rose to dance around the fire. Soon they had their clothes off and were dancing and laughing and singing songs the younger ones had never heard, their bare feet pounding a permanent circle around the metal disc and fire.

Caleb shook his head, smiling and thinking he would never understand these people and the time they had come from. As the fire died down, the couples retired to their shelters and Caleb could hear them making passionate love. He chose to stay awake, watching over them and looking into the clear night sky and the countless stars. After checking on the horses, he settled down and finally drifted off to peaceful sleep himself.

The sound of mourning doves woke Caleb although he found their soft cooing a comfort. It was said that the doves mourned for those who had died and no one knew. A sad thought to such a soothing sound, he thought. It was then that he heard his mother softly crying from inside his parents' shelter. Caleb slowly picked up the shelter side. His mother held his father's head in her lap as she slowly braided his long gray hair in an act of love, tears rolling down her cheek. "Mother, what is wrong, why are you crying?" Caleb softly spoke.

"He is gone, my son." She turned Gary's head slowly to show the puncture marks where a rattlesnake had struck directly into the jugular vein of his neck. "He probably did not even know it had happened."

Caleb's shout of "NOOOOOOOOO!" woke the others, who came at a rush. Neville held Caleb tightly as he sobbed hysterically. The others sat down with Sue and wept quietly. Jungsuk finally asked Sue what she wanted to do. After some thought, Sue remembered, "He often spoke about the Mongols and how they leave their dead out on the steppes to be eaten by the birds. We will leave his fleshly body here, at the center of the earth, he would have liked that. His consciousness will be with us always."

They propped his naked body up in a cross-legged position on the metal disk. Each person said goodbye as they passed one last time. The ride back to Ash Grove was slow and silent with everyone one remembering and dealing with the loss in their own way. Sue would look back often until the intervening hills blocked the line of sight. In the distance they could see a rider approaching. It was Acoba and he was coming fast.

When he reined in, he was so excited he did not notice the somber mood of the small party. "We have made contact with another community of survivors in a place called Boulder, Colorado," he gasped. "It is only about 450 miles away, the closest of any group we have ever made contact. They want to meet with us and will make contact again tonight." Acoba said with excitement. When he saw the response, he looked from face to face then asked, "Where is Papa?"

"Papa is gone," Caleb said slowly. "He died of a snake bite last night."

"I cannot believe this," Acoba said. "Take me to him."

Caleb looked to his mother, who gave a nod. Caleb turned his horse to return to the center of the earth and Acoba followed.

The rastas proceeded slowly as the talk of their loss and the possibilities before them intermingled.

Balance.

29996433R00150

Made in the USA
San Bernardino, CA
04 February 2016